CRITICAL PRAISE FOR THE NOVELS OF ARTHUR NERSESIAN

For *Unlubricated* (2004)

"Nersesian is a first-rate observer of his native New York."
—*Publishers Weekly*

"Reading *Unlubricated* can make you feel like a commuter cata-pulting herself down the stairs to squeeze onto the A train before the doors close . . . In his paean to the perplexities of dislocation and discovery—both in bohemian life and in life at large—Nersesian makes us eager to see what happens when the curtain finally rises."
—*New York Times Book Review*

For *Chinese Takeout* (2003)

"Not since Henry Miller has a writer so successfully captured the . . . tribulations of a struggling artist . . . A masterly image."
—*Library Journal* (starred review)

"One of the best books I've read about the artist's life. Nersesian captures the obsession one needs to keep going under tough odds . . . trying to stay true to himself, and his struggle against the odds makes for a compelling read."
—*Village Voice*

"Thoroughly validates Nersesian's rep as one of the wittiest and most perceptive chroniclers of downtown life."
—*Time Out New York*

For *Suicide Casanova* (2002)

"Every budding author should read this book. Stop your creative writing class on the technique of Hemingway and study the el-egant gritty prose of Nersesian. Stop your literary theory class on Faulkner and read the next generation of literary genius."
—*Cherry Bleeds*

"Sick, depraved, and heartbreaking—in other words, a great read, a great book."

—Jonathan Ames, author of *The Extra Man*

For *dogrun* (2000)

"Darkly comic . . . It's Nersesian's love affair with lower Manhattan that sets these pages afire."

—*Entertainment Weekly*

For *Manhattan Loverboy* (2000)

"Best Book for the Beach, Summer 2000."

—*Jane*

"Best Indie Novel of 2000."

—*Montreal Mirror*

"Nersesian renders Gotham's unique cocktail of wealth, poverty, crime, glamour, and brutality spectacularly."

—*Rain Taxi Review of Books*

"*Manhattan Loverboy* sits somewhere between Kafka, DeLillo, and Lovecraft—a terribly frightening, funny, and all too possible place."

—*Literary Review of Canada*

For *The Fuck-Up* (1997)

"The charm and grit of Nersesian's voice is immediately enveloping, as the down-and-out but oddly up narrator of his terrific novel, *The Fuck-Up*, slinks through Alphabet City and guttural utterances of love."

—*Village Voice*

"For those who remember that the '80s were as much about destitute grit as they were about the decadent glitz described in the novels of Bret Easton Ellis and Jay McInerney, this book will come as a fast-paced reminder."

—*Time Out New York*

THE
SWING VOTER
OF
STATEN ISLAND

A NOVEL BY
ARTHUR NERSESIAN

AKASHIC BOOKS
NEW YORK

Published by Akashic Books
©2007 Arthur Nersesian

Map by Sohrab Habibion

ISBN-13: 978-1-933354-34-7
Library of Congress Control Number: 2007926051

First printing

Akashic Books
PO Box 1456
New York, NY 10009
info@akashicbooks.com
www.akashicbooks.com

For Margarita Shalina

And when you shall come to the mountains, view the land, of what sort it is, and the people that are the inhabitants thereof, whether they be strong or weak: few in number or many: The land itself, whether it be good or bad: what manner of cities, walled or without walls: The ground, fat or barren, woody or without trees. Be of good courage, and bring us of the fruits of the land.

—13:19, Book of Numbers

"Walk to Sutphin Boulevard . . ." Morning sun. "Catch the Q28 to Fulton Street . . ." Low-level warehouses. "Change to the B17 and take it to the East Village in Manhattan . . ." Empty truck bays. "Wait outside Cooper Union . . ." Nothing. "Until Dropt arrives . . ." No one around. "Shoot him once in the head . . ." Who? Where am I? "Then grab a cab back to the airport and catch the next flight out . . ."

His thoughts started breaking through his nonstop chant.

"Walk to Sutphin, catch the Q28 to Fulton Street, change to the B17, take it to the East Village in Manhattan, wait outside Cooper Union until Dropt arrives, shoot him once in the head, then grab a cab back to the airport . . ."

He couldn't stop chanting. In fact, Uli wasn't fully aware that he was even repeating anything aloud. He had just left JFK Airport and was shuffling like a sleepwalker up Rockaway Boulevard in Queens.

A sharp pinch compelled him to look down. A big hairy rat was biting him. No, it was a runty dog with protruding ribs and hips trying to angle its little jaws around his right ankle. Uli shook the little mutt off and considered hailing a cab, but his thoughts instructed him otherwise: *Walk to Sutphin, catch the Q28 to Fulton Street, change to the B17 and take it to the East Village . . . until Dropt arrives . . . once in the head, then a cab back . . . Walk to Sutphin, catch the Q28 to . . .*

As he moved along the barren avenue, he felt it again. The small dog was calmly trying to eat Uli's leg as he walked. He kicked the little beast away, and it dashed off yelping. Looking up, Uli nearly bumped into a wooden post with three arrow-shaped signs. Each one pointed in a different direction: *Woodhaven Boulevard*, *Atlantic Avenue*, and *Sutphin Boulevard*.

"Walk to Sutphin, catch the Q28 to Fulton Street . . ." He now remembered that a white-haired man with a brown lap dog had hastily imparted the crucial instructions—the chant.

Turning left at the next corner, Uli spotted something odd a half a block up the long sandy street. Raised five feet above ground with a small ladder attached was a wooden platform that looked like a boat pier on dry land. He noticed an attractive middle-aged woman with short chestnut hair and big orange-tinted sunglasses seated at its base.

She was leaning tiredly against a post, scribbling in some phone book–sized document. As he approached, he saw a floppy-eared dog with strangely large hind legs pressed up against her.

"Run!" a loud voice yelled from no place visible. Something was very wrong. Uli's throat was parched and his shirt was drenched in sweat. He sensed some kind of drug was in his system, dulling his thoughts and inhibiting his flight reflexes. Suddenly, a pack of wild dogs burst out from behind a warehouse a couple hundred feet away and raced toward him.

Uli's shoes sunk and slid along the sandy road, and he finally grasped that the raised wooden platform was the Q28 bus stop.

The woman saw him sprinting her way with the pack in hot pursuit. She heaved her thick document up onto the platform, then slipped her strange dog into a shoulder bag. As she climbed up the ladder onto the wooden landing, her derrière blocked Uli's frenzied escape.

He jumped up along the side of the five-foot structure, seizing onto a banner that read, MOVE 4 SHUB, just as a Doberman leaped at him. He rolled onto the wooden scaffold, winded. A large pit bull pounced up onto the first two steps of the ladder, but couldn't ascend the remaining rungs.

"They're a lot . . . quicker than . . . they look . . ." Uli said, trying to catch his breath. The dogs were barking and lunging up at them from every direction.

The woman ignored him and continued filling out her form. He saw that her pet wasn't a dog at all.

"Where'd you get the wallaby?" he asked, staring at the large-eyed marsupial peaking out of her shoulder bag.

"He was sitting on the road next to his dead mother who had been hit by a car," she finally replied, still scribbling.

"I'm sorry, I didn't get your name."

"I don't want to be rude," she said, "and I'm sure you don't either. I just have a lot of work to do before this day is done."

A half hour later, Uli began wondering how much longer he could sit still on this plywood platform, hardly bigger than a kitchen table, with an antisocial bitch and her orphaned kangaroo.

"I respect your desire for peace, but I just need to make sure the Q28 stops here."

"About a dozen buses stop here—eventually. The problem is, they all take forever and, as I'm sure you know, this is one of the most dangerous spots in the city. So if I were you, I'd get on whatever bus comes first and take it to a more populated transfer point." She immediately returned to her forms.

Over the next hour or so, whenever Uli stole a glance, he saw her flipping through her mammoth document, reading, revising, and making notes. The worst aspect of this silence was the *Walk to Sutphin* chant that kept looping through his head.

"May I ask what exactly it is you're doing?" he eventually inquired.

"Filling out forms."

"I just arrived here, so I don't really know what's going on."

"You *just* got here?"

"So it seems, I can't really remember anything. What are the forms for?"

"Okay, well, there are two major political parties, or gangs: The Piggers got Bronx and Queens, and the Crappers control Manhattan and Brooklyn. They run this place."

"Why would any group name itself *Piggers* or *Crappers*?"

"The Piggers were initially called the *We the Peoplers* and the Crappers were the *All Created Equalers*. Somehow over the years those titles got corrupted. Anyway," she returned to her goliath document, "I'm doing administrative work for them."

"What kind of work?"

Letting out a big sigh, she said, "Okay, I serve on the November 9th Commission to Combat Citywide Voter Fraud. I have to conform the figures recorded here to the number, model, access, and quality of voting equipment and booths in the two dozen or so districts that comprise eastern Queens—which I just inspected—for next week's mayoral and presidential elections. And if it's not filled out and submitted by 3 o'clock tomorrow, the Crapper Party loses all rights to appeal. Any other questions?"

Though nothing she said made any sense to him, he nodded nervously.

"If I seem a little curt," she added, "up until about ninety minutes ago, I had a private bodyguard and a nice new car."

"What happened to them?"

"Who knows? I went into the Howard Beach polling center for five minutes, came out, and both were gone. So I'm not in the best of moods."

The baby kangaroo suddenly jerked forward in her shoulder bag and plopped down five feet to the earthen street.

"Shit!" she shrieked just as the Doberman snatched up the joey in its jaws. Without thinking, she jumped down off the platform. "Give it back, fucker!" she yelled, grabbing the kangaroo by its jerking legs.

A Rottweiler was about to leap up on her, when Uli dropped down squarely on its broad back, stunning the canine. He pulled out the small red-handled pistol that the man at the airport had given him and put a bullet through the snarling Doberman's large skull. The woman lurched back from the blast, then scooped up the traumatized marsupial and scurried up the ladder to the platform. When a large German shepherd lunged at him, Uli tried shooting it as well, only to find that his gun was out of bullets. Dropping the weapon, Uli caught the animal by its long snout, then used its own momentum to fling it across the sandy roadway. Some smaller dogs barked furiously at him while backing away.

"Where the fuck did you learn to do that?" the woman asked as he climbed up the platform.

"Haven't a clue."

"You look familiar," she said, peering at him closely for the first time. "Where are you from?"

"The airport," he replied, then absentmindedly explained, "I was told to walk to Sutphin, catch the Q28 to Fulton Street, change to the B17, take it to the East Village in Manhattan, wait outside Cooper Union until Dropt arrives, shoot him once in the head, then grab a cab back to the airport and catch the next flight—"

"Is that some sort of joke?" she snapped. "My husband was shot by an assassin. He was paralyzed from the neck down."

"I have no idea who I am or what I'm doing here," Uli replied, exasperated.

"You really look familiar," she said. "You don't have a sister, do you?"

"Other than that chant, all I remember is being on a cargo plane . . . Or maybe that was a dream . . ."

"No, you probably came in on a drone. They fly them in several times a day. They drop off supplies and take off again, see?" She pointed to one circling overhead.

"I vaguely remember some chubby white-haired guy with a high voice."

"That sounds like Underwood. He's Commissioner of Supply Stock under Shub. Underwood probably found you in one of the drones and guinea-pigged you into an assassin."

Still slightly out of it, Uli watched closely as the woman resumed filling out one of her forms.

<u>KEW GARDENS VOTING DISTRICT</u>
23,631 registered voters

<u>Voting Equipment</u>
Finger ink: Y or N?
    If so, how much? _____
Paper ballots: Y or N?
    If so, how many? _____
Hole-punching voting machines: Y or N?
    If so, how many?_____

_____
Signature of Inspector

—982—

After filling in the form with numbers and checks, she signed her name—*Mallory*.

Looking tiredly at the distant hills around him, Uli said, "I don't exactly remember JFK as being in a mountain range."

"Those are the Nogales Mountains. You're in Nevada now, the first designated Rescue City. This is all federal territory."

"I thought this was Queens."

"Queens, Nevada. Actually, we're almost in Brooklyn." She pulled off her orange-tinted glasses.

"What do you mean by *Nevada*?"

"The army gridded up the Nevada desert and gave each massive box a number. Someone told me that this was Area 41 through 51." She pulled at her chestnut hairdo. It turned out to be a wig, which she shoved into her handbag. Then she wiped the sweat off her brow and neck. "They started building this place during the last World War. They finished it during the Cold War. There were seven or eight central target areas throughout the city. It wasn't originally designed for people, just for aerial and troop training. You'll see signs of warfare all over the place."

Glancing over the woman's shoulder, Uli spotted a small cloud of dust rising in the hot, wavy distance. "Mallory, is that a bus?"

"How did you know my name?" she shot back.

"I saw you sign it in your book."

"Do me a big favor and don't ever say my name again. I'm not too popular out here."

"Why?

"Long story. I used to be on the City Council."

As a small bus approached, Uli could see that all of its windows, including the windshield, were bound in a wide metal mesh. It looked like a cage on wheels with a few arms branching out the windows to the roof.

"Shit!" Mallory muttered.

"What?"

"Of all the buses to arrive, this one takes me furthest from where I'm going."

"Then why take it?"

"Cause there's no telling how long I'll have to wait for the next one."

Uli waved nervously to the vehicle and the dogs below went into a renewed frenzy of snarls and snaps. The pack was caught by surprise as the bus sped right into it, nearly crushing one of the bigger canines under its front wheels. The dogs scurried away, barking angrily.

The minibus flung open its door.

"You okay?" asked the driver, a large light-skinned black guy with only one arm.

"Now we are," Mallory sighed.

10:52 a.m.

"Where you heading?" the driver asked Uli after Mallory paid and took a seat.

"Walk to Sutphin," Uli said calmly. "Catch the Q28 to Fulton Street."

"That's this bus."

"Change to the B17, take it to the East Village in Manhattan, wait outside Cooper Union until Dropt arrives, shoot him once in the head—"

"I didn't ask for your freakin life story," the driver replied as he zoomed onward. A large handwritten sign said, 1/16. In his pocket, Uli found a rectangular piece of paper that had neither numbers nor a president's face on it. It simply said, ONE FOODSTAMP. Uli handed it to the driver, who counted back the change—fifteen neatly sliced parts of another foodstamp.

Two men—one bald and thin, the other thick with long, curly hair—and a woman were the only other passengers. Each had an arm stretched out the mesh-covered window.

"What's up with them?" Uli asked the driver.

"The solar panel's loose on the roof."

"You have photoelectric cells generating this bus?"

"They generate all the vehicles here, and if it slides off, we got no battery—ride's over."

Seated behind the driver, Mallory returned to her mega-form. Upon taking a seat toward the rear, Uli slipped his arm out the window like the others. He felt the unsteady piece of paneling on the roof and pressed his hand down on it.

"Howdy," said the thin male passenger. He had a bald head and squinty eyes. "The name's Jim Carnival." He was holding what looked like a World War II mine detector with his free hand. Between his knees was an old bucket. "This is the wife Mary and our boy Oric." The woman appeared slightly younger, but the heavyset "son" seemed to be around the same age as his father. Through Oric's shaggy curls of hair, Uli spotted a small metal cross protruding from the back of his cranium and tried not to stare.

"Is that the former First Lady?" Carnival shouted over to Mallory, who hunched forward, annoyed. "Don't worry, we'll keep it on the hush-hush, ma'am. I worked briefly for your husband."

Mallory nodded without stopping her frantic scribbling.

"So where are you from, pal?" Carnival asked Uli.

"New York, I think. I just got here." Whenever he tried to remember anything, all that came to mind was, *Walk to Sutphin, catch the Q28 to Fulton Street, change to the B17 . . .*

"Hold on," the guy said. "You just arrived from old New York?"

"I think so. I'm totally disoriented."

"You look familiar," the wife spoke up. Uli shrugged.

"Howard Beach 9!" the supposed son, Oric, blurted for no apparent reason.

Amid the trash littering the floor of the bus, Uli spotted a newspaper entitled, *The Daily Posted New York Times*. Picking it up and flipping through the articles, Uli read the last page: *Weekly Police Blotter*. A subcategory read, *Number of Car Bombings: 4*. Without listing the names of any victims or any other colorful details, the article gave bare-bone descriptions of the four harrowing bomb blasts. One car was blown up on the Little Concourse in the Bronx, killing twenty-one people and wounding fifty-four. An alleged former member of a group called S.N.C.C. was suspected. A second car bomb exploded in the Upper West Side, killing thirty-four and wounding twelve. A third one detonated in Brighton Beach, killing four, wounding eighteen. The last bomb that week had gone off near the Chrystler Building in Queens, killing six and wounding thirteen.

Under *Conventional Crimes* some details were offered: Five former F.A.L.N. suspects died in police custody in the Morrisania section of the Bronx. A family of seven was found murdered during a home invasion in Astoria, Queens. One of them had been an associate of the Black Cubs, a splinter group of the Black Bears, which in turn had splintered off from the Black Panthers. A solarcar was hijacked in Staten Island and the driver, a known B.M.T. operative, was murdered. In Sheepshead Bay, Brooklyn, ten seniors, possible fundraisers for the March 29th Army, were killed when a suspicious fire swept through their retirement home. Six former S.L.A. suspects were shot dead during a concert in Bed-Stuy, Brooklyn. There was a massacre at a Crapper club in Boerum Hill, Brooklyn, which claimed twenty-five lives.

Underneath that, Uli read:

WEEKLY CITYWIDE ELECTION RESULTS

MANHATTAN:
> Total Pigger districts: 1
> Total Crappers districts: 9
> No change from last election

STATEN ISLAND:
> Total Pigger districts: 0
> Total Crappers districts: 0
> Total Independent districts (Verdant League): 10
> No change from last election

THE BRONX:
>   Total Pigger districts: 9
>   Total Crapper districts: 1
>   No change from last election

BROOKLYN:
>   Total Pigger districts: 3
>   Total Crapper districts: 17
>   No change from last election

QUEENS:
>   Fresh Meadows (Crapper) invaded
>   2,345 Crappers, 3,392 Piggers
>   Outcome: Pigger
>   Councilwoman Diana McNair (C) removed
>   Councilman Abraham Hodges (P) elected

>   Hillcrest (Pigger) invaded
>   6,331 Crappers, 6,323 Piggers
>   Outcome: Crapper
>   Councilman Larry Mahonney (P) removed
>   Councilman Earl Grims (C) elected
>   Total Pigger districts: 18
>   Total Crapper districts: 2
>   Two changes from last election

"It's good to see communities standing up against in-vading gangs once in a while," Carnival commented, star-ing at the paper over Uli's shoulder.

"These invasions occur every week, do they?" Uli asked.

"Just like with car bombings—every time *they* do one, *we* do one."

"And who are *we* again?" Uli asked.

"This is Crapper territory and we're Crappers," Carnival responded proudly.

"Speak for yourself," his wife murmured.

"Hey! We're losing our plate!" the driver shouted back to the passengers.

Uli pressed the solar panel harder against the roof. He peered out of the window across the barren urban landscape. On the far side of a huge lake, he spotted a cluster of tall, liver-colored buildings in the distance. He could see lines of dark-suited people filing into several buses.

"That's Pud Pullers up in Howard Beach," Carnival said. "You definitely don't want to go there."

"Pud Pullers?"

"Its real name is Pure-ile Plurality. That's the only good thing about this stinking place," his wife retorted. "It's a haven for family unity."

Carnival shook his head in disgust. The couple were clearly not of one mind.

The bus turned a corner and moved past a row of buildings with plastic garbage bags dangling from them. Down a side street he was surprised to see a single-humped camel sticking its long neck into one of the suspended garbage bags, rooting for food.

"They figured that by releasing all these desert animals out here we'd somehow become more lovable," Carnival said. "Instead we have mountains of strange dung."

Some of the buildings were clearly abandoned and covered with crudely painted images of male faces. Captioned underneath each one were apparent birth and death dates, as well as brief epitaphs, like *Crapper Hero* and *Killed 8 Piggers*. Doing the math, Uli realized that few of them had made it to the age of twenty. The semi-abandoned neighborhood was like a large cemetery where the amateurishly rendered portraits on the collapsed structures served as large headstones.

"Flatlands," the driver announced as they entered what looked like a new neighborhood.

This area was bordered by a row of four-story apartment buildings with street-level stores that had been converted into flimsy bulwarks and slapdash fortifications. Interspersed through these principal structures were poorly built garages, usually just corrugated tin roofs affixed between uncemented cinder-block walls.

"Correction! Howard Beach 9!" shouted Oric, the manlike child, rocking back and forth.

At that moment, the bus hit a bump and Carnival's old mine detector fell toward Uli, who caught the large pan base before it could brain him. A long beep sounded.

When he handed the contraption back, the man looked at him strangely, then leaned it toward Uli's head. The machine elicited a second beep.

"You got a deal with some CIA pointy-heads?"

"What do you mean *deal*?"

"You got an electronic bug in your skull."

"Underwood probably inserted it there," Mallory spoke up.

"What are you talking about?"

"Greenpoint 22!" Oric shouted.

"It means someone is tracking you," Carnival replied. "Go to the Manhattan Crapper headquarters—if anyone can corkscrew that thing out of your head, they can."

Uli thanked Carnival for the advice and asked where he and his family were coming from.

"Rockaway Beach," Carnival said. "The wife and I met in old New York's Rockaway when we were kids."

"Correction! Rockaway 6, Greenpoint 22. Correction!"

"What the hell is he talking about?" Uli asked.

"Don't mind him," Carnival said, "he's a little mushy in the penthouse, but the wife and I love him all the more for it."

"So what were you doing in Rockaway?" Uli asked.

"We were digging for clams." The man lifted the bucket between his legs and revealed a collection of rusty and sand-encrusted bullets. "These clams are worth money. Bunch of them got buried in the sand down there during the parachute drops years ago."

"Do you have guns for the bullets?"

"Everyone has guns, but no one has any ammunition left. Hence, bullets are expensive. I can get about five to ten stamps for each one."

The conversation was interrupted by the driver shouting through his window: "Get the fuck out of my way!"

Some vehicle was slowing down in front of them. The one-armed man swung the bus onto an empty sidewalk and pulled ahead of the car. As they sped past, Uli could see a strange-looking man in the vehicle shouting upward at the bus driver.

"Fuck you!" the driver yelled back.

"What's going on?" Uli asked nervously as they sped down the sandy street.

"Some damn Flatland motherfucker is trying to hijack us."

Uli could hear the man shouting from the car behind them: "Just give him back!"

"How far along are they in the cleanup anyway?" Carnival asked.

"Cleanup?" Uli replied, his confusion mounting once again. As Carnival rambled on about the operation, Uli got a clear view of the guy in the car behind them. Other than his fashionable goatee and a trimmed widow's peak, the man looked uncannily like Oric.

"One way or another," Carnival said, "I'm getting back to old New York."

Suddenly the car slammed into their rear bumper, sending Mallory and her document to the floor.

"Oh shit, he's got a gun!" Carnival's wife shrieked, seeing the man holding something out his window. A blast exploded through the rear window and out the roof of the bus.

"This guy's going to kill us all!" Carnival cried out, grabbing his mine detector in both hands as if it were a rifle.

"Okay, everyone, hold onto the damn panel!" the driver shouted. All did.

Without slowing down, the bus made a sharp left turn and slid across the unswept sands of King's Highway. All the buildings on the north side of the street were bleached white by the Nevada sun while the structures along the south side were carbonized black by some bygone fire.

"Shit!" the driver yelled, peaking into his rearview. "That Flatlander's serious. He ain't letting up."

Seeing that Oric was starting to cry, Uli tried to break the tension by asking Carnival, "How are you planning to leave this place?"

"I'm stuck here just like you," Carnival replied, staring out the window.

"You said that one way or another you were going to get back to New York. How do you plan to do that?"

"I said that?"

Mary shot her husband a stern look.

"I just meant I'm nearing the end of my appellate process—what do they call it, the Road Out Program. Eventually, when they see that I wasn't supposed to be sent here in the first place, we'll get flown out."

"There's an appeals process?" Uli vaguely recalled filling out some forms while he was with the white-haired guy at the airport.

The pursuing car, which had now edged next to them, slammed into the side of the bus. The two vehicles drove neck and neck, scraping and slowing each other. Carnival's wife jumped out of her seat and positioned herself next to the driver, trying to help him turn the wheel against the car, but it wasn't working. Their bus was slowing down. Pretty soon they'd be forced to a halt.

Mallory nervously pulled her chestnut wig back over her head, then grabbed a heavy flannel shirt out of her bag and slipped it on.

As Carnival's shrieking wife kept the steering wheel turned against the mad driver from Flatlands, Uli watched the bus driver reach under his seat for a bottle of wine, which he uncorked with his teeth. With his one good hand, he calmly shoved a napkin down the bottleneck. Then flipping open a lighter, he lit the napkin and tossed the bottle out the window. It exploded along the top of the car. "Hold on!" he shouted, grabbing the wheel from Mary and slamming on the brakes, which sent the other vehicle flying into an abandoned building. The bus driver turned left and sped away.

"That was too damn close," Mallory muttered.

"I wonder what they wanted," Uli said.

As the bus turned up Flatbush Avenue, the sand that had been covering the road began to thin out. The quality of the roadway was still poor, but the one-armed driver gracefully dodged potholes without having to slow down. Eventually they made a left on Church Avenue, where signs of life began returning.

"Welcome to Japtown," Carnival said with a sigh.

The neighborhood was covered with delicate wooden buildings that had tiered levels and swirling pagoda-style bamboo roofs.

"This area was designed to resemble Japan for ground and aerial training," Carnival explained.

Little shops with twirling mansard roofs dotted the area: a tarot card psychic, a barbershop, a scratch-and-match vendor, a sushi bar, an Optima cigar stand. When the bus turned down a side street, Uli saw a mini–restaurant row—a group of food vendors toiling over smoky barbecues and hibachis. Directly across from them, a line of people gathered outside a movie theater that looked like it might originally have been a Buddhist temple.

With an apparently limited supply of red plastic letters for the marquee, the establishment had improvised: W9zT S1OE StoR7.

11:12 a.m.

After ten more blocks, the cute japonica architecture ended, and with it, all signs of civilization. Streets were again barren, and the buildings took on a harsher, colder style. Soon they came upon a complex of larger buildings that looked like skeletons of the Soviet housing made popular under Khrushchev. The structures appeared empty and most were burned out altogether.

Six passengers who had boarded the bus along Church Avenue had already gotten off, leaving only the five original riders.

"Welcome to Borough Park," Mallory said. "Once a thriving Hasidic community."

"What happened?"

"It was a dignified Pigger neighborhood eight years ago—before the Crappers took over Brooklyn. The local residents kept supporting their own Pigger leader, Moss Leere, and the Crappers persecuted them until they couldn't take it anymore and moved to Queens."

The bus passed a partially collapsed cupola with a big Star of David on the front. It looked like something out of Czarist Russia. According to Mallory, the destroyed synagogue had once been the spiritual center of the area.

"Shit!" the driver suddenly shouted. "He's back."

Turning around, they all saw it. Smoke from the burned paint on the roof was streaming off. The car from Flatlands was gaining on them. In a desperate effort to lose it, the bus driver veered off his route and sped deeper into the desolation of Borough Park. Soon, though, the Flatlander once again slammed into their rear bumper.

"I can't outrun him," the driver conceded, trying to

block the car from getting around.

"Maybe we should stop and give him our money, or just slow down and see what he wants," Uli suggested.

Carnival noticed a cinder block propped under a broken seat in front of him. He pulled open a hole in the mesh covering his window and hurled the large concrete weight onto the front of the pursuing car. The block shattered the solar panel affixed to the vehicle's hood, bringing it to a slow halt.

"Good job!" the bus driver yelled back to Carnival, then turned at the next corner to try and get back to his route. Amid the maze of sandy streets blocked by debris, they had difficulty finding their way. The driver came upon a narrow yet clear street that ran loosely parallel to his route. Following it as far as he could, the driver turned again, only to find a shiny new car blocking the street. A group of burly young men were standing around it. The bus driver stomped on the brakes and tried turning his vehicle around. "We're trapped!" he said. "These guys are probably in cahoots with the Flatlander!"

"I don't think so," Uli replied. He noticed Mallory desperately hoisting her thick document and official identification badge up under the solar panel above the bus. Still in her wig disguise, she slipped contact lenses over her pupils. The driver had only completed the second part of a three-point turn when some kid raced over from the shiny car, dragging a long spike strip before the front wheels. The bus driver jammed on the brakes, causing the solar panel to shoot forward and crash to the pavement.

"Fuck!" Mallory yelled, as her huge election document tumbled to the ground as well.

The driver groaned and threw the bus into reverse, crashing into a dead fire hydrant.

The rest of the burly boys dashed over to them. Four unsynchronized bursts erupted and the bus sank down several inches—they had popped the tires.

"I'm Officer Chain! Open the goddamn door, we're Pigger gangcops!" the oldest and fattest of them shouted, flashing a gold badge. He was stocky and bald, with wire-frame glasses and a square-linked chain wrapped around his thick neck like a glittering, unknotted tie. Some strange mechanical object that Uli didn't recognize was affixed to his forehead. As the man came closer, Uli saw that the forehead appendage resembled a bent scope from a sharp-shooter's rifle.

The driver stepped out of the bus, leading Mallory, Uli, and the Carnival family behind him. Five large men with machetes surrounded them. A sixth gangcop raced on board and brought out some of the items they had left behind.

"May I ask why, if you're a Pigger officer and this is a Crapper neighborhood—" Uli started.

"May you ask?" Officer Chain cut him off. "Who are you, the fucking King of Siam?"

"He just arrived here," Mary explained.

As two gigantic men silently pushed everyone face-forward against the side of the bus, Oric nervously whispered, "Rockaway 6, Greenpoint 22, Howard Beach 9."

One of the gangcops searching for weapons lecherously patted down Mallory's breasts and groin.

"Where'd you get the kangaroo?" Chain asked her. Both Carnival and Uli leaned toward her protectively.

"Found him along the side of the road."

"You look familiar as shit," Chain replied, as his sharp chain swung up against her arm.

"Never had the pleasure," she replied icily.

"What's your name?"

"Frances," Carnival spoke up before she could say anything. "She's my child."

"What are your affiliations?" one of the men asked her.

"None of us are wearing any colors," Mallory replied, as though citing a key rule of engagement.

"That's right. You don't have the right to ask nothing!" the bus driver declared.

"How about you, New Yorker?" the bully said to Uli, scanning his eyes with his scopic horn. A red ray shooting out from its tip led Uli to believe it was a lie detector. "You pro-life or pro-choice?"

"He doesn't know the issues," Mallory answered for him.

When one of the assistants edged up toward Mallory again, Uli stepped forward, compelling the man to lift his blade. Mallory raised her hand, urging restraint.

The lead cop swung his cyber horn into Mallory's eyes, but before he could ask any questions, Carnival punched the device.

"Motherfucker!" Chain groaned, grabbing his forehead.

One of the other gangcops immediately brought his machete up against Carnival's long lean neck. Chain tapped his horn until the red light flickered back on, then leaned forward so that the scanner pointed directly in Carnival's face.

"What's your name, asshole?"

"Chad."

"Are those yours, Chad?" Chain pointed toward the old bucket and clunky mine detector.

"I found them."

"What gang are you all with?"

"We're from different parties," Carnival's wife replied.

"Not anymore you're not," Chain said. He gestured to one of his assistants, who pinned Carnival's arms behind his back.

"Don't you dare touch my husband!" Mary screamed.

"Or whatchu gonna do?"

"I used to be a Pigger Councilwoman, asshole," she shot back.

Chain scanned one of her eyes with his instrument. "How do you like that? She's not lying. Well, you're lucky, honey, cause as you know, our party would never permit us to make a woman a widow or turn a child into an orphan."

"The family must be kept together at all costs," added one of the other gangcops, as though he were reciting an axiom.

Chain began laughing and two of his lackeys grabbed Carnival's wife and Mallory, who they seemed to actually believe was his daughter.

"Hold on!" Mallory yelled. Her little kangaroo was struggling to get out of her arm bag. She grabbed its furry legs and asserted, "We're not related!" With her free hand, she fumbled through her purse and brought out an identity card.

Pushing his cyber-eye up against her right pupil, Chain concluded, "You don't look Jewish."

When the gangcop handed back Mallory's ID card, Uli peered over and read the name on it: *Alison Lowenstein—INDEPENDENT.*

"Chad and his Pigger wife are under arrest," Chain announced. "The rest of you—scram!"

"Wait!" Mary screamed.

"They're *my* passengers," the bus driver objected. "I demand to know what you're arresting them for."

"His metal detector is a rifle." Chain kicked off the pancake base of the instrument, revealing that it was in fact disguising the barrel of a gun. Lifting the plastic bucket, he added, "And here are the rounds."

"What the hell?" Mary shouted at her spouse.

"Pa!" their idiot son cried fearfully. "Howard Beach! Correction!"

"I'm so sorry, babe," Carnival mumbled to his wife.

"This guy called that guy *Pa*," said one of the gangcops, grabbing Oric's chubby right arm. "He's in the family."

Uli clutched Oric's other arm. "Come on, he's mentally incompetent and obviously older than that guy. How the hell can this be his son?"

One of the men pressed his machete to Uli's throat as the other shoved Oric up against the bus. Another gang-cop fingerprinted the fat man and ran the print through a scanning machine in the shiny car's glove compartment. A moment later, he reported back, "The guy's clean," and shoved Carnival's son toward Uli.

The driver started back toward his bus, but was stopped by Chain. "We're confiscating your vehicle."

"Officer, where can we post bail for them?" Mallory asked, before the driver could protest. As a response, one of the gangcops grabbed the joey from Mallory's bag and tossed him to the sandy sidewalk, then shoved her back up against the bus.

"You're interrupting a vital Pigger mission," Uli said as they pinned his arm back. "I work for Council President Underwood."

"Oh sure," Chain replied with a sneer, shining his scope in Uli's eyes. "I really believe this New Yorker is one of us."

"Call Underwood. Tell him you're holding the guy who was supposed to walk to Sutphin, catch the Q28 to Fulton Street, change to the B17 to the East Village, and shoot Dropt."

Registering no lie, Chain walked back to his shiny car. He snatched the radio phone from his dashboard and made a call. After a minute, he beckoned Uli over and handed him the black phone.

Uli heard the strangely familiar high-pitched voice: "S'that you?"

"Yes, sir."

"Tell me your mission again."

"Walk to Sutphin, catch the Q28 to Fulton Street, change to the B17 and take it to the East Village in Manhattan, wait outside Cooper Union for Dropt to arrive, shoot him once in the head, then grab a cab back to the airport and catch the next flight—"

"And why isn't this being carried out, soldier?"

"These guys hijacked my bus and falsely arrested two people."

"I don't give a shit about that, just tell me you still have the gun I gave you."

"Yes sir, I was heading to Manhattan when these guys hijacked the bus—"

"All right, listen, I just got a call from the blond lobbyist." Uli had no idea who Underwood was talking about. "She's impatient, so she's going to help you. Proceed to Jay Street in downtown Brooklyn and meet her at the bus stop."

"Fine, but there's this fat bald guy who illegally arrested some friends of mine—"

Chain snatched the radio phone out of Uli's hand and slammed it down. "Get walking before I change my fat bald mind."

Uli, the bus driver, Mallory, and Oric began heading down the road. Seeing her bulky election document amid the shards of shattered solar paneling, Mallory bent down and scooped it up, never breaking her stride.

"If they're Piggers," Uli asked softly, "why do they have jurisdiction in a Crapper borough?"

"Since they work as Council cops, they have citywide jurisdiction," Mallory explained.

After several blocks down the long sandy street, the driver stopped, looked back at his hijacked bus, and groaned. Two corpses swung by their necks from a broken light post. Oric dashed about thirty feet back toward his murdered parents before Uli tackled him. The challenged man collapsed in the sand and wept.

As Uli stared at the murdered couple in the distance, he blurted out, "Wait a sec, I don't think it's them."

The driver put his finger over his lips, indicating silence.

"But whoever is hanging up there looks black," Uli protested. "The Carnivals were white."

"The light's just playing tricks with your eyes," Mallory assured him, and making the sign of the cross she added, "They're back in old New York now." She handed Uli her election document, then removed the billowy shirt and wig she had used as a disguise. Pausing, she quickly popped the contact lenses out of her eyes and slipped them into a tiny plastic case. She took Oric gently in her arms and helped him to his feet.

The four of them walked further down the succession of barren streets, away from the swinging bodies. Soon they sat down near a small empty square under the long shadow of a statue that appeared to be Lenin.

Oric began mumbling, "I didn't see it coming, I didn't see it coming, I didn't see it—"

"It's not your fault!"

"They were my brothers!" Oric retorted inexplicably.

Mallory held the man-child's hand as he whimpered softly.

"If all of Queens votes for the Piggers," Uli asked, tiredly toting Mallory's giant book, "who exactly are you protecting with this document?"

"After eight years in office, Shub has disappointed even most of the hard-core Piggers. Hell, he was so damn powerful that he wouldn't allow any other Piggers in the primary."

"So what exactly do you hope to do?"

"I was appointed to a bipartisan commission that sends officials to monitor the elections at different polling sites. They're the ones responsible for making sure the right equipment is available and accessible. If I can just make sure that the hardware is there, we should get a reasonably fair mayoral election, and we might actually have a shot at beating the son of a bitch."

"Do you know anything about that Chain prick?" the bus driver asked her.

"Yeah, I know him. He would've recognized me with that scope if I didn't have the contact lenses. Nine years ago, when my husband was mayor and Horace Shub was head of the City Council, that bastard was his chief of security," Mallory explained. "Hor eventually fired Chain to appease the Crapper moderates—the man was a known sadist. About five years ago, the Slope had a mini uprising because they resented Shub's Pigger policies. Chain was appointed to oversee Council security for central Brooklyn."

Several minutes later, Uli asked the driver, "What color did Jim Carnival and his wife appear to you?"

"There's an expression round here," he replied. "You don't really know a person till he's dead . . ."

"And by then what does it matter?" Mallory added, still holding Oric's hand as they got up and marched onward.

4:02 p.m.

Oric's mental limitations did not extend to his sense of love or grief. The Carnivals' adopted and orphaned son continued weeping over his "dead brothers" as they headed down the middle of empty streets, passing abandoned and damaged buildings. By late afternoon, when they had crossed a desolate intersection marked *Ditmas Avenue*, they came to the outskirts of a new neighborhood that bore the sign, *BEN HUR*.

Moving into the northern end of Bensonhurst, they approached a battery of a dozen or so older blue-haired women and six male amputees working in the street. Some of the crew were digging with shovels. Others were stooped on their knees upon squares of cardboard. Each person was an arm's reach from the next. They moved in a straight line at their own slow pace, scooping sand into wheelbarrows.

"What the hell is this?" Uli asked.

"Sandstorms," Mallory replied. "They hit about twice a month this time of year. The locals dig them out—refundable sand."

The four bus refugees stumbled past as the locals harvested the coarse brown sand dropped during the last storm.

"You should get your children to help you," Uli suggested to one lady who seemed to be the group leader.

"Fuck off!" she barked.

"Didn't no one tell you bout the epidemic?" the bus driver asked when they were out of earshot.

"What epidemic?"

"The EGGS epidemic," the driver said. "Something in the ground water messed up their plumbing."

"Roughly one-third of all women of child-bearing age died within the first five years of coming here," Mallory chimed in as they labored along down the street.

MY JAW'S SORE, announced the canary-yellow T-shirt of a brightly lipsticked woman they came upon who appeared to be a malnourished hooker. She was leaning invitingly from the window of a tenement on New Utrecht Avenue, though she wasn't much to look at.

Uli heard an emaciated man on a corner chanting in what sounded like Spanish, "Sí . . . sí . . ." Then he realized the scary creature was actually hustling something. "What exactly is c-c?" he asked the driver.

"There are two main drugs here: choke, which you smoke, and croak, which you shoot or swallow. Pigger gangsters control croak because Underwood grabs it from JFK."

"What other drugs are shipped out here?"

"Aside from painkillers and sleeping pills, one of the main drugs of choice is methadone. A lot is sent in."

"Is choke shipped in?"

"No, it's made from indigenous plants—pot, peyote, what have you. Crappers handle the choke production in Hoboken. They harvest fields of it across from Manhattan, using the river for irrigation."

Lapsing back into silence, Uli smelled a foul odor and realized it was coming from Oric. He sped up a little and walked with Mallory, the other two trailing behind.

"You know that guy chasing us in Flatlands?" Mallory said after a while.

"What about him?"

"Did he look familiar to you?"

"Yeah, he looked like him," Uli said, tipping his head toward Oric.

"Did that couple, the Carnivals, seem odd to you?" she asked.

"Everything here seems odd to me. Do you think they abducted Oric?"

"Why would anyone abduct a mentally retarded man?" she asked. Uli shrugged. "In any event, there's a city-run home for the mentally impaired out in Willowbrook, Staten Island."

"Maybe we can drop him off," Uli suggested.

They began to hear lively carousing in the distance. A group of people were gathered around an energetic band that consisted of two youths drumming on upside-down spackle buckets, accompanied by various homemade wind and string instruments. Beautiful women twirled like dervishes with equally handsome guys. Half a block further down, a group of older men standing around a barrel filled with greenish flames was sucking on stinky cigars. A vendor was turning chunks of skewered meats over a small flame. A sign on his cart said, *GB-ways!* Smelly, oil-bearing smoke trailed down the block. Oric paused at the food stand.

"Come on," the one-armed bus driver said, and led everyone into a small empty shop that had a large rickety table with a row of grills in the center. Against the wall was a stack of old milk crates. He went up to the worn wooden counter where there was a large can of old soup spoons, along with napkins and four plastic squirt bottles, each with a different color paste inside.

The driver took a crate and dropped it on the floor at

the table's edge. Everyone followed him, taking napkins and spoons. A small Asian woman with the face of a bat appeared at the rear door smoking a corncob pipe.

"One-stamp size," the driver said, holding up his index finger for emphasis. Uli saw that there was only one item on the menu; its size was determined by the price. The woman disappeared into the back, presumably the kitchen.

Several minutes later, the woman reappeared wearing oven gloves and carrying an old pot filled with flat noodles in steaming water, which she carefully placed on the grill. Underneath she slid a small can of some sort of gel. She lit the Sterno can with a match, creating a small but persistent blue flame.

A boy who appeared to be her son followed her out with a cardboard box containing raw vegetables and several dull knives. He returned to the rear room and came back with a tray of sizzling chunks of meat, which he dumped into the boiling pot.

"Food here don't make you sick," the driver commented, "but you got to work a little." Since he had only the one arm, he instructed Uli to chop up the browning celery and wilted carrots. Mallory was told to dice an onion the size of a small cantaloupe and Oric was given the task of shredding lettuce, cabbage, and basil leaves. Everyone dumped their sectioned vegetables into the bubbling pot.

The driver picked up a bright red squirt container and was about to squeeze it into the pot when Mallory said she didn't like it spicy and that everyone had the right to season their own bowl.

"Fine," the driver said, putting down the hot sauce.

When the flame in the can finally burned out, Mallory began doling out hearty bowls of soup. Everyone quietly slurped down their food. Oric and the driver had another two bowls. The driver and Mallory both said they were getting low on cash, so each of them pulled out a quarter-stamp. Uli made up the difference with a half-stamp, which they paid to the lady. Then, tiredly, they resumed walking.

The sun began to set about ten minutes later, when Mallory spotted the silhouette of a tall man with extraordinarily wide hips wearing a skipper's cap—a bus dispatcher. The official stood like a statue before the only illuminated building on the block. When Mallory asked if he knew when the next bus was coming, she was told that some driver just had his bus hijacked.

"His passengers were hung by the neck," the dispatcher said, "so all bus service is being suspended in southern Brooklyn until morning."

"They only hung two folks over in Borough Park," clarified the driver as he slowly approached. "That was my bus."

"Sorry to hear it. No more buses or cabs neither tonight," the dispatcher replied flatly. "Best chance you have is bedding down right here." He pointed his thumb behind him at a run-down building with an old sign that read, HOTEL BEDMILL. "He has several rooms available, and cause of your tragedy he'll probably cut the price."

Mallory led the little group inside a dim, paint-peeled lobby where several questionable characters sat on crates in the corner like human mushrooms. A large bug-eyed man wearing an old derby was sitting at a counter next to a wood-burning stove, listening to the radio.

"Half a stamp per night. You can do two per room," the clerk said. Everyone started digging through their pockets.

"Give me something quiet," the driver said, slapping a half-stamp on the worn-down counter top. The clerk gave him a towel and explained that the bathroom was in the hallway. "Checkout's at 9 a.m. sharp."

"You snore, boy?" the driver asked Oric, who was leaning up against him at the counter. The heavyset man shook his head and farted. The driver asked for a second towel.

Mallory politely asked if Uli could spare some cash.

"This is it." He held up his last half-stamp.

"I thought I'd be back home by late this afternoon, or I woulda . . . All I have is a quarter-stamp," she said. "Want to share?'

"Do you snore or fart?" he half-joked.

"If I do, my husband never told me about it," she replied. "Then again, he was usually sleeping with some underage, overweight assistant."

Uli put his half-stamp down and said, "Keep your cash and buy me coffee tomorrow."

The clerk handed him a key and two towels.

They marched up two flights of steps and down a corridor filled with various creaks and bangs coming from the rooms they passed, until they located their door. Inside they found a narrow, ancient bed with a ridiculously springy mattress.

Feeling sore all over, Uli didn't want to sleep on the filthy floor, especially considering he had paid for the room. Before he could prepare some suitable compromise, Mallory kicked off her shoes, unbuttoned her shirt, and said, "You want the wall or the outside?"

"Either's fine," Uli replied gratefully.

She stripped down to her bra and panties and brushed an accumulation of sand off the bed. Then she jumped on the mattress, pulling a threadbare sheet over her. For a moment there was an awkward silence as each of them listened to the other's slow breaths. Uli tried once again to remember anything about his past, but all he could think of was his assassin's mantra—*Walk to Sutphin Boulevard, catch the Q28* . . . It was driving him nuts.

"So how'd you like your first day in Nevada?" she finally murmured with her back to him.

"Carnival and his wife or whoever that couple was, they didn't look black to you?"

"No, the light was just playing tricks on you," she answered with a yawn.

"How did a national refugee camp turn into this polarized prison yard?"

"During the first year they talked about building a monorail connecting us to Vegas. Hell, we could even make calls off the reservation. Then, while monitoring phone calls, they discovered they had accidentally shipped half a dozen different terrorist cells here, but they didn't know exactly who or where they were. The attorney general's explanation was that the baby *was* the bathwater. He eventually used it as the basis to end our right to communicate with the outside world until they could figure out who the bad guys were."

"How did they get professionals out here? Doctors, lawyers, and so on?"

"A.S.—Alternate Service volunteers."

"Alternate Service?"

"The government allowed conscientious objectors to serve here instead of Vietnam."

A moment later, now much more at ease, Uli yawned. Within ten minutes they were both fast asleep.

The strange nude woman was holding his naked body so tight that he had stopped trembling and was starting to sweat. Although she was beautiful and he sensed that she liked him, she was reluctant to be intimate. Lying in her arms, he was wildly attracted to her. They were watching some strange wild animals in the darkness. He wasn't sure what the creatures were doing, but while watching them, he felt himself slipping and thrusting into this tall beautiful woman.

Awakening, Uli found he had become intimate with Mallory—though she wasn't the woman from his dream. He was grasping her thighs and slamming himself against her while she slept.

"Oh god!" she gasped. Before he could apologize, she reached around, clutching his hips, clawing his ass cheeks, and pulled him into her. Her head turned and their lips locked together. She was plunging her tongue into his mouth. He unclasped her bra as she pulled off his boxers, then he tugged off her panties and they pressed on feverishly.

"No . . . I don't want you to get pregnant," he muttered, remembering that it could be a death sentence in this strange place.

"My tubes were tied long ago."

They spent the next hour screwing. There was something incredible about this woman, even though he couldn't recall ever having sex before. Finally, in unison, they trembled into a shivering orgasm. Uli knew he probably wasn't a virgin, yet he couldn't imagine a more intense and joyful experience. Holding each other tightly, they fell fast asleep.

10/28/80

*W*alk to Sutphin, Uli thought as soon as he woke up, *catch the Q28 to Fulton Street, change to the B17 and take it to*— He couldn't remember where. Opening his eyes, he saw that Mallory had already dressed and left the dank room. After using the communal bathroom for a quick sink-bath, Uli dressed and went down to the shabby lobby. There, surrounded by prematurely old retirees and a bizarre number of amputees, he found Mallory sitting next to two gawking seniors, feverishly working on her endless election form.

"I would've woken you up with a frothy cappuccino," she said without looking up, "but they don't have room service here at the Bad Smell."

"That's Bedmill!" shouted the same bulbous clerk who had checked them in the night before.

Oric and the driver appeared moments later, before either Mallory or Uli could so much as mention last night's indiscretion.

"If you're all heading up to Manhattan, the nearest bus stop is over in south Sunset Park," the driver offered. "It's not too close, so we should probably get started."

The four spent the next twenty minutes hiking alongside the drab semi-occupied, Soviet-style projects of New Utrecht Avenue, which grew increasingly desolate. At one demolished intersection there was evidence of a major gun battle. Uli couldn't tell if it was from an old military training exercise or a recent gang conflict.

Mallory, who was walking ahead of the others, abruptly froze and seemed to stare up at the blue sky. Uli saw, however, that her eyes were closed. She was smelling the air. Without warning, she bolted full force down an empty street.

"Hey!" the driver shouted.

Fearing that she was in some kind of danger, Uli dashed after her. He seized a rusty pipe on the ground in case he needed a weapon. Mallory came to a dead halt roughly two blocks away, before a sandy field that looked like it had once been the parking lot for an old factory of some kind. There, she dropped to her knees as if she were about to be executed. Uli looked up, trying to spot the enemy, but the vast industrial complex was eerily deserted.

"What's going on?" he cried out.

She signaled over to him frantically, instructing him to back away. He approached timidly, nonetheless, trying to follow her sight line. That was when he spotted it, about ten feet away, hopping slowly toward her. It was a small kangaroo, possibly the joey she had lost yesterday. It was unlikely that the baby marsupial could have hopped all the way to this neighborhood without being attacked by dogs or hit by solarcars, yet the animal seemed to know Mallory. Uli watched as it tentatively sniffed her face. She picked it up and set it snugly into her bag.

"What the hell is that?" Uli asked, pointing to the three stone smoke stacks rising from a long, flat building that looked like some kind of plant. A hooded conveyor belt angled out of it in the distance.

"It was modeled after a famous steel mill in Leningrad and used for battlefield simulation."

Moments later they returned to New Utrecht Avenue, where Oric and the bus driver were waiting for them. They resumed walking.

"Is there any connection between these various military training zones?" Uli asked.

"I think they were built as three different scenarios," answered Mallory. "The Japanese architecture is back that way, and the Soviet structures are clumped here in western Brooklyn. Manhattan is largely Germanic."

"What about Bronx and Queens?"

"There were no rivers or swamps back then, so they were both long stretches of land. The Air Force did a lot of bombardment there. Because the area was so heavily blitzed, it had to be redeveloped later on from the ground up. So for the most part, those pricks got all the best houses."

"Where are the newest houses?"

"The newest are here—they were hastily built when we were still coming in—but the the best ones are up in Queens. They were built in the fall of '71."

"How do you know all this stuff?"

"Construction workers were still working when we arrived. We struck up friendships with some of them when we got here, and they told us all about their work."

"How about Staten Island?"

"They have gorgeous houses over there along the shoreline. People believe they were meant for Feedmore administrators and the military. Proof that they had intended to stay and oversee Rescue City."

"And when were those built?"

"That's the funny thing. The workmen claimed they were built during the first wave of construction in '71, but after the flooding, when the water went back down and some of the houses collapsed, we found newspapers behind the walls and in the floorboards that were dated from as early as 1968."

"Why is that funny?"

"Manhattan was hit in 1970—why would they build housing *before* the bombing?"

"Maybe they needed an administration center back then."

"I suppose."

"So when the administrators and military pulled out, who moved in?"

"Pigger officials mainly, but that didn't last too long. When the sewer got blocked and the area flooded, the homes became uninhabitable, even after it drained. The rest of the borough is strictly Third World. I stayed down there for a while after Shub came to power . . ."

The first sign of Sunset Park was a food stand where for a sixteenth-stamp the driver bought a piece of deep-fried dough covered in powdered sugar—a donut without a hole. Although Oric and the others watched him eat, no one else ordered anything.

After another block they passed a strip mall of small businesses: a body-art parlor called Tattoo You; a barber shop, Unkindest Kuts; a homemade brewery, Fine Fermentations; and a diner called Hamburgeriffic. Lastly, there was a Chinese takeout place, operated by two scantily clad Asian women, entitled Food Ho's.

"They got awful versions of every major cuisine here," Mallory told Uli.

If there was a sauce covering their beefy bones, Uli thought, it'd be chocolaty, curried, MSG'd, chilied, oreganoed, all under a milky base. Everyone seemed a bit ethnically homogenized. All the blacks he'd seen were fairly light-skinned. Whites looked tanned. Asian eyes appeared relatively oval. If any details established clear heritage, it was the styles of dress and the haircuts, which varied wildly from person to person. Caesars, crew cuts, dreadlocks, ricebowls, as well as age-old mullets all defined individual cultures more clearly than skin tone.

Throughout this area Uli spotted betting parlors. In addition to the Council-operated OTDs—off-track dog races—Uli saw slot machine and blackjack parlors, not to mention scratch-and-match tickets for sale everywhere.

"This place has a serious gambling problem," Uli observed.

"The five mob families that ran things in the old city had wiseguys who came here and divided up everything," the driver imparted as they marched westward.

"Did you lose your arm in Vietnam?" Uli asked. The two of them were walking ahead of Mallory and Oric.

"Why, you find one there?" the driver countered. When Uli didn't laugh, he said, "About eight years ago I got into an alley fight and shanked some dude."

"Must've been a heck of a fight," Uli muttered.

The bus driver led the tired group to an establishment with a sign that read, SIXTEENTH-STAMP STORE. The driver and Oric entered.

Next door was the Sunset Park Crapper headquarters. Mallory dashed inside. Explaining her vital mission and dire situation, she was able to appropriate ten stamps for official business. Then she entered the general store and surveyed the largely addictive impulse items lining the shelves. Candy, mentholated cigarettes, and various liquors—all of which fit into sample-sized wrappers or narrow containers so they could be sold for a sixteenth-stamp apiece. Mallory purchased fruit-named soft drinks for everybody.

As Uli sipped his bright pink "strawberry" beverage out front, a beat-up minivan screeched to a halt and the driver hastily tossed out a small bundle of the *Daily Posted New York Times*.

Uli surveyed the headlines: *Big Antiwar Rally Today*. A smaller article announced, *Antiwar Folksinger Fillip Ocks Hangs Self in Rockaway, CIA Involvement Strongly Suspected*.

Uli read the latest listing of crimes and their terrorist links. Like in the issue he had read on the bus, they were all supplied by nameless sources. A truck bomb had blown up in Rego Park, killing eighteen. Members of the Shining Path were suspected. Six middle-aged women from Howard Beach—who had somehow pissed off members of an extremist cyclist group, the August 30th MassCritters—had been raped and strangled. The Symbionese Liberation Army was suspected of shooting and killing a dozen people in Far Rockaway. According to the paper, the Black Liberation Army had engineered a string of jewelry heists in Staten Island. The list went on.

The single detail that the *Times* failed to mention, Uli noticed, was how these crimes—particularly the violent ones—served each of the revolutionary organizations' higher ideals. How could raping middle-aged women from Howard Beach help the cause of the notorious August 30th MassCritters? What did the B.L.A. do with cheap bracelets, paste-gem amulets, and imitation diamond tiaras to further its cause of racial equality?

Inexplicably—since there was no official communication between the residents of Rescue City and the rest of the world—the newspaper also included a lively page of national and international news. One misspelled headline screamed, *Reagan Orders Secret Bombing of Louse and Terroran!* A second article proclaimed, *Religious Cult in Go'on'ya Commits Mass Sewercide.*

Uli turned to the sports/politics page:

WEEKLY CITYWIDE ELECTION RESULTS

MANHATTAN:
> Total Pigger districts: 1
> Total Crappers districts: 9
> No change from last election

STATEN ISLAND:
> Total Pigger districts: 0
> Total Crapper districts: 0
> Total Independent districts (Verdant League): 10
> No change from last election

THE BRONX:
    Total Pigger districts: 9
    Total Crapper districts: 1
    No change from last election

BROOKLYN:
    Greenpoint (Pigger) invaded
    2,124 Crappers, 2,122 Piggers
    Outcome: Crapper
    Councilman Guido Basilicata (P) removed
    Councilman Antonia Basilicata (C) reelected
    Total Pigger districts: 2
    Total Crapper districts: 18
    One change from last election

QUEENS:
    Far Rockaway (Pigger) invaded
    2,438 Crappers, 2,435 Piggers
    Outcome: Crapper
    Councilman Ted Kostiyan (P) removed
    Councilwoman Carmen D. Sapio (C) reelected

    Howard Beach (Pigger) invaded
    1,335 Crappers, 1,332 Piggers
    Outcome: Crapper
    Councilman Newton Underwood* (P) removed
    Councilman Dwight Valone (C) elected
    Total Pigger districts: 16
    Total Crapper districts: 4
    Two changes from last election
    *Former President of the City Council

The Crappers had won in both Howard Beach and Far Rockaway by only three votes. And in Greenpoint, they had beaten the Piggers by two votes. All were paper-thin victories. Yet the number of people killed in those three districts nearly mimicked the figures that Oric had been nervously barking out during the previous day's trip through Brooklyn.

The newspaper report set Uli's thoughts into a paranoid tailspin: If that cross-shaped object buried in the back of Oric's shaggy-haired skull was harnessing the man's psychic abilities so he could predict the slim margins of Pigger victories, then the late Jim Carnival—the overzealous Crapper—could travel into the designated neighborhoods and "correct" the Pigger constituencies, disguising the casualties as typical crimes, thus altering the outcome of the local elections.

And if Oric did have special abilities, this potentially answered the question of why the Flatlands pursuer had been coming after them.

Uli reentered the sixteenth-stamp store and discreetly guided Oric out to the street, then delicately asked, "What exactly does *correction* mean?"

Oric looked at Uli strangely. Without warning, the man bent over and grabbed Uli around the waist and playfully pulled him down.

"What are you doing, Oric?" Uli said, shoving him away. "Stop it!"

"Don't worry, I won't let go," Oric replied.

"Listen to me," Uli tried to regain the challenged man's attention, "what does *correction* mean?"

Oric paused a moment, then pointed his chubby index finger at Uli and said, "*Bam!*"

"What's going on here?" Mallory asked as she came out of the store, seeing the incompetent man shooting off an imaginary pistol. While she fed the baby kangaroo a succession of celery stalks she had just purchased, Uli filled her in on his little theory.

Taking a deep breath, she said, "The majority of this city is registered as Crappers, yet through strategic invasions and pork-barrel patronage, the Piggies under Shub have managed to stay in charge for the past decade."

Uli considered this, then asked, "Why are you sharing this with me?"

"Well, since you openly stated you were programmed to kill Dropt, I can't accuse you of guile. In fact, after risking your life to cover for me with Chain, and having monitored your actions over the past twenty-four hours, I think I can trust you."

"Trust me with what?"

"I have to get *back* to Queens to turn in this Affidavit of Electoral Inventories by the 3 o'clock deadline, so that Dropt will have a shot at getting a fair election next week." She held up her fat book. "This theory about Oric kind of changes things. I need you to bring him to the Manhattan Crapper headquarters in the Lower East Side pronto."

"You want me to bring him to the guy who I was programmed to kill?" Uli said, amazed.

"You won't be going anywhere near Dropt. You'll just bring Oric to the heavily guarded building and then leave. And only because I have no one else to turn to. This bus fiasco has been a major setback. I've been trying not to show it, but I'm starting to really freak out about the election. I can give you some stamps to cover your expenses and put a little cash in your pocket."

"Sorry, but I can't abide by the notion of murder to win an election."

"If that Carnival character was actually killing people, I guarantee it wasn't sanctioned by us. We're the party that wants people to make up their own minds. If we know we might lose by a slim margin, we can reallocate our funds, campaign harder in specific districts, and try to convince the wobbly margins to vote."

"This is all way too—"

"There's something else," she added, lowering her voice

to a whisper. "What I'm going to tell you is highly classified: We have reason to suspect that the Piggers have had their own election psychic for years. He's just a kid, supposedly the only person actually born in this hellhole."

"Are you lying to me?"

"A high-ranking Pigger who defected told us about him. They call him Karove. He's one of the reasons they've been able to hold power for years. Study the election results over the past decade and you'll see that the Piggers pulled off nearly eighty-five percent of the the paper-thin victories. We can't locate Karove, but we're pretty sure he exists. Maybe with Oric we can balance the scales."

Uli let out a long sigh. "So how exactly do I get to the Manhattan Crapper headquarters?"

"I'll go with you to Fulton Street and put you on a bus to the Lower East Side."

"What do you think of that?" Uli called over to Oric. "Would Mallory lie to us?"

"Mallor— Mallor— Mallor—" The challenged man seemed to be having difficulty pronouncing her name. Finally he just blurted out, "Mayory!"

"I seem to be fated to go there," Uli conceded. First Underwood had tried to program him to assassinate the rival candidate there, then Jim Carnival had told him it was where he could get the tracking device extracted from his head.

11:12 a.m.

When the group finally reached the Sunset Park bus stop, the dispatcher there immediately reassigned their one-armed driver to a southbound route. The others waited at the end of a long line for the northbound vehicle. Nearly an hour later, when the bus finally pulled up, it was already packed. Mallory let the baby marsupial stretch its legs and relieve itself one last time before slipping it back into her shoulder bag. Then she squeezed on board and they started north.

The new bus chugged up Fort Hamilton Parkway toward Flatbush Avenue, and here the street became pure asphalt—apparently the local assemblage of sand refunders had swept the street down earlier. When the bus made a stop on 39th Street, a cluster of seats opened up in the rear.

Uli hastily grabbed a seat next to a window, pulling Oric with him. Mallory sat across from them. The bus moved through bumper-to-bumper traffic until they came to a standstill alongside the western edge of the Greenwood Cemetery. All got an up-close view of some closed-coffin funeral in progress.

"What can I say about the passing of my own brother?" a bearded minister asked a crowd of gray ponytailed men and women. "From a divine point of view, we live in a devil's playground where each person's greatest and darkest temptation is truly tested. And while we live, only God can see through our meager disguises." The minister looked up and over the crowd. His gaze suddenly locked onto Uli through the bus window. "But lo! From where I presently stand, I too can see the shame and pain that a single man can inflict upon an entire nation! And that man is . . . you lee!"

"What's that, padre?" someone yelled out from the crowd.

"He's the reason we're all here!" The minister began pointing at Uli, and called out some name that Uli didn't catch.

"Which one?" he heard someone in the crowd shriek.

"That one sitting in the back of the bus!"

The mourners turned, almost as one, and stared up at him, then started racing over to the bus. Uli slid his window shut, but their collective hands, arms, and torsos began rocking the vehicle as though it were hit by a wave.

The bus was frozen in traffic, so the many wrinkled and arthritic fingers working together were able to pop out the emergency back window. Uli tried to rise to his feet but Oric was squeezed up next to him, making a quick retreat difficult. All at once, a dozen hands and arms thrust in and grabbed him. He punched at them, furiously trying to defend himself, but it was too much. In another moment, overpowered, he was being yanked out headfirst, through the aluminum window frame. Before being fully extracted from the vehicle, however, something caught his ankles. Horizontally, still in the air, he exchanged punches with the elderly mob below. Oric was holding onto him, anchoring himself between Uli's legs, braced up against the bus seat. Crackling voices screamed at him:

"You monstrous son of a bitch!"

"Die in hell, you scumbag!"

Uli felt his shirt and jacket pulled from his chest, and his body flopped down against the outside of the bus just above the wheel.

"Get that cocksucker!"

While one man was whacking his cane furiously at Uli's head, pruned hands scratched at his face and tore his clothes. Just as an elderly lady was about to thrust the pointy end of a parasol into his face, someone grabbed its handle and knocked the woman down. A vaguely familiar blond man was fighting to defend Uli. The guy kicked the knee out from under another old woman clawing at Uli's exposed chest. Her fingernails felt like ten little fishing hooks tearing down his flesh. Once released, Uli tried to wiggle backwards.

"What the fuck are you doing here?" the blond man screamed at him.

"I don't know!" Uli shouted back. "Who am I?"

Someone clipped Uli along the side of his skull with a small bat. The blond man grabbed the improvised weapon and yanked it away before the swinger could take a second shot. With all his might, the stranger shoved Uli upwards, back into the bus.

"Get that yellow-haired fucker!" someone yelled.

A large bald man carrying a machete came running up toward Uli's protector just as the traffic jam finally opened up and the bus started moving. The blond man jumped up onto the side of the bus, folding his arm precariously inside the windowsill. Uli tried to pull him up, but he was barely inside the bus himself.

The bald man led the chase along the sidewalk, with a group of surprisingly agile seniors racing along the avenue.

"I can't hold on, my arm is slipping!" the blond man gasped.

"Who am I?"

"Huey!" the guy screamed in pain. "Meet me at Rockefeller Center."

"I'll get off *now!*" Uli shouted.

"No, just meet me at Rockefeller Center at 3!"

The blond man pushed away from the bus to avoid falling under its wheels and rolled onto the ground. In another moment, the bus zoomed on and Oric and Mallory pulled Uli all the way back inside. Everyone sitting around him stared in shock.

"What the hell did you do?" Mallory asked, cradling her kangaroo in her bag.

"Haven't the foggiest," he replied, trembling. He modestly folded his arms over his aching and exposed chest, which was red with scratches and welts.

Some guy pulled an old shirt from a laundry bag and said, "I was going to toss this anyways."

"Thanks," Uli said, taking the wrinkled garment and pulling it on over his clawed torso. It read, *Rescue Me from My Rescuers.*

Upon finally calming down, Uli thanked Mallory for her concern and Oric for saving him. Slowly the other passengers stopped staring. His paranoia still engaged, however, he decided not to say anything about the strangely familiar blond man. Mallory took a seat behind him and resumed working on her never-ending form. Uli sensed that the best chance of getting to the bottom of his situation was by going to Rockefeller Center at 3 o'clock and meeting with the blond guy.

As the bus inched uphill, Uli noticed the green dome of a narrow tower peeking out in the distance. Though the building couldn't have been much taller than ten floors, with its lime-covered cap and distinct red clock face it was the tallest building he had seen since arriving.

"What's that?" he asked Mallory, pointing to it. He was beginning to vaguely recognize some of these landmarks.

"The Williamsburgh Savings Bank," she muttered back.

"They have banks here?"

"No, it's actually the municipal building that houses the criminal justice system," Mallory replied. "It's where Shub works."

"Is Rockefeller Center the same place here that it is in old New York?"

"Yeah, midtown Manhattan. Why?"

He shrugged and stared off dismally, so she didn't press. Soon the bus merged into a four-lane boulevard. Uli spotted a street sign that said, *Flatbush Avenue*, and under it, *Jackie Wilson Way*.

"Wasn't Jackie Wilson the first black baseball player?"

"That was Jackie Robinson," Mallory explained without looking up. "He was a pop singer, but this is a different Jackie Wilson."

Uli closed his eyes and tried to rest.

"Last stop!" the driver shouted after another half hour, flapping open the front door. As people tumbled out, Mallory grabbed Oric's hand. She quickly led them to a line of people at a connecting stop a block away. A sign said, *B17 Bus to Lower Manhattan & Staten Island*.

"My bus is leaving in just a few minutes or I'd wait

with you. Yours is leaving in twenty minutes," Mallory said, gently stroking the short snout of the joey peeking out of her bag. Handing Uli five stamps, she added, "Buy Oric some food and take him to the bathroom before boarding. Traffic in Manhattan is unbelievably slow."

"Do they know we're coming?"

"I'll call from Queens. Just ask for Dr. Adele and tell him I sent you. He'll take care of Oric." Glancing at her wristwatch, Mallory assured him she would be there as soon as she submitted the updated Affidavit of Electoral Inventories to the Election Commission in Astoria, Queens and paid a quick visit to her paralyzed husband up in a Harlem hospice. Uli wished her a safe trip. She nodded back tiredly. It was almost as if the prior night of intimacy had never occurred.

1:34 p.m.

"Very hungered," said Oric soulfully, as they roamed through the chaotic Fulton Street Mall near Jackie Wilson Way.

Having survived the incident at Green-wood Cemetery, Uli now appreciated why Mallory carried a disguise. From among the racks of cheap garments and bins of sundry merchandise, Uli purchased a new shirt, a short brim hat, and sunglasses. Whoever he or Huey was, some people obviously knew and despised him.

Spotting a noisy crowd across the street mall, Uli and Oric headed over to see what all the hubbub was about. The gathering was pressed up against a rope held by two brawny security workers. Uli made out an oddly thin young woman with distinctive eyebrows, who was screaming, "Come shake hands with the protector of freedom and godliness—Horace Shub!"

Another security guard placed a microphone stand in the middle of the clearing. A moment later, a small simian-faced man with abnormally large hands walked up and tapped the mic to make sure it was on. It was indeed Shub, the Pigger mayor.

"My opponent, Dropt, remains immobile on dynamically fluid issues," the man said in a tinny meter. "He doesn't waver when you need the wavering." Shub made a flapping motion. "He's intractable in a business that requires a lot of tractoring!" The bugle-eared mayor issued a series of tight little gasps that Uli realized was self-satisfied laughter. Shub then started working the rope line, shaking the grimy bouquet of outstretched hands.

The extent of Shub's animal magnetism was fully evident to Uli when he saw Oric suddenly break loose and dash toward the mayor, knocking down others.

"Oric, no!" Uli shouted. "Wait! No!"

"Terrorist with a bomb!" someone screamed, and all hell broke loose. Within seconds everyone had retreated in panic. Shub was huddled off to his armored car and a phalanx of beefy security guards pushed forward, slamming Oric to the pavement.

"No! Please be careful, he's got something coming out of his skull," Uli called out. Oric's curly hair obscured the strange metallic cross.

The thin young woman rushed over and watched as the men pinned Oric's chubby arms up against his fat back, cuffing his wrists together.

"This is what happens to those who try to interfere with God's plan!" the woman announced victoriously. "Take him away, boys!"

"No! Please!" Uli appealed to her. "He didn't mean anything. He's got the mind of a child."

A security guard took Uli into custody, checking his fingerprints and asking exactly how he knew the would-be assassin. Two other bodyguards frisked Oric, pulling his pants down and shirt up, while a third inspected his headcross. Another fingerprinted him to verify his identity. Discovering that Oric was a registered Crapper, they rushed him into a black van to interrogate him about his gang loyalties and possible terrorist ties.

After an hour of Oric continuously weeping and finally wetting himself, they realized Uli wasn't kidding and released the mentally deficient man to his custody.

"We can still have you arrested for not controlling him," the girl threatened Uli, who noticed fresh bruises along Oric's face and neck. *REELECT SHUB!* announced a brochure now protruding from Oric's back pocket. The tagline read, *A Vote on Earth Is a Win in Heaven.*

Once they were alone, Uli apologized to Oric and led him back toward a line of food carts on Jackie Wilson Way.

"So hungered," Oric whimpered.

Some meat on a skewer called *God Be Ways* seemed to be as predominant as hot dogs in Rescue City. A maimed vendor was standing before his homemade cart with a crude sign, *ONE-ARMED BANDIT*, alongside a picture of a slot machine with a jackpot of hot shish kebabs. Inspecting the charred chunks of fat and muscle speared on a wooden stick, Uli asked exactly what it was.

"*Be Ways* means *backwards*, so the question you want to ask is what's *God* spelled backwards." The vendor held up one of the barbecued meat skewers. Uli thanked him and kept walking.

The various other deep-fried objects crammed into pita pockets seemed better options than man's best friend. Still, there were few fresh fruits or vegetables on offer. Uli told Oric to get what he liked most, and the oval man waddled hastily toward the corn dog cart. Uli bought four dogs on sticks and selected two baked yams with butter instead of some sugary dessert. The vendor bagged it all and handed it to him.

As they crossed the street to return to the bus stop, they passed an older woman with a basket of bananas on her head.

"I'll take some of those, if you're selling," Uli said.

"An eighth of a stamp for three," she replied, as he selected the fruit. When he handed her the eighth-stamp, she reached up and snatched the sunglasses right off his face. "Oh shit! It *is* you!" She stumbled backwards as though she were looking at a ghost.

"Tell me," he appealed, grabbing her, "who am I?"

"Let go," her voice became soft. Uli could see that she was so terrified that her diaphragm wouldn't contract. People started looking over, so Uli grabbed Oric and vanished into the crowd.

Uli and Oric cautiously returned to the B17 bus stop, where Uli noticed an unusual blond woman across the street checking him out. In addition to a raccoon-like application of eyeliner and stiff golden hair, she wore a black miniskirt.

He casually peeled a banana as she walked over and asked if he was who she was looking for.

"Sure," Uli replied. She seemed too fashionable to be a prostitute.

"I'm Dianne Colder." She shook his hand with a firm grip. "I have been waiting for you since yesterday. That's when Underwood said you'd be here."

"I got stuck in Sunset Park," he said. Oric immediately started getting fidgety, so Uli added, "Dianne, this is my pal—"

"Kid!" Oric shouted out before Uli could utter his name.

"So, I heard you tried taking out the mayor, Kid," she replied with a grin.

"—nap," Oric blurted.

"He wants to take a nap," Uli added weakly.

"What's that thing sticking out of the back of his skull?" Oric's hair was matted down with sweat, so the strange object protruded like a tiny TV antenna.

"It's a skull plate," Uli replied. "He was wounded in Nam."

"That explains a lot." She sniffed at him and wrinkled her nose.

"Who exactly are you?" Uli inquired.

"I'm a lobbyist for the Feedmore Corporation," she said, handing him a click pen with some sort of corporate logo on it. "I come to Rescue City about once every six months to make sure everything is as it should be. That way, when I go to Washington, I can tell them all is well."

She knows the way out of here, Uli thought.

"So hungered," Oric said again. Uli opened the bag of food and handed him a greasy corn dog. Oric gobbled it down while staring at Dianne like a wild animal. When Uli took one out for himself, Dianne made a disgusted expression and asked, "You're not really going to eat that, are you?"

"Manhattan—*boom!*" Oric shouted through his mouthful of corn dog.

"What?" Dianne asked, startled.

"Big boom bang!"

"Hmm . . . I'll be right back," she said, then abruptly dashed down the block. The Manhattan-bound bus immediately pulled up and opened its flapped door. It took a few minutes for everyone to board. Uli and Oric grabbed seats at the very rear. Others behind them crowded into the aisles. To Uli's relief, the driver closed the door and they began rolling.

In a few minutes the bus was crawling over a causeway supported by two narrow stone towers. Those structures, along with the faux span webbing overhead, were a sad homage to the original Brooklyn Bridge.

With his first real view of multiple boroughs, Uli could see how they were graded and contoured. Brooklyn and Queens seemed to be built on one level; Manhattan was slightly lower, allowing for water to spill around it; and Staten Island was the lowest. The water level was oddly higher around Staten Island than Brooklyn. A lengthy wall of what appeared to be slick brown stones was constructed around the lower lip of Manhattan.

A blond head suddenly emerged through the wall of standees. Uli's heart sank as Dianne Colder smiled at him and held up a brown paper bag.

"This is the best chow you're going to find floating in this toilet bowl," she said as she approached. "I felt bad watching you eat those corn dogs."

He tried hiding his dismay. "What exactly is it?"

"A cactus burrito. I only got one since Pogo obviously relishes the shit they serve here."

The bus moved at a snail's pace over the low bridge and Dianne launched into some weird tangent: "Einstein's Theory of Relativity, you can prove—light bends, zing! Ha ha! But Darwin's Theory of Evolution is a whole nother story! What are you gonna do? Wait around till the next monkey talks, right?"

Oric nodded nervously in agreement. To pacify him, Uli handed over the rest of the corn dogs and opened the wax paper containing the cactus burrito. The tortilla shell stuffed with local vegetables and topped with a spicy chipolte sauce was heavenly.

"Remember when the Crappers started a school in the Village? They didn't teach Johnny reading and writing, you know why? Cause they'd teach him *fisting*." She shoved her clawlike hand in Oric's face. "A word every bit as ugly as it sounds, ha!"

Uli tasted something acrid. Dipping his fingers into the sauce and holding it up to the light, he detected a powdery substance and felt a wave of fatigue. She had slipped some kind of narcotic into the food.

"Blist bags!" Oric shouted furiously through the food in his mouth.

"Big breasts?" Dianne asked, modestly covering her own flat chest.

"Big blast! Big blast!"

Dianne turned to face Oric. Though Uli was on the verge of passing out, he tossed the remainder of his burrito out the bus window.

Oric's fingers digging into his side awakened Uli to the fact that they were slowly descending off the bad imitation of the Brooklyn Bridge. Rather than hooking into City Hall like the original bridge, this new one tilted onto 14th Street. After several minutes, the bus pulled up at the northeast corner of Second Avenue. The driver stood up and called to the back of the bus: "We ain't going one more stop till lil' Miss Miniskirt pays her damn fare. I couldn't pull over on the bridge, lady, but I ain't moving another inch till you pay up just like everyone else."

"Oh damn," Dianne said, "I got on so quickly I forgot." She rose and angled her way through the crowd to the front of the bus.

"Come on," Uli said, and punched open the rear emergency window. Uli helped his heavy companion down to the pavement. Before Uli could join him, Oric waddled toward a large pastry shop with a sign that said, *Veniero's*. The bus turned south on Second Avenue as Uli hit the ground.

Checking a wall clock through the shop window as he caught up to Oric, he saw it was already 2:00. Too late to drop off Oric first.

"Blig bast!" Oric said nervously.

"We're getting as far away from that scary lady as we can," Uli explained.

"Blast, big boom!" Oric repeated as they walked west.

"Where blast?"

"I'll never know."

"Why won't you know?"

"You know, you're me." He touched Uli's forehead.

Still concerned that they were being pursued, Uli took the challenged man's hand and hastily led him westward along 14th Street. They joined a stream of young hippie types heading in the same direction. A growing crowd was visible several blocks down.

Onion Square, declared a psychedelic hand-painted sign at the corner of Fourth Avenue. Just as Mallory had said, all the buildings in the area had a distinctly European flavor. A small German restaurant called Luchow's was the only establishment here that triggered a distant memory from old New York.

The crowd of longhaired kids was centered around a large makeshift wooden stage in the middle of a barren field—Onion Square. Old-fashioned bullhorn speakers were blasting a speech: ". . . If these bastards aren't going to end this war, we've got to end it for them!"

All cheered.

Glancing up at the stage, Uli saw a slim Mediterranean man with a springy Afro wearing an American flag on his shirt.

"Remember, it takes two eyes to spell FBI and CIA." He spoke with a slight lisp. "And they're always watching!" All cheered once again.

"Do you know where Rockefeller Center is?" Uli asked some post-adolescent with peach fuzz and pimples standing next to him.

"Up that way," the guy replied, throwing his arm northward.

"Who's that speaking?"

"Abbie Hoffman."

"What's he talking about?"

"The *war*," the kid answered.

"What war?"

"Vietnam!" the fuzzy-faced youth replied, then walked away in disgust. "It's an antiwar rally."

Uli had this strange feeling that he had already served in Vietnam. Something told him that he was in favor of the war, but he had no clue as to why.

Next, an older, wild-bearded man with black-framed glasses, a top hat, and a waistcoat took the stage. He began reciting rhymes: "Communism's / shooting jism / on top'a Asia / We'll invade ya / Napalm bomb / And all is calm / It's a mock, you see / our Democracy . . ."

"Who's that?" Uli asked another unsuspecting youth whose neck was ringed with turquoise beads.

"Ginsberg!" the youth shot back, not wanting to miss a single word of the rant.

"Beware / she's there!" Oric pointed at a thick shag of blond hair on the western edge of the crowded square.

A beat-up city bus was turning onto Park Avenue through the tangle of longhaired war protesters. Uli impulsively grabbed Oric's hand, raced across the square, and flagged it down. The driver pulled past them to the curb and opened the doors.

"You go by Rockefeller Center?"

"*Rock & Filler* Center," the driver corrected as Uli paid their fares.

"Rock and Filler?" Uli asked. "Sorry, I just got to Rescue City so I don't know my way around."

"By Crapper decree, all the names in Manhattan and Brooklyn have been corrupted."

"Why?"

"To remind us that this is not the place they want us to think it is. It's *word protest*." That explained Onion Square.

"How about in Queens and the Bronx?" Uli asked.

"The Piggers are proud to be here, so they've kept most of the original names intact in their areas."

As the bus sped up Park Avenue, Uli and Oric sat down behind the driver, who took the opportunity to keep playing tour guide.

"Many of the buildings you see around here have been rebuilt two, even three different times. The Air Force held multiple bombing exercises here. The Army Corp of Engineers would repair buildings, like restacking bowling pins, then the Air Force would knock them down again. They were initially modeled after Gropius's Weissenhof houses. This gray building coming up to your left was bombed and rebuilt at least four times; it's based on a famous building designed by the Taut Brothers."

Reaching 51st Street, the bus made a left and came to a halt on a low-rent stretch of Fifth Avenue, before a small gothic European church with a missing spire. A smattering of worshipers were entering it.

"This is the stop for Rock & Filler," the driver said.

Uli and Oric got off along with a handful of others. Uli began heading down toward Rock & Filler Center, but Oric dashed into the church. Uli raced after him.

Inside, he was surprised to find that the house of worship was actually a hollowed-out brownstone. Its upper floorboards had been removed, revealing only unmilled crossbeams and a high, peeling ceiling. Rows of benches faced forward to a large fold-out picnic table. Behind it was a big wooden cross. Clean holes at the ends of the tall crucifix suggested that the Jesus had been set free.

Oric was staring at some lady photographing a colorful mural on a large wall that looked like a little girl riding a dog. On a tray in front of the image was a coffee mug that said, DONAT, behind which was a row of unlit, half-melted votive candles. Off to the side of the dog-riding girl were sketches of three homeless men, and above them, a yellow starfish. When Uli stepped back, the tableau pieces all locked together.

"Oh, it's the manger scene," he declared. The little girl was actually a boy, and the dog was a donkey. "That's God," he explained to Oric.

"Huh?"

"That's who your mom and dad are with," he elaborated.

"In there?" Oric said, looking at the unevenly plastered wall.

"No, they're *with* the kid in the painting—the baby Jesus." Uli reached into his pocket and took out a sixteenth-stamp. He instructed Oric to light a candle for his murdered parents, then asked him to stay put. "I'll be right back."

"I wait for my brother." Oric pointed to the wall.

Uli asked someone outside where Rock & Filler Center was. He was pointed to a traffic jam of cars and people squeezing around an empty mall between two large buildings. Instead of Saks Fifth Avenue, Uli noticed a six-column archway across the street. Approaching the plaque affixed to it, he found himself standing before a quarter-scale replica of the Brandenburg Gate.

He moved tentatively toward Rock & Filler Center, looking around for the blond stranger from the cemetery. At 50th Street, he spotted a familiar figure down by 49th, but it wasn't the blond guy. His body clenched up as he realized it was the Flatlands pursuer, the one who resembled Oric. The man's clothing was singed and wrinkled.

No sooner had Uli turned away, when he heard, "Hey! Wait a sec—"

A loud explosion knocked Uli and a dozen others backwards to the ground. As he rose to his feet several moments later, he saw a large plume of black smoke suspended in the air before him. It appeared that the goateed pursuer, along with a cluster of others, had been blown to smithereens.

"Fuck a duck!" one of the seniors behind him shouted.

Once the ringing in his ears had subsided, Uli limped through the smoke to the edge of a small crater. Smoldering body parts from at least a dozen victims were strewn about the twisted frame of a destroyed minitruck. Gasping for breath, he heard others screaming in shock, and realized that he must've seen a lot of this kind of thing, since his heart hadn't so much as skipped a beat.

With the Flatlands pursuer dead, Uli resumed his search for the blond stranger. Rock & Filler Center had two paved walkways on either side of a raised stone garden that ended at a drop-off. Walking to the edge, still gasping for breath, Uli found himself standing on the precipice of a large empty ditch. It was roughly thirty feet deep by thirty feet wide, with a muddy puddle at the bottom. At the far side of the hole, a man was taking a piss on a pile of white stones.

"What the hell happened over there?" the urinator called out to him.

"A truck bomb."

"Pigger faggots!"

"Yeah," Uli replied tiredly. Behind the urinator was a narrow four-story office building that looked nothing like the surrounding structures.

"Do you know what that building is?" Uli asked.

"Yeah. Number 30."

As Uli walked over, he saw that the front of the building looked like it had been chiseled down. Inside the lobby, two men in dark-blue blazers were checking people's IDs and whatever bags they carried. A sign read, *Manhattan Municipal Government Offices*—hence the bomb blast?

Uli headed back to Fifth Avenue where arriving EMS workers triaged the injured as a growing crowd watched. Uli wondered if perhaps the goateed man had killed his nameless blond friend before being blown up. *How else would the Flatlander know I'm here?* he pondered. *I should've gotten off the bus after that cemetery in Brooklyn.* When the first gangcops finally arrived and started rounding up witnesses, Uli decided to leave before he could be detained.

He found Oric back at the church, rubbing the wall frantically, while other worshipers stared at him.

"What are you doing?" Uli asked, trying to pull him away.

"I saw him! He's with them."

"Who is?"

"My brother, but he said . . . he said they ain't mine, so . . ." Oric looked confused and then distressed.

"I think maybe you had a bad dream."

"No dreams. My brother, he just came here, see, and . . . he said you take me to him."

Uli gently led Oric outside the church and across the street. As Oric continued with his nonsense, more emergency vehicles came to take care of the wounded. Uli led him to the bus stop at the corner of 51st. Glancing eastward, he could see a row of towers across the slim waterway separating Manhattan from Queens. There was something odd about them. It was as though a Hollywood producer had shot a big-budget film there and left this elaborate set behind.

"What exactly are those?" Uli asked a tall man wearing a pointy bamboo hat who was also waiting for the bus.

"Just backdrops," the guy replied. "They're nicer than the ones across from Wall Street."

A southbound bus eventually pulled up. With his mission to meet the blond man a failure, Uli's next move was to drop Oric off at the Crapper headquarters.

Uli paid their fares and watched as a balding gangcop waved all traffic past the explosion site. Oric started whimpering again, and then murmured, "See you soon."

The buildings down Fifth Avenue, though occasionally singed and almost all run down, looked occupied. Small-business owners had loaded piles of merchandise onto the cramped sidewalks, forcing pedestrians into the street.

Growing impatient, the driver angled the bus along the far right side of the street. Straddling one tire on the edge of the curb and the other in the gutter, she drove down a new lane of her own creation.

At 42nd Street, Uli saw a big sandy mound where he had expected the stately New York Public Library. It seemed that not all of the city's landmarks, or their German-inspired replicas, had made it into the final imitative plans.

Passing 34th Street, Uli spotted a strange building soaring up six majestic flights with a sign that read, *Vampire Stake*

Building. It didn't have swastikas emblazoned on it like some of the other midtown buildings, but was instead covered with leering gargoyles and hieroglyphics that suggested powers of the occult. A string of sightseers cued up at the front door.

At 23rd Street, when a group of people finally got off, Oric and Uli grabbed a pair of seats across from a cute girl with curly hair and glasses. She smiled, revealing a mouthful of black teeth.

Uli greeted her with a smile of his own. "Hi, I just arrived yesterday from old New York and I'm totally lost."

"I'm jealous," the woman replied with a chuckle. "Unlike everyone else here, I never really lived in New York. My name's Kennesy. You guys go to the rally earlier today?"

"Yeah," Uli said. "How bout you?"

"Yeah. Now I'm heading down to CoBs&GoBs for a benefit show." She spoke with a slight Southern twang.

"What's that?"

"A musical palace. I'm a deejay for a rock show on the local radio station."

"Where exactly are you from?" Uli asked.

"Mississippi."

"How'd you wind up here?"

"When I was a kid, we lost our place to Hurricane Camille and were offered temporary asylum in New York. No sooner did we arrive than the attack happened and we were offered refuge out here."

"So which gang are you with?"

"That's a rather indiscreet question," Kennesy replied coyly, "but I'm still a Crapper. At least until they fragment into a half a dozen other parties."

"Why do you say that?"

"Go to the next Crapper convention and see for yourself."

"What would I see?"

"Well, recently they broadcasted the Pigger convention

in Queens. It was like watching a high mass. Everyone talks softly, one at a time, and they all applaud politely. But the Crapper convention, wow! They held it at the Coliseum on Columbus Circle last year. I did a radio show from there, and I swear, I couldn't hear myself think. Five thousand screaming voices. Fistfights in the aisles."

"Amazing that they've been able to hold two boroughs together."

"Yeah, but in the last month they've lost three Brooklyn neighborhoods and one in Manhattan," she said. "Inwood just elected its first Pigger Councilperson, Julie Rudian. And it was done by internal dissent. All the Crappers just voted for her."

"Sounds pretty messed up."

"That's the wave of the future, and the Crappers don't get it," she said. "It won't be gang warfare that'll decide the future of this place, it'll be the *sentiment* of the people. Folks in Manhattan are growing more and more Piggish."

"Why do you think that is?"

"Pure-ile Plurality—they're this quasi-evangelical out-reach organization." Uli thought he remembered seeing their headquarters in southern Queens. "A lot of Piggers work for them. They're always hiring people. You know that expression, *If you win their hearts and minds* . . . Well, P.P.'s food trucks won the stomachs of Inwood, then they went down to Harlem. Now they're going all the way to the East Village. They start with food, then it's clothes and basic medical treatment. Soon it'll be free movies in the park."

"So is P.P. an arm of the Piggers?"

"Technically no. If any evidence is found showing they are swayed by any one gang, they could lose their government funding—"

"Would you mind keeping your brilliant insights to yourself?" interrupted an older woman a few seats away.

Kennesy rolled her eyes, and without lowering her voice she resumed: "The only thing I respect about the Piggers is their pro-life stand. They've accepted this as the life they are fated to, instead of always waiting for the day they get to leave—that's the pro-choice position."

"How can someone actually want to live in this hell-hole?" Uli said quietly.

"Just ask anyone here what it was like being homeless. After being evacuated when Camille struck, we were given housing in Queens shelters. Then when the bombs went off, we were moved out into a hangar at LaGuardia Airport. Try living there on cots with thousands of people and tell me this isn't better." She took a deep sigh. "Besides, if you don't like it here, you can always file an appeal."

"Why couldn't they just give us subsidies and let us stay in Flushing or Prospect Park?" burst the older woman who had just tried silencing them. "That's what they did during the San Francisco earthquake! Why the hell did they ship us out to a radioactive desert in the middle of nowhere?"

"You didn't have to come here," Kennesy replied, and explained to Uli, "I don't know about you, but everyone here *applied* to get in. There's still a lot of poor people living in old New York."

"What do you mean a radioactive desert?" Uli asked the older woman.

"There's no scientific proof of radioactivity," Kennesy shot back.

"This is where they set off all the A-bombs back in the '50s," the lady explained to Uli.

"And in case you don't remember," Kennesy countered, "they did try subsidies. They handed out supplies in the streets of New York. Everyone got in line. Do you remember who eventually wound up with the bulk of stock?"

The older woman made a sour face.

"The Mafia, that's who. No one has ever starved or frozen here. Hell, we even got cars and other basic luxuries."

"We can't travel or have children!" the lady barked.

"People were *homeless*. They couldn't afford to travel anyway. And why the hell would someone who doesn't even have a home want to have a homeless baby?"

"So only the rich should reproduce, is that it?"

"Look, you want to blame someone for sticking us out here? How about the terrorists who hit the city!"

Before Uli could intervene, the driver called out, "Eighth Street, Crapper HQ. Last stop."

Uli and Oric got off with the cute hurricane evacuee, who bid them farewell and headed south down Lafayette Street.

Uli and Oric moved eastward to Astor Place. Suddenly, two hands grabbed Uli's elbows from behind. A thick arm looped over his head and across his neck. Back-kicking his assailant's kneecap, Uli grabbed the arm and flung a fat bespectacled kid up over his back and onto the pavement. Just as quickly, a third and fourth pair of beefy hands grabbed at his arms. The fat kid pressed a wet rag against Uli's face. Another pair of hands grabbed his knees and lifted him. As Uli struggled, he smelled the chloroform compound and held his breath. Twisting his head around, he realized that the person holding the rag to his face was the guy from midtown with the pointy bamboo hat. Uli struggled to free one hand, but he felt his consciousness thinning out.

"Ma! Da! Ma-Da! I miss you!" he heard Oric yell.

Dazed, Uli was now being lifted into a van. The geeky fat boy kept the rag pressed tightly over his mouth. Uli found himself fading to Oric's screams.

10/29/80

W *ake up now! Wake up! GET THE HELL UP! GO!*
"What?" The sun was bright in the doorway, so it had to be the next morning. Uli was hanging upside down with his hands bound together.

She's going to torture you! You're going to have one chance and that's it!

"Help me!" Uli shouted back.

Where are you? It was the blond man. Yet the voice was female. How could this be?

"I don't know," he said aloud. Looking around, he saw that he was alone and dismissed the interaction as the afterwash of a bizarre dream.

An awful sulfuric stench pulled him to full consciousness. He appeared to be in a barnyard. His lower section was numb with pain. He could still hear Oric's shrieks nearby.

"How do you know about the blast?" Uli heard a woman's voice shouting.

During an interlude of silence, Uli figured something sinister was underway. Sure enough, Oric started screaming terribly.

"Talk, you fat fucking retard!"

"Great Neck," Oric groaned. "Little Neck. Great Neck, Little Neck!"

"What are you talking about? What's this neck shit?"

"Dark, dark," Oric heaved. "Then light!"

"You are going to tell me what that *Great Neck*, *Little Neck* shit means or you're going to . . ."

He recognized the voice. It was Dianne Colder, the Feedmore lobbyist. Uli could hear her engaging in some kind of strenuous activity. Maybe she was punching Oric. It didn't last long. To the frenzied squeal of pigs across the barn, Oric was shouting, "No, please! Don't hurt Oric no more!"

Uli mustered all his strength, flexing his waist to catch a glimpse of the knot around his knees. Then he heard a loud thud.

"Shit! You fat fuck!"

"Brother, brother!" Oric was continuously screaming now.

"Scat! Get out of there!" he heard Dianne shouting over the shrieks. "Serves you right! You should have told me!"

In a moment, her footsteps were marching toward Uli. He dropped his arms back down and laid limp, pretending to be unconscious. The lobbyist paused before him, then poked him hard in the stomach—he didn't budge. As she crouched low to inspect his lifelessness, Uli sprung his body outward and wrapped his bound wrists over her blown-out, highlighted hair.

"Wait a sec!" she screamed, immediately trying to negotiate. "Ninety-two percent of all Crappers—"

He yanked her head sharply forward, dislocating her vertebral column. With a crunch, she fell into a perfect seated position and just stared straight ahead.

"Oh my god," she slowly said. "I can't move— I—"

He had paralyzed her. Only her mouth still worked. Like a broken robot, she manically recited statistics underscoring how Piggers were morally, intellectually, and economically superior to Crappers. She was a true partyist.

Uli twisted on his rope like a large marlin on a hook. Behind him, hanging from a nail, he saw a rusty scythe veiled under years of dusty cobwebs.

"I didn't mean to hurt him."

Uli swung backward and caught the wheat cutter in his bound hands. He squeezed the wooden handle up between his knees. Oric's shrieks were unbearable now.

"I was only trying to scare him."

"What'd you do?" Uli asked as he frantically rubbed his knotted wrists over the rusty tool.

"He was yelling strange shit! He kept saying, *Great Neck, Little Neck.*" She paused. "I guess he was talking about *my* neck!"

"He's psychic," Uli explained candidly, since the woman was clearly headed nowhere.

"Well, if he wasn't so fat, I wouldn't've dropped him in the pig pen," said the talking blond head. As Uli continued sawing away at his ropes, she added, "The average Pigger is 12.8 pounds lighter than the average Crapper. Did you know that?"

"That's a lie, so you've probably been lying all along," he replied, cutting through the final strands.

Once free, he began sawing through the cords holding his ankles together. The dried-out rope snapped and Uli fell to the ground, collapsing on top of the paralyzed body of Dianne Colder.

"You are a truly despicable human being!" she shouted painfully.

"Even if that were true," he countered, "I'd still be a hundred percent better than you."

A car screeched to a halt outside. Uli grabbed the rusty scythe, hid against the side of the barn, and waited.

"Help! Quick!" Dianne squealed, now lying flat on her back. "He's in here!"

A large man rushed inside. Uli swung the scythe deep into the front of the guy's neck, severing his jugular. It was the man in the goofy hat who had been with the fat boy when they kidnapped him at Astor Place. He grabbed his neck wound, dropped to his knees, flipped over, and gurgled slowly to death. Uli removed the scythe and dashed out to the pen.

Four large wild hogs were chewing on the tied-up limbs and torso of Oric's bloody body. Uli could see their teeth tearing through the poor man's flesh as though it were raspberry pudding. When he kicked one of the animals away, it tried to bite him. He slashed and stabbed at their fat hairy backs with the rusty weapon. When the biggest one charged him, Uli jabbed it right in the eye. The hog squealed insanely with blood shooting forth, causing the others to dash off. Uli used the opportunity to heave Oric out over the rails of the bloody pen. Among his many wounds, Oric's right shoulder was eaten clean to the bone. The hogs had chewed into his belly and bit into his scalp, inadvertently pulling the long t-shaped device out of his skull.

Oric was still slightly conscious. Placing him gently on his back, Uli tried to tie a tourniquet around his gnawed arm, but two of the worst bites on his torso had severed major veins and arteries. The poor man was bleeding to death and there was nothing Uli could do.

"I'm so sorry, Oric," Uli said sadly.

"It's okay, friend," the dying man muttered. "The Carnivals abducted me and had some goddamn scientist shove that thought-cuff into my skull."

"What . . . ? Why?"

"They knew I had some basic psychic gifts. And by retarding me they could enhance those abilities."

"Oh my god."

"You're the only one who figured it out. He was using my predictions to change the outcomes of—" Oric was losing it. "That was my twin brother in Flatlands trying to rescue me . . . I'll be joining him now."

"I didn't know."

Oric was gasping for breath and consciousness. "You . . . you have . . . too!"

"Have what?"

Oric moved his mouth, but nothing came out.

"DO I HAVE A CROSS IN MY HEAD?"

Oric stared at him.

"A TWIN, DO I HAVE TWIN?"

Oric just kept staring. It took Uli a moment to realize he was dead. He heaved the man over his shoulder and walked out to the front yard. There he saw an old sports car with only two seats. The keys were still in the ignition.

"No, wait, please don't leave me here!" Dianne cried out faintly as Uli checked Oric's pulse for the last time. He was about to drive off and just abandon the paralyzed lobbyist, but then remembered that she was the only person he had met here who mentioned routinely leaving the place. She had to know some way off the reservation. Racing back inside the barn, he scooped up Colder's limp body and carried her out.

"Thank you. Bless your soul."

"We have to get you to a hospital right away," he said, hauling her up on the roof of the old car so that she was lying belly-down with her head facing forward.

"There aren't any good hospitals here," she blurted. "These animals can barely handle basic bruises."

"We have to get you and Oric out of here. He's going to die."

"The retard's already dead. Help me and I'll get you a million dollars!"

Uli glanced around and spotted an old burlap sack slung over a laundry line running from a wooden post to the end of the barn. He pulled the cord down and grabbed the sack, which he slid under the corporate shill's skinny body. He tied the line tightly around Dianne's left wrist, strung it through the windows, and knotted it to her other wrist so that she was pressed flat against the roof of the car.

"What do you think you're doing?"

"Underwood sent you to kill us," he answered while securing her legs.

Letting out a deep sigh, she said, "You got it all wrong—
he works for *me*. The only reason I'm here is to protect the
company's interest—" She cut herself off, realizing that in
her muted agony she had imparted too much information.

"How are you protecting its interest?"

"Just making sure that everything is running smoothly,"
she said simply.

"I'll give you one chance," he reasoned. "If I think
you're lying, I'm feeding you to the pigs. Now tell me
what's really going on."

"Oh, what the hell. I was sent in to sway the election."

"The mayoral election?"

"Fuck no, the presidential election. It's tightly split
along party lines. I'm here to tilt it right."

"Just how do you hope to do that?" She didn't respond.
"Your only chance of survival is by talking quickly."

"The five boroughs work almost like the electoral college. Each borough gets a single vote. Three out of five
boroughs throw a single electoral college vote from Rescue
City, Nevada to the presidential election."

"Are the boroughs divided?"

"Queens and the Bronx are Pigger. They customar-
ily vote for the Democratic Party. Brooklyn and Manhattan are Crapper. They go with the Republicans. Staten
Island is the wild card. They went Democratic in the last
election, but the Staten Island borough president has the
power to ratify or veto the vote of his constituents at his
own whim."

"Really?"

"Yeah, and the only reason I was sent here was to make
sure Staten Island swings the vote to the Democrats."

"So you're a Democrat?"

"I'm whatever they tell me to be!"

"How exactly did you hope to alter the vote?"

"I already did it—with a large quantity of bullets. Look,
if this really matters to you—"

"It doesn't. These people can all kill each other for all I care. I just want out."

"Then undo my ropes and within thirty minutes I'll have you sitting in a Jacuzzi in a Vegas hotel with two underage girls."

That was the best offer he'd had since he found himself sleepwalking near the airport two days ago.

"Where do we go?"

"Take me to the corner of 4th Street and First Avenue in Manhattan," she commanded. "Let's get the fuck out of Staten Island!"

Before untying the cord, he propped up Oric's dead body in the passenger seat. He had rescued Uli yesterday from the geriatric mob at the funeral in Sunset Park, and now this blond bitch had brutally killed him.

Uli jumped into the sports car, turned the key, and hit the gas. In his rearview as he left the compound, he saw a sign that read, *CALYPSO PIG FARM*. Dianne Colder began screaming from the roof of the car like a human siren: "Treason! Treason!"

After twenty minutes of bouncing over the dunes of Staten Island, following rusty signs directing him to Manhattan, crisscrossing streams of waste water along Hyman Boulevard, he had to clamp his nose due to the stench. Driving past the rows of gorgeously designed buildings he had heard about, situated along the banks of the borough, he saw that they were indeed uninhabitable. Some were still submerged up to their roofs, just as Mallory had said. These flooded structures were evidence of how high the sewage water had risen.

He soon reached a two-lane ramp marked *Staten Island Ferry Bridge*. The wooden bridge swayed as he drove from submerged foundation to submerged foundation. The guard rail was a string of rotten two-by-fours. Fearing he would skid right off the aging planks into the toxic waters, Uli slowed to a crawl. To the southeast, he spotted a short, arching red bridge connecting Staten Island to Brooklyn. Nearer to his right, a dark angle of land narrowed to a point, then turned into a tall, reinforced concrete wall. The liquid sewage reached almost to the top of it. Below him, the black muck oozed south from the western side of Manhattan. At the other side of the dam were cleaner waters streaming northward up around Brooklyn.

As he approached Manhattan, Uli saw up close what he had spotted from the Brooklyn Bridge the day before. A tight wall of sandbags around four feet high and ten feet wide had been constructed next to the concrete dam wall running along the southeastern edge of Manhattan. The bags moved westerly around the Battery and up the west side of the borough. Conical orange sentry booths, like gi- ant traffic cones, lined the bagged wall.

Uli sped through lower Manhattan, ignoring the pass- ing motorists who gawked at the screaming blonde roped like a deer to his rooftop. He made his way onto Houston, turned left on First Avenue, and screeched to a halt at the corner of 4th Street, in front of a building with a shingle that read, *CLASS-A LADY HOTEL.*

"Is this where you live?" he asked, getting out of the sports car with Oric's motionless body still slumped for- ward in the passenger seat.

"You've performed . . . high crimes . . . and misdemean- ors . . . against the Feedmore . . . Corporation." Dianne at- tempted to spit bugs out of her mouth as she spoke.

"Exactly how much are you getting paid to destroy American democracy?"

"You think I'm evil because I work for a corporation . . . but let me set you straight, mister!" she said with baited breath. "Everything great and powerful about this nation was made . . . not in the halls of Congress, but by the laissez- faire system . . . Corporate interests *are* American interests!"

"Just tell me what to do to get the hell out of here."

"Upstairs in my hotel room, on my bedside table, is a piece of paper with Newt Underwood's phone number. Call him, tell him where I am, and I'll have you out of here tonight."

"What's your room number?"

She glared at him uncertainly. "I smell a Crapper. Untie me and carry me up there."

"That's absurd."

At that moment, a large man in a City Council Police Department uniform turned the corner and walked toward them.

"HELP! Pol—" Dianne started to scream.

Uli kissed her hard on her bright red lips. The officer walked past without even noticing that the woman was strapped to the roof of the car, or that a dead man was slumped in the passenger seat.

"So what room are we in?" he asked again, as he frisked her for her room key, finding nothing.

"I'm not telling you shit, asshole!"

For the first time, Uli noticed a strange bump on the front of Dianne's neck. He tapped it gently.

"What do you think you're—"

"How come I didn't see this before?"

"See what?"

"You have an Adam's apple."

"What are you talking about?"

Uli reached around behind her legs, lifted up her skirt, and pulled her panties aside, revealing a set of small pink testicles. He didn't know how he could have missed it before. The lobbyist was a transvestite.

"High crimes, high crimes!" Her voice had been growing deeper since her injury.

Uli pulled the burlap sack out from under her and shoved the end of it in her mouth, slipping the rest of it over her head and torso. Ignoring her muffled cries, he entered the lobby of her grungy hotel.

"Wanna room?" asked a bored desk clerk who was listening to Elvis crooning "Viva Las Vegas" over an ancient radio.

"Actually, I'm looking for my wife."

"Who is she?"

"A tall thin blonde with too much mascara—Dianne Colder."

"What a bitch," the clerk muttered. "No offense, but every time she comes here she complains about something— the smell, the view, the furniture. I'm not responsible for the whole world, you know."

"Just try living with her," Uli replied, as the man looked up her number.

"Room 2-A, second floor in the back."

"Would you have the key?" Uli asked, seeing hotel keys dangling out of almost every mailbox behind the counter.

"I can only give that to her."

"Well, she's probably up there anyway," Uli said and headed upstairs.

"Hold on, I'm not supposed to let anyone up." But the clerk was too lazy to pursue him.

The hallways had an old embossed wallpaper pattern that looked like a series of mushrooms. A funky, mildewy smell probably accounted for the hotel's vacancies, Uli thought, as he sped up the two flights. Her door was locked, but that of the adjacent room was ajar, with the bed unmade. Uli went inside. A fire escape in the back connected the two units. He opened the window and climbed over to her window, which was locked. He pulled off his shirt, wrapped it around his fist, and shattered the glass pane. Then he reached in, unlocked her window, opened it, and climbed through. The first things he saw were several fashionable skirts and a cabinet full of mascara, along with an advance galley copy of a book entitled, *Boo Hoo, My Husband's Dead: Whiny Vietnam War Widows* by Dianne Colder.

Shit, he thought, *the only way I'm going to find out how she's getting away from here is by forcing it out of her*. Stepping out into the hallway, he heard a distant ruckus. Racing down the stairs and into the lobby, he found the desk clerk slumped over his radio with the red handle of a longneck screwdriver sticking out of his right eye. The cash drawer was emptied out.

The victim moaned softly when Uli leaned him backward. He was still slightly conscious.

"What happened?"

"I gave him all my stamps," the man groaned. "He didn't have to—"

"What'd he look like?"

"He wasn't human, he—" The clerk passed out before he could say anything further. Uli laid him down to die in peace, then dashed outside. His sports car was missing.

An old guy standing on the corner asked, "Was that your two-seater?"

"Yeah, did you see where it went?"

"Some kid just ran out of the hotel, jumped into the driver's seat, and took off."

Uli sighed. The sadistic thug who had needlessly stabbed the clerk to death had also stolen the car with an even bigger sadist still strapped to the roof and poor Oric's body inside.

Stepping around the clerk's body back inside the Class-A Lady, Uli's only regret was not giving his friend a proper burial. He picked up a phone and dialed 911. It rang and rang for about five minutes before an answering machine clicked on. The message said: "*If you wish to report an emergency of some kind, please leave the nature of the crime, the location, and the time. Oh, and your name*—beep."

Uli reported that a robbery and homicide had just been committed, then hung up, failing to leave his name or the location. He went back upstairs to Dianne Colder's empty room. Looking carefully through her stylish clothes and the usual personal items, he found nothing particularly helpful. Wrapped in her sheets he discovered a possible weapon—a small black plastic item shaped like a pickle. Uli slipped it into his pocket. Just before leaving, he pulled the mattress up. He noticed several objects dangling from the hollowed underside of the old box spring. Taped there were a face mask, eye goggles, a tank marked *Charon*, and a small plastic box containing a full syringe of some unknown substance. Uli took the four items, slipped them into an old shopping bag from the woman's room, and hit the street just as a police car turned the corner.

He started running west. From the corner of 4th Street and Third Avenue, he spotted a brown three-story building with a small clock tower—Cooper Union. He vaguely remembered that the original one had been some kind of school and that Abe Lincoln was somehow affiliated with it, perhaps he had gone there.

Entering the large lobby of the building, he approached a group of fierce-looking guards sitting behind a long table and explained that he had an appointment with a woman named Mallory. One guard picked up the phone and called upstairs.

"You were supposed to be here yesterday," Mallory said, marching toward him five minutes later. "Where the hell is Oric?"

"We almost made it," he said somberly. "We were right over there, about a hundred feet away, before we got grabbed." He pointed out the big bay window to the corner of 8th and Lafayette.

"Oh my god, the Piggers got him?"

"They tortured him. I don't think they intended to, but they killed him."

"Fucking bastards!" she shouted.

The security guard rolled Uli's fingerprints on a card and slipped it into a bulky electronic scanning device. A few minutes later the results appeared on a small screen.

"He's got no record, which means he's a security risk," the head guard announced.

"This is a special situation. He's not going into any high-security areas," Mallory assured him. "I'll take full responsibility."

"We'll have to put him under escort," the guard said.

"Fine."

"What's in there?" the guard asked Uli, referring to the shopping bag from Colder's room.

Uli took out the small metal tank and the plastic case holding the hypodermic needle. "Oric's killer had them in her room. I thought maybe you could tell me what they're for."

Mallory looked at them closely before shrugging.

"You can pick them up on the way out," the guard said, putting them back in the bag and then into his desk drawer.

Uli was directed through a metal detector. Flanked by two guards, he followed Mallory upstairs into a small conference room. The guards stood outside and closed the door. Upon the table was a pot of warm coffee and a tray of Spam-and-Velveeta sandwiches from a meeting that had just broken up. When Uli mentioned that he hadn't eaten since yesterday, Mallory offered him the food. He gobbled down a sandwich in three bites and a cup of coffee in a single gulp.

"So, exactly what happened?"

"This blond bitch intercepted us at the Fulton Street bus station just after you left," Uli explained, cramming the second Spam-and-cheese sandwich into his mouth. "Her name was Dianne Colder."

"Colder?"

"First she said she was a lobbyist for Feedmore, then she said she was the coordinator of this place and that the Piggers were *her* agents."

"Ah yes, the sexy blonde who compulsively lies for the Piggers."

"I wouldn't say *sexy*. Actually, she's a transvestite."

"You're lucky you weren't her target," Mallory said.

"She leaves a trail of dead men behind her. So, she abducted you?"

"Not then—she accompanied us after you left. Of course, Oric had to blurt out one of his crazy predictions, which made her suspicious as hell. But she seemed to think I was on her side, and I didn't want to alarm her, so when the bus reached Manhattan we jumped out the rear window and snuck away."

"What was Oric's final prediction?" she asked intently.

"*Big blast* was all he said."

"I wonder where."

"While dodging her, we went through midtown and I saw someone blow up a truck in front of Rock & Filler Center. I think that was probably it. Anyway, they chloroformed me."

"*Who* chloroformed you?"

"There were at least four of them," Uli replied. "One was the man I ended up killing in Staten Island—and there was also a chubby boy with bangs and glasses."

"Do you remember him having any scars or identifiable marks?"

"No, I don't think so . . . Actually, he had a missing tooth," Uli suddenly recalled.

"A front tooth?"

"No, it was *here*," Uli said, pointing inside his own mouth. "An incisor."

"Oh god! Did he speak with a—"

"I didn't hear him speak, but I could probably identify him again."

Mallory grabbed the phone. "Security, get me Manny Lewis!"

"You're holding him?" Uli asked.

"No, but he's an intern in my office. He knew I was expecting someone important all day, but he didn't have any details."

"How could he have helped my assailants?"

"He must've told them you hadn't arrived and to keep a team in the area—" The ringing phone interrupted her. Mallory listened quietly for a moment, then cursed and hung up. "Shit, he didn't come in today."

"Maybe he's sick," suggested Uli.

"He's never missed a day. He's gone—but we'll find the cocksucker." Mallory ran her hands through her hair. "Tell me what happened after you were abducted."

"Well, when I woke up, I was dangling upside down like a side of beef in some barnyard in Staten Island." He remembered an odd detail: "The only reason I woke up was because I heard some voice in my ear screaming at me."

"Whose voice was it?"

"I can't really describe it," he replied. "I heard it my first day here, when I was being chased by dogs. I thought it was my wife, who I don't really remember, and then I thought it was this blond guy I saw in Brooklyn yesterday, but it's probably just a recurrent daydream."

"This place is a little bizarre."

"Yeah, it's like everyone's a terrorist," he said, remembering the newspaper articles.

"Before I came here, I was in one of the splinter groups of the Weather Underground called the May 19th Brigade."

"Really?"

"Why would I lie to you?"

"So I guess this place *is* full of terrorists. Are most of them Crappers?"

"No. In fact, one of the big fallacies about Rescue City is that all the former terrorists up and became Crappers. A bunch of them, mainly the younger ones, sold out and went Pigger."

"Hold on a second. What exactly did your May Brigade do?"

"The usual: protested the war, visited Cuba, blew up draft offices, ROTC offices, recruiting centers. Stuff like that. You have to realize that a lot of disenfranchised groups saw terrorism as a legitimate alternative. Anyway, did you get some sense of what the blond lobbyist was after?"

"She said she was here in Rescue City to bribe the borough president of Staten Island."

"Bribe him to do what?"

"To cast the swing vote to give the Democrats the one electoral college vote this place has for the upcoming presidential election."

"Yes, it all makes perfect sense. The Piggers are terrified of Ronald Reagan."

"The actor?" Uli asked.

"He was elected president in '76 after Nixon," Mallory said. "His reelection is our one great hope."

"Why?"

"They don't think we know. That's why the Feedmore Corporation doesn't ship in radios or TVs."

"But I've seen people using them."

"Those government-issued radios and televisions don't pick up reception beyond about two miles or so. Hell, they can barely pick up the stations transmitted here. But using parts from them, some people have managed to rig together shortwave radios, so we can occasionally catch news from the outside world."

"And what have you heard?"

"Reagan has been going head-to-head with the Russians, outspending them on defense."

"So?"

"He's cut every social program in order to come up with the cash for his arms race."

"That's awful."

"Actually, it's good for us. The money that goes into Rescue City is one of the biggest expenses in the national budget."

"What are you saying?"

"In order to pay for his military buildup, Reagan's been talking about closing this place down. It's supposed to be a close presidential election," Mallory continued. "If Reagan gets reelected and cuts funding, we'll all be returned to New York."

"So if the Staten Island borough president votes Democrat and Reagan loses his reelection," Uli concluded, "we're stuck here."

"It's going to be murder to try to reason with Rafique."

"Why, who is he?"

"When you were being held in Staten Island, did you smell anything funny?" she asked.

"Yeah, the pig farms."

"That stink isn't from pigs. It's because the river is blocked with sewage. Jackie Wilson did it years ago in order to seize control. It's a long story, but the sewage makes the borough nearly uninhabitable."

"What does this have to do with the borough president?"

"A number of years ago, Adolphus Rafique broke off from the Crappers and started this weird anarchist cult in the East Village district. He named it the Verdant League. Its members rejected the newly implemented capitalist model with the food stamp currency that the Piggers had come up with. The VL evenly distributed all food and housing in the Lower East Side among themselves. When the rest of us objected to Rafique, he and his renegade band moved out to Staten Island, becoming the new majority there since it was so underpopulated."

"How do they deal with the stench?"

"Most of those who joined his cult have had their sinuses cauterized. It knocks out a lot of the taste, but you don't smell a thing. They call themselves the Burnt Men. Anyway, because of the deadlock between the two Pigger and two Crapper boroughs, Rafique usually becomes the tie-breaker, so he's now a major player." Mallory paused. "What could the blond lobbyist have bribed Adolphus with?"

"Bullets," Uli remembered. "That's what she said. She gave him a bunch of bullets."

"Of course. Rafique is constantly under attack from both gangs, and bullets are one of the things that Feedmore doesn't provide anymore." Mallory paused again. "You have to help me."

"Do what?"

"Try to convince Rafique not to throw his vote to the Democrats."

"Nothing personal, but I already did you a big favor and got poor Oric killed. I'm not even a Crapper."

"That's one of the reasons I need you," she said. When Uli smiled dismally, Mallory explained: "Rafique won't let any party affiliates into his precious Verdant League headquarters. But more importantly, it's just a matter of time before the Piggers catch up with you. Help me and I'll tell you a possible way out of here."

"What exactly am I supposed to do?"

"Rafique may be an anarchist, but he's also very smart. Just tell him that the blond woman who bribed him works for the Feedmore Corporation. He's opposed to corporate funding."

"Can't you offer him your own bribe?" Uli asked.

"Like what?"

"Give him more ammo?"

"We can't do that," she said, "though come to think of it, we did get a huge shipment of water-purification pills, and I know he hates being dependent upon us for water. Offer him unlimited pills."

"I'll consider approaching him, provided you get this thing out of my head and help me get out of Rescue City."

Mallory said she'd do her best to meet his conditions, but that she couldn't make any promises. She then mentioned that she had made some inquiries about Carnival and his wife. There was no record of either of them from before they arrived. While here, though, Jim had run for a

City Council office nine years earlier as a Crapper candidate. "This was back when Manhattan was still bipartisan. After losing several successive elections, he finally stole an election down in East New York. In order to placate the Piggers in his district, he ended up marrying the former Pigger Councilwoman, Mary."

"It sounded like she was a Pigger," Uli recalled.

"This was before the Piggers took orders from Feedmore."

"Did you find out anything about Oric?"

"No one ever reported them having children."

"Oh, they didn't. Oric reverted to normal when he was dying. He said the Carnivals abducted him and had some scientists turn him into an idiot savant."

"You're kidding!"

"Nope. Remember the guy chasing us in the Flatlands? He was Oric's twin."

"That explains a lot," Mallory said. "Twins have a great significance here."

"What do you mean *here*?"

"I mean out here in the desert. This is a sacred Indian site. It has something to with duality. Twins have certain powers."

"Are you kidding?"

"It's not a coincidence that they put us all here."

"What does that mean?"

"The federal government was able to kill two birds at once—creating a refugee city along with turning this into a research lab for psychic studies."

"What are these psychic experiments?" he asked.

"They're probably part of the arms race with the Soviets. Apparently, the Russians poured millions of rubles into trying to develop telepathic communications with their cosmonauts."

Suddenly the door flew open and a secretary with a strange unicorn-horn hairdo led a group of men into the room.

"Where is he?" someone called out.

"No, wait!" Mallory shouted.

In quick glances through the arms and shoulders of bodyguards, Uli recognized the tall lean man from posters all around town.

It felt as if something sleeping inside of him had sprung to life. Before he knew what he was doing, he had hurled himself through the four guards and pushed himself up to James Dropt. All he could think was, *Walk to Sutphin, catch the Q28 to Fulton Street, change to the B17, take it to the East Village in Manhattan* . . .

His hand, which was already in his pocket, pulled out the single-chambered pistol and pointed it at Dropt's head. He squeezed the trigger and blacked out.

1:58 p.m.

Uli awoke to find himself on the floor in the conference room with his wrists cuffed and a squad of bodyguards standing over him.

"What the hell . . . ?"

"I had this damn room screened!" Mallory was shouting to the captain of security. "Goddamnit, I informed them downstairs that he was a risk, and no one, certainly not Dropt, was supposed to come in!"

"Help!" Uli called out with his face pressed against the floor.

"He didn't," the captain stated.

Another security guard came in and tossed an amateurish Dropt mask on the desk.

"He heard that your buddy got Underwood's Manchurian Candidate experiment, and since the subject was carrying no detectable weapon, Dropt wanted us to test him in case he ever wanted to do his own experimenting."

"You could've told me," Mallory replied angrily.

"What did I do?" Uli asked.

"You went into a fugue state," one of the guards politely explained. "Your eyes glossed over and you tried to kill Dropt with this." He held up the soft-edged oblong piece of rubbery plastic. "We initially thought it was some kind of explosive, but after doing some quick tests, we determined that it was what is commonly referred to as a *marital aide*. Where'd you get it?"

"Oh, in Dianne Colder's bed," he recalled.

The door swung open again and a team of armed guards rushed in. Uli, still in handcuffs, watched as the real James Dropt entered. The candidate looked at Uli for an instant, testing to see if he'd revert back into his altered state. Whatever demonic possession had him a moment ago, he was free of it now.

"So," Dropt spoke directly to Uli, "we hear you were jumped, and the seer was killed."

"Yeah. I'm really sorry about it," he said earnestly.

"Did Mallory inform you that we suspect the Piggers have a secret seer of their own?"

"She did."

"Any idea why you were interred in Rescue City?"

"Not a clue."

"You were probably part of the antiwar movement incarcerated for indefinite detention. Despite my service in Vietnam, that's how I got here."

"I was going to take him downstairs to see Dr. Adele, to find out if Underwood really did put a bug in his head," Mallory said.

"Oh, Adele is out sick today," Dropt informed her.

"Then you'll have to come back tomorrow," Mallory told Uli.

He thanked her and wished Dropt good luck with the upcoming election. Mallory escorted him out into the hall, where the guards uncuffed him.

"I'm sorry about all that," she said. "I honestly had no idea they were going to do that."

"No harm done. And if you still need my help, I'll try to get Rafique to consider throwing his vote to the Republicans. But only if you show me a way out of this place."

"Let me clarify that my offer is not a hundred percent. What I have in mind . . . no one has ever come back to say it works."

"If there's any chance at all, I'll take it," Uli replied, as they passed the security detail and exited the building.

"Your mission, then, is right behind you. About a hundred yards down is the southbound M3 bus. It goes directly down Bowery, then along Water Street, and right over the Staten Island Ferry Bridge. You're going to ride down to the very bottom of Staten Island. The Verdant League headquarters is the last stop."

"Wait a second. If you're trying to reason with him, why don't you just call him on the phone yourself?"

"Well, even if he takes the call, which I highly doubt since he refuses to interact with anyone affiliated with either party, a face-to-face appeal is much more persuasive."

"Then when I come back here tomorrow, I can see this Dr. Adele?" Uli asked.

"Absolutely, and afterwards I'll give you detailed instructions about a possible way out through the desert."

"Fine."

"Lucky you," she said, pointing up Third Avenue. "There's your bus."

He said goodbye and hurried toward the bus stop as she returned inside.

As the M3 pulled up, a loud grinding of engines compelled him to look back. A convoy of large trucks with *Feedmore Road Repair* stenciled on their doors was pulling up next to the Crapper headquarters.

Uli paid his fare and squeezed between an overweight woman with purple hair and a bony elderly guy.

The first blast shattered the windows of the bus, sprinkling the passengers with fragments of glass. Two other explosions quickly followed. The final and most powerful one lifted the bus in the air and knocked it onto its side.

An incredible weight slammed into Uli's chest. For a moment he blacked out. When he came to, gasping for breath, he realized that three or four people were piled on top of him, including the large purple-haired lady. Beneath him, bent backwards over a seat, was the thin older man, who appeared crushed to death. Those who were still conscious were moaning and writhing in pain. Uli wormed around bodies until he was able to climb up the side of the bus to an emergency window, which he pushed open.

One by one he started pulling people out. When the driver, some of the sturdier passengers, and a man on the street began pitching in, Uli climbed off the bus and sprinted over to the demolished Crapper headquarters.

Approaching the smoldering rubble, he could hear sections of the building collapsing internally. Uli searched for the original entrance, but couldn't locate it. Yesterday's midtown bombing looked like child's play by comparison. From one spot in the wreckage he heard a faint banging and muffled cries for help. Immediately, he started grabbing stones and debris and heaving them into the street.

"Over here!" he yelled. "There's a person trapped down here! Someone help me!"

Several nearby men and women joined in, pulling wood and stone from around the pulverized site. After fifteen minutes, tunneling roughly ten feet into the wreckage, they unearthed a pair of squirming legs. Uli was able to carefully free the upper torso of a shaggy-headed man.

"My buddy's trapped right there." The guy pointed into the hole he had just been pulled out from.

Uli peered in and through the dusty darkness could make out the bottom half of another man twisting in pain. After twenty more minutes of excavating, Uli and the others were finally able to pull the second man free.

"My name is Bernstein," said the first rescuee, shaken and dusty.

"I'm Woodward," coughed the second man upon catching his breath. Someone handed him a bottle of water which he gulped down. Patting the chalky dust off his clothes, he added, "Those bastards at Rikers did this."

"Did you see Mallory?" Uli asked frantically, surveying the destruction around them.

"No, we were doing research in the records room on the third floor," Bernstein said. "Next thing we know, the floor is dropping below us."

Uli excused himself and walked around the smoldering block-long, block-wide mountain of rubble. Though a couple of other people had been pulled out, the vast majority were still trapped inside. Hard as he listened, Uli could hear no other muted cries or dull sounds.

Over the next hour or so, firefighters arrived from Brooklyn and Manhattan, as did gangcops, to make sure the Piggers didn't try to exploit the chaos.

Soon, the gangcops and a few Council officers had to hold back the screaming family members of those buried inside. For fear of further collapse, the Manhattan Crapper fire chief, who had taken charge of the situation, waited for an engineer to arrive before trying to put together a comprehensive excavation plan.

Gas mains and electricity were shut off. At the engineer's recommendation, four teams were set up to start digging into the disaster from all sides at once. Someone improvised a crude diagram detailing the main Crapper offices. Uli volunteered to work with the northern crew, which was focusing on Dropt's office, where he was supposed to be holding a meeting at the time with eight of the borough's twelve Councilpeople. Uli believed that was where Mallory had been heading when she left him. Two rescue dogs were called in. The engineer deemed it too soon for heavier equipment, so a small crane and tractor were brought over.

Uli soon realized the full ramifications of the explosion. Aside from the fact that the upper echelon of the Crapper leadership, including Mallory, had been wiped out, gone too was any possibility of him leaving Rescue City.

He worked feverishly with his team at the northern wall, hoping against hope that they might still find Mallory alive. Each group created a human chain of thirty or so people passing buckets of bricks, two-by-four studs, hunks of broken dry wall, and miles of electrical wiring.

The blast had occurred around 2:30. By 4:30, half an hour after his team had assembled, they located the first cluster of victims—four crushed bodies: the Councilman from Chelsea, his top aide, a clerical worker, and Dropt's secretary with the unicorn-horn hairdo. By 5:30 Uli had stripped down to his T-shirt and was passing the buckets from a middle-aged man named Lucas to a guy named Marky behind him. Uli learned that both had come to Rescue City to fulfill Alternate Service requirements—instead of going to Vietnam—and had been working with the Crappers on local social programs.

"First we get evacuated due to a terror attack in the old town," Lucas said. "Now we're getting it here."

Over the ensuing hours, as the three became friends, Uli explained that he suffered from acute amnesia and asked, "What exactly happened to the original New York?"

"A terrorist attack," Luke said with fatigue, handing an empty ten-gallon spackle bucket to Uli.

"A series of around fifty contamination bombs went off in lower Manhattan," Marky elaborated.

"A missile attack?"

"No," Marky replied, after cutting through a section of piping with a chainsaw. "Pitchblende, an ore they use in some old fluoroscope machines. About two tablespoons of it was stuffed in small sections of lead foil, using an M-80 as the detonator. Extremely low-tech, but lots of them."

"How many dead?" Uli asked.

"None immediately," Luke replied. "The worst part at first was that Manhattan had to be evacuated. A lot of poorer neighborhoods in the outer boroughs were flooded overnight by the newly displaced middle class."

"Albany was quick to respond," Marky reminded him with a smirk. "They immediately suspended all rent stabilization and control laws, so that within two years almost all rents skyrocketed."

"Keep in mind the city was near bankruptcy," Luke elaborated. "They were terrified of losing their dwindling middle class, even if it meant screwing over their poor."

"Within a year or two, almost all tenants who had been living in low-income neighborhoods for decades couldn't afford the rents anymore," Marky continued. "Illegal evictions were epidemic. The working poor found themselves forced into the streets."

"You'd see piles of furniture dumped out onto the sidewalk."

"What did the city do about them?" Uli prodded.

"Initially, they were sheltered in Shea and Yankee stadiums," Marky said, "but things quickly degenerated. Angry mobs started moving throughout the city, breaking into stores and shops. The National Guard and the city tried to make smaller encampments, turning the city parks into trailer parks—"

"Don't forget upper Manhattan," Lucas cut in. "Harlem became a massive tent city."

"When did the federal government get involved?"

"July of 1971 was incredibly hot," Marky replied, scooping up a bucket of crumbled plaster board. "When the big blackout first struck, all the poor just went bananas. For three days everyone rioted. They broke into all the new businesses that had finally resettled after the Manhattan attack. Within three days the city was totally trashed all over again."

"So everyone was just rounded up and brought here?" Uli concluded.

"There was a big class-action lawsuit that was going nowhere in the courts," Lucas said. "But after the blackout, Lindsay and Rockefeller appealed to Nixon for help. The federal government had a plan, but things got screwy."

"Many agreed to come here because they were promised that once Manhattan was scrubbed down, they'd be brought right back," Marky added.

"And all the poor out here were told they would be given priority housing in Manhattan as a kind of restitution."

"Who initiated this?" Uli asked. It didn't sound like something Nixon would do.

"The Democrats started it," Luke recalled, "but then critics kept hitting on things like Kennedy's War on Poverty and LBJ's Great Society and wasting money on the poor . . . so the Republicans wound up taking the lead—"

A severed foot emerged out of the debris before them. Sifting onward, they soon located a new clump of mangled bodies. For the next twenty minutes the three of them silently pulled out limbs, torsos, two heads, three more feet, and then what appeared to be a very large mouth.

By 7:30 their group had recovered six more bodies. Along with the other three crews, the total came to twenty-eight dead. In the hands of two corpses they found scribbled goodbye notes, indicating that some people had survived the initial explosion only to bleed to death while waiting to be rescued. This compelled everyone to work harder. Floodlights were brought in.

As it grew late, Marky, Luke, and the others on Uli's line were gradually replaced. Only Uli remained from the original group. He was intent on staying until they had located Mallory. By 11 p.m. he started dropping his buckets and seeing double. His coworkers finally ordered him to get some sleep.

It was an unusually hot night for the Nevada desert. A series of food tables were unfolded on 7th Street between

Second and Bowery. Outdoor showers and portable toilets were unloaded on 6th Street, as were a row of shower stalls. For volunteers who lived too far away to commute home, cots were brought in and lined up under the stars down 6th Street.

Uli dropped exhausted onto a hard cot, barely able to kick off his shoes.

10/30/80

Flashing lights, shouts, and various engines revved up. Uli awoke to the news that the dead body of mayoral candidate James Dropt had just been located. The bright lights of the Crapper TV crew shone down on the catastrophe. Uli wandered over to Bowery just as the recovery team wheeled the gurney with Dropt's mangled body past. All four crews stopped working and quietly lined the sidewalk to catch a glimpse of their fallen leader. With Dropt's corpse found, the last vestiges of hope had vanished. Even Uli felt it—not so much sadness as a general despair from those all around. The possibility of the first Crapper victory since Mallory's husband had been shot was blown asunder.

Dropt's body was slid into the back of an ambulance, which departed slowly under a single police escort. Most of the crew workers either went back to work or returned to their narrow outdoor cots. As Uli thought about the leader he had only briefly met, he could hear men in the neighboring cots weeping. Following a shallow sleep, he arose with the first rays of the sun.

Sitting elbow-to-elbow, knee-to-knee with others at a community table over a bowl of flavorless cereal, Uli learned both good and bad news. Just an hour earlier they had discovered four people still alive, buried in the basement. Unfortunately, they had also unearthed twenty-two more crushed bodies, which included the last of the Councilpeople. They had accounted for all but two people, and one of those was Mallory.

Passing by the makeshift morgue set up near the rear of the headquarters, Uli spotted something that made him cringe. It was the crushed body of the baby kangaroo that Mallory had taken such pains to rescue. Seeing the little marsupial's body, Uli knew in his heart of hearts that she was dead.

In the early afternoon, Uli saw a crowd gathering around a small TV. The Honorable Horace Shub, Jr. was in the middle of a speech denouncing the bombing and begging for reconciliation between the various gangs. Apparently, vengeful Crapper gangs from northern Brooklyn had ventured into weaker Pigger neighborhoods in Queens the night before and burned stores and slaughtered over twenty Piggers before order was restored.

"James Dropt was a greatly good man," Shub said in his weirdly earnest way. "He believed in a peaceable resolution to our manifold problems. I am calling upon the Councilpeople of New York, both the Created Equalers and the We the People Party, to put an end to the anger and join me in working together and bringing peace to our greatly good, God-fearing municipality . . ."

1:22 p.m.

Uli didn't stick around to see how the mayor's speech was going to end. As he walked down Bowery, his thoughts reverted to Mallory. He decided that as a tribute to her, he was going to do what he had initially set out to do for personal gain: He would venture down to Staten Island, locate the borough president, and try to convince Adolphus Rafique to cast his decisive vote in favor of the former matinee idol Ronald Reagan.

Over the next fifteen minutes or so, exhausted young volunteers for the Crapper recovery effort gathered with

Uli at the M3 bus stop. A number of them were still coughing and hawking up dust particles.

"How long is it to the very last stop?" Uli asked the
driver when the bus finally arrived.

"A little over two hours, but I better warn you that
Shub ordered a curfew because of the rioting, so there's
only one more bus going down there. Then they're cancel-
ing service for the night."

"What time is the last bus leaving there to head back
this way?"

"Six o'clock sharp."

Uli thanked the driver and took a seat, hoping to catch
some shut-eye. Tired as he was, though, he couldn't stop
looking at the strange revisionist city passing around him.

He was able to remember more of the places from
old New York that were missing here. Little Italy, SoHo,
and Chinatown had all been consolidated into one tiny
neighborhood—LittleHoTown. TriBeCa and Wall Street,
on the other hand, were gone without a trace.

As they ascended the wooden bridge over the sand-
bagged wall protecting the Battery, foul odors began to
rise.

There was something depressing about the low-level
skyline of European buildings behind them that made up
this odd simulacrum of Manhattan.

An old man slid his hand along the overhead aluminum
bar as he walked down the aisle peddling something. Uli
figured it was gum until he spotted a middle-aged woman
with a bad dye job giving the fellow a sixteenth-stamp. In
return he handed her a small padded clothespin that the
woman duly clipped over her flared nostrils.

"Holy shit," the man said as he approached Uli.
"You're—" Something behind Uli caught the solicitor's attention, and he hastened past. Uli turned and saw a cardboard sign slung around the man's stooped back: *NOSE
PINS!*

"Excuse me," Uli called out. "What were you starting to say?"

"I was just looking at that." The old man pointed out the window over the swampy waters of New York Harbor. Standing on a cluster of black rocks was a plastic lime-colored lady, about six feet tall—a mockery of the Statue of Liberty. In her outstretched arm someone had taped an empty beer bottle onto the torch. Over her arm where she held the Bill of Rights someone had strapped a golf bag with a single rusty club sticking out. Inasmuch as the entire place seemed like a miniature golf course done in a New York City theme, it sort of made sense.

Behind him, four young bucket-passers from the devastated Crappers headquarters were asleep across the rear seats.

"Want a nose pin?" the solicitor asked.

Uli purchased one, and as he clipped it on, the bridge they were passing over started swaying back and forth.

"Why is this thing so damn shaky?" Uli asked the pin seller, and added, "I'm new here."

"The Feedmore Corporation gave us ten old ferry boats, but Staten Island here is a lot closer than in old town and the water is far shallower, so the local engineer submerged the ferries, laid planks over the tops, and turned it into this ratty-ass bridge." The pin seller studied Uli's face closely.

"But the sewage level is rising, isn't it?"

"Not anymore. But at its worst, the water level came right up to the bridge. That was when Rafique decided to dig the canal, and in one day the water dropped six feet."

When they reached Staten Island moments later, Uli noticed another bridge, dull and red with abruptly arching spans shooting northeast. "Is that the Verrazano?"

"Name's been shortened like the bridge," the man replied. "Here it's just the *Zano*."

The bus headed slowly down Richmond Road, past the row of submerged and semi-submerged luxury houses, all uninhabited. The paved street turned to packed dirt and sloped steeply downhill. A handmade sign read, *Hyman Boulevard*. It was the same street he had driven up with Dianne Colder strapped to his roof.

For the first mile or so, in the low swampy parts of the borough, more abandoned houses sprang up. They almost looked like homes on a military base. Though the land was mostly dry now, earlier flood waters had wrecked the area.

Crossing sporadic flows of black sewage, the bus stopped at various points along the succession of tiny Staten Island communities, all of which looked more barren than anywhere else he'd been on the reservation.

The further down they drove, the more primitive the little settlements appeared. Many of the structures were made from old packing crates and pallet wood, probably from when the Staten Island airport had been functioning. In one instance, Uli noticed a small circle of huts with thatched roofs that looked like they had been made with dry grass and stripped bark.

Whenever they went down a sharp incline, the smell worsened and the road would be washed out by an inlet of lumpy black water. The driver had to gun the engine to slice through the hazardous streams. Clearly the entire borough was one big environmental disaster zone.

Just like Manhattan, hand-painted planks corrupted the original names of deserted little outposts with their ramshackle huts: *Doggone Hills*, *New Dope Beach*, *Great Killers*, and so on. Large rodents, perhaps prairie dogs, sat on their haunches staring at the passing bus.

As the bus ventured to the southern tip of the borough, the road grew worse with ever fewer shanties. Occasionally, Uli saw people walking about. Most of them appeared grungy and sickly, much like the borough itself. On several occasions when people boarded the bus, Uli wondered how they could stand the smell. Looking over the swampy streams and arid dunes he kept wondering how much further the route continued. Sometimes when the bus lumbered uphill, they'd catch a desert breeze and there would be a fleeting reprieve from the heat and smell, but then the road would slant downhill again, through the liquid shit.

When the bus finally came to its terminus, only one passenger remained on board with Uli, a skinny kid curled up in the rear. How he could sleep through such stinking turbulence was a mystery.

"Tottenville—Nut Central!" the driver shouted, as he folded open the door. Uli wished him a good day and stepped off. The kid followed, then walked away in the opposite direction.

A huge terminal that had fallen into disrepair was balanced all alone on the edge of a hill. This was the southern demarcation of Staten Island, Nevada. Below it was a dusty recreation field that looked like it might once have supported a little league team, a haunting reminder of the absence of children. Beyond that a swamp of sewage covered the old airfield.

The oxidized copper ferry building was an homage to the old St. George Landing, even though it was at the opposite side of the borough than in old New York. In front of the station was a big hand-painted sign: *The Dastardly Notorious VERDANT LEAGUE—Adolphus Rafique will debate with anyone at any time (subject to availability)!*

The terminal was covered with old paneled doors and large unwashed bay windows reinforced by wire netting, but there didn't seem to be anyone inside. Uli followed a faded red arrow pointing around to the back of the building, where he heard a muffled ruckus. Semi-naked forms danced sweatily in the sun, chanting through plumes of smoke to the steady beats of handmade drums. They looked like a strange fusion of American Indians and urban homeless. Uli figured they were the tribe of environmental extremists that Mallory had mentioned—the Burnt Men. Semi-domesticated barking canines dashed about and chickens squawked. A smoky bonfire burned in the center of it all. An old man in a loincloth and white facial paint stopped dancing and stared at Uli. The banks of the swamp behind the dusty rec field were a honeycomb of tents and cardboard partitions.

Uli reached a set of open double doors in the rear of the terminal and came upon a heavyset security guard. He was sitting at a desk with a phone and several strange clerical-looking machines reading a worn paperback copy of Tolkien's *The Hobbit*.

"If you're here for the Turning Toxic into Organic class, it's been canceled till next week," the man said, "but if you're here for the Fantasy Literature course—"

"Actually, I was hoping to debate with Mr. Rafique."

"Do you have an appointment?"

"No, but the sign says he'll debate with anyone at any time," Uli said.

"*If* he's not out campaigning," the guard amended. "He's running for mayor and for the presidency, you know."

"Is he available?"

"That depends. Are you Pigger or Crapper?"

"I'm neither."

The security guard held his finger up asking for patience, then lifted his phone and dialed a number.

"Why does that sign say this is Templehof Airport?" Uli asked while waiting.

"That was the main airfield for the Berlin airlift. Before it was flooded, this was where the piloted flights landed with all the supplies, so they . . . Hello." The guard asked if Adolphus Rafique was available to debate "an unregistered walk-in." After another moment, he hung up and said, "Rafique's there, but you have to have your paw prints checked and get cleared here first." He took out a blank index card and an ink blotter.

"I can save you some time by telling you that there is no record of me."

"Which means you're potentially a detainee, which in turn means a possible terrorist," the guard said, pressing Uli's thumb and middle finger onto the blotter and then the card. He fanned the card till it was dry, then slipped it into the slot of a machine that looked like a black cigar box. Wires connected it to a small monitor, upon which boxy green digits appeared. "As you say, you're not registered with either party," the guard deciphered aloud.

"That's why I want to talk to Mr. Rafique."

The security guard told him he'd have to strip down to his underwear.

"Can't you just frisk me?"

"Adolphus Rafique has survived ten attempts on his life. Twice he was shot in the head. A few years ago some guy stuck a wooden spike right through his heart."

"How'd he survive?"

"The Indians down in the swamp claim that it's his private *mana*. A lifetime of losing election after election yet always coming back has made him a survivalist."

"I could use a gift like that," Uli replied, as he started peeling off his shirt and pants. After having every inch of his naked body checked, Uli put his clothes back on. The guard stuck an adhesive pass on his shirt pocket and told him to report to Room 310.

Just inside the building, a plaque said, THE VERITAS VERDANT LEAGUE. *What you don't know* is *hurting you*.

Although most of the fluorescent bars overhead appeared to be burned out, the large bay windows running along the side of the building caught the sunlight and the white marble floors made maximum use of it. Uli walked through empty halls until he spotted a young olive-skinned man dressed in loose black formal wear. He had scraggy facial hair with tortoise-shell glasses taped together over the bridge of his prominent Roman nose. Long white strings of cloth flowed from his sides.

"Excuse me!" Uli called out to him, but the man rushed away.

He continued down the hallways, from empty room to empty room, until he happened upon what appeared to be a yoga class in session. The practitioners were bent forward on one knee, arms in the air, striking warrior poses. But there was something wrong. The class looked strangely out of sync. It took him a moment to realize that everyone in the room was missing a limb. It was amputee yoga. Hearing more sounds down the hallway, Uli moved along and peaked into another classroom.

A young dark-skinned teacher was addressing a lecture hall of older students. Uli stepped into the doorway and tried to listen to the young man speaking in a thick unidentifiable accent: ". . . Da streme leftward gave the streme right a chance to tip the wobbly middle, and they did it. Conned away from the crucifix retards who gave away their votes on trinket issues and working-class gestures, losing their basic well-being, not to mention the future of their dumb kiddies. Billions of bucks that could've gone to health or education were wasted in unwinnable slapdowns half a world away, so major corporations could secretly lift their little wallets. Dumbocracy is dead, and we're living proof of the need for a new criterion for voters based on a standard level of education and skepticism to protect the sentimentally feeble-minded . . . If mankind or America is to survive, we need a Smartocracy! If we can mobilize our forces, then in ten or twenty years, after we've returned to New York, we can try to instigate our own revolution to take power by—"

Turning abruptly, the man spotted Uli watching him from the doorway. Uli smiled as the foreign ideologue closed the door on him.

Uli headed on to a huge staircase at the end of the hall-

way and found a glass-framed directory that listed different departments:

DePartMeNt OF PRo7EcTEeS & DeTAiNEeS

DEpARtMEnT Ov EgG6 EPiDEmIc & AcUte Ammezia

Tw1n TeLePaTnY & ShAPeShiF7IhG

WoWoKa Profisies—CLoseD 1ndEf1nit7Y

dePaRtMent oF tErRORist oRgANiZaSHUns & tHeIR
maNY SPlIntERy gROvPs

At the bottom was listed, STATEN ISLAND BOROUGH
PRESIDENT, Room 310.

Uli marched up the three flights. Glimpsing the tiny
gold numbers on each door, he located Adolphus Rafique's
room. A heavyset secretary handed Uli a clipboard with an
extensive questionnaire on it. "You got to fill this out if you
want to speak to him."

Uli looked over the form: *Name (both Nevada & New York),
Address (Nev. & New), Birth Date, Employment, (Nev. & New)*. On
the back of page two, under *Personal Convictions (optional)*,
quirkier questions appeared, starting with, *Past and Present
Gang & Party Affiliations*, and moving on to, *Personal Stands on
Hot-Button Issues*, including, *Pro-life or Pro-choice*. Next was
Criminal Record.

Before he could even finish reading it, an older man
with a slightly wandering eye peaked into the waiting area.
"Mr. Rafique's ready for you."

When Uli entered the borough president's office,
Rafique shook his hand and took his blank form, then
asked, "Why do you look familiar?"

Uli shrugged and said, "I didn't have a chance to write
anything—"

"My eyes are shot anyway," Rafique said. "Just have a
seat and tell me about yourself." The man tossed his old
suit jacket against the back of his chair.

"Well, I found myself walking outside of JFK, chanting about killing Dropt, without a clue of how I got here. Though I'm beginning to remember some things, I suffer from general amnesia—"

"I just heard over the Crapper radio station that they blew up Cooper Union," Rafique said. "I don't suppose *you* killed him."

"No."

"What do you want to talk about?"

"Do you remember meeting a tall blonde in a fashionable miniskirt?"

"Ahh, the lobbyist," he sighed. "She gave me this." Rafique exposed his hairy wrist—a brand new digital watch. On it was the Feedmore logo: a brown-skinned baby suckling a light-skinned breast. "Also a big coffee mug."

"May I ask what you talked about with her?"

"It started out as an intellectual discourse on conservatism versus liberalism, and the next thing I know she's trying to unzip my trousers."

"Then what?"

"When I explained that I was a Buddhist celibate, she offered me bullets, provided I override my constituents and throw my presidential vote to the Democrats."

"It makes complete sense that she's trying to get you to vote for the Democratic party," Uli said.

"Uh, yeah, I already figured all this out," Rafique replied.

"If you vote Republican, I can get you an unlimited supply of water-purification pills—"

"Ever taste water after purification pills have been dropped in it? Yuck!"

"Look, if Spencer Tracy is reelected—"

"Ronald Reagan," Rafique corrected. "Not that it matters, cause there's no way he's getting reelected."

"Why not?"

"I heard over a homemade radio that a bunch of Iranian students recently grabbed the staff of the American embassy in Tehran and have been holding them hostage,"

Rafique explained. "Reagan hasn't taken any action and the American people don't forgive things like that."

"Not true," Uli replied. He didn't know how he knew, but he knew this: "When a Democrat doesn't use military force, people regard it as weakness. When a Republican doesn't use force, it's viewed as restraint."

"We'll just see about that," Adolphus Rafique said, amused.

"The point is, if Reagan is reelected to office, he's going to cut all excessive government spending. He's going to shut this place down and dump everyone in some Jersey ghetto—Orange or Newark, probably."

"How exactly do you know that?" Rafique asked him.

"It was Plan A," Uli answered without thinking, then froze. The dam of amnesia apparently had hairline fractures: He began remembering snippets of administrative and congressional hearings on what to do with the New York refugees. His mind flooded momentarily with flow charts delineating costs and projecting expenses. Congresswoman Chisholm and Senator Javitz from New York cosponsored a bill. Television pundits and critics from both sides of the aisle were arguing heatedly on all the political talk shows. Everybody was for Plan A because it didn't involve isolating anyone or suspending any civil rights. The plan was simply to transport the displaced New Yorkers to several economically distressed cities in the Garden State, where housing stock was plentiful yet dilapidated. Mass-produced trailers could take up the slack. That way the federal monies would help the struggling local economies as well as the newly afflicted homeless population. For a while it looked like the plan was going to fly. However, it required first passing a local referendum in New Jersey. That was when a coalition of lobbyists let loose a paranoid television and radio barrage demonstrating how such a plan would turn eastern New Jersey into a permanent ghetto. The referendum failed, and just as quickly the lobbyists initiated what became known as America's First Rescue City, where unfortunate people could slowly get back up on their feet without dragging down surrounding communities.

"Look," Rafique said, "you seem fairly smart, so I'll simply say that we Staten Islanders want to live in peace. Over the years we've had marauding gangs from both sides attack our people and use our borough as a dumping ground. We've had our food trucks hijacked and the water pipes from Jamaica Bay shut off. Hell, even after we built the canal that rescued Manhattan, we've still been attacked by the Crappers. We don't have the same resources as the others. That's why we need those bullets."

"Did you know Mallory?"

"The Councilwoman who was married to the former mayor?"

"She died in the explosion as well."

"Too bad. I liked her. She stayed out here awhile, with Leary's group."

"She asked me to speak to you before she was . . ." Uli paused. "Before she was murdered, she wanted me to try to get you to change your vote."

"If the Crappers were as honorable as they want to appear, they would've unblocked the sewer years ago." Adolphus had clearly made up his mind.

Glancing at the wall clock above Rafique's desk, Uli noticed with a start that it was five minutes to 6 o'clock. "I don't mean to be rude, but the last bus out of Staten Island tonight is leaving in a few minutes."

"Go ahead."

Uli said goodbye and dashed down the stairs, through the halls, and out of the large and drafty terminal. He ran about a hundred feet up toward the dusty road before he looked up and saw it lying on its side with its long brown tail flipping in the breeze.

A large cougar, probably down from the surrounding

mountains, slowly rose to its feet and stared at Uli, then started slinking over toward him. In the distance, Uli could see a rising plume of dust. The 6 o'clock bus was crossing the final stretch of roadway toward its terminus.

Uli took a deep breath and considered cutting across the rocky field toward the road to intercept the vehicle, but the cougar was still approaching. Keeping roughly forty feet between himself and the massive feline, Uli started retreating back to the VL headquarters. He watched helplessly as the last bus of the day reached the end of the road and, seeing no one there, drove in a big circle and slowly headed back toward Manhattan.

"Hold on!" Uli yelled out, and waved to the vehicle.

This only drew the big cat to him quicker.

"Fuck!" he muttered, as he pushed through the front door.

"What's up?" a security guard asked.

"A cougar is stalking me!" Uli said nervously, looking out the door.

The guard opened a side door and asked, "You see a cougar around here?"

"Yeah, it just took off," said a soft female voice. Uli turned to see a tall attractive woman with light brown skin standing behind him.

"That was a big one," said an older man with white cream on his face, who appeared through the same door as the tall woman.

"It kept me from catching my bus," Uli said. "Now I'm stuck out here for the damn night."

A very old hunchbacked man, clearly blind, tapped up to them with a white cane. He gently placed his wrinkled palm on the tall woman's back.

"We'll put you up," offered the older man with the white face.

"No, I can't, I have a bit of a problem." He didn't want to go into the whole amnesia mess.

"We know about your situation," said the woman, who looked about his age. She had long powerful legs and was barefoot.

"Besides," the man added, "the Piggers just blew up Crapper headquarters. They're rioting out there. Added to which it's a full moon. Spend the night here, and let them all kill themselves."

"Look, I just want to get the hell out of here," Uli replied.

"Maybe you should be more concerned with why you were sent here," said the tall woman.

"What do you know about me?"

The ancient blind man started rocking back and forth, mumbling something incoherent.

"What's he saying?" Uli asked.

"Wovoka summoned you," she replied.

"He said that?"

"No, he's deaf, blind, and mute," the woman explained, then repeated, "Wovoka summoned you."

"For what?" Uli asked.

The white-faced elder shrugged. "We might be able to help you discover who you are, but there are no guarantees."

"I appreciate your concern, but I really don't believe in any Indian mumbo-jumbo. And I should also add that I don't have any money or anything, if that's what you're after—"

"Since you're stuck out here for the night anyway, you have two choices," said the apparent chief with the cold cream on his face. "You can walk back to the city, which is a serious hike *if* you know where you're going. Or you're welcome to join us on a little trip while there's still some light. It might reveal some of the mystery about why you're here. Afterwards, we'll have dinner and put you up for the night."

"Where exactly is this trip to?"

"A hole in the earth's skull, through which you can visit

memories past and future," said the tall woman. "It's believed to be a nexus between this world and the other."

"It's also a really pretty rock formation," said the Indian chief.

"How far away is it?"

"About an hour each way," said the woman. "If we leave
here now, we should make it back for a late dinner."

"Why are you so eager to take me to this place?"

"I was instructed to," the chieftain replied.

"By who?"

"Look," the woman said as if reading his thoughts,
"your fear is understandable, but this is one of those moments in life when it really pays to have a little faith. We're
under a serious time constraint, but I guarantee you'll be
safe, and you might come to understand why you're here.
In the meantime, we can answer all your questions in the
boat."

Under any other circumstances the idea of venturing
out with a group of obvious nuts would have been simply
out of the question, but it seemed unlikely they would go
through all this just to kill him. Besides, if they were going to execute him, they'd have the entire night to do it
anyway.

"Let's go."

The chief gave a sharp low whistle, then led Uli downhill toward the embankment of the smelly basin. A long,
leaky wooden canoe was being paddled across the fetid
waters by a muscular man. The chieftain with the white
cream caked on his face and the tall muscular woman
grabbed the sides of the boat when Uli got in. The blind
elderly guy stood on the shore as the woman and man
started paddling across the quagmire that had formerly
been the old airfield. The putrid smell alone was almost
enough to make Uli hallucinate.

Only when they were far from shore, as Uli accidentally
rocked the boat, did the chief mention that this little body

of water was known as the Bay of Death; if any of them fell in, they'd perish before the day was done.

"I guess a life preserver wouldn't make a difference anyway," Uli replied, pinching his nostrils, then asked, "So, are you a born-again Indian tribe or something?"

"Actually, I'm a Buddhist," the man smiled. "I was formerly a Harvard professor of Psychology."

"How'd you get stuck out here?"

"I experimented with some mind-expanding drugs, advocated others to do so, and finally got arrested. Nixon himself sent me here," he said almost proudly.

"How about the others in your tribe? I heard something about environmental terrorists."

"We all care about the Great Mother," the woman spoke up, "but most of us are former Diggers from the Bay Area or Yippies from New York. My name, by the way, is Bea."

Uli shook her hand and turned back to the man. "You're the head of this shindig?"

"No way. They voted a pig as the head of the tribe, kind of a joke on the Piggers, but he died a few years back. I'm Tim."

"This place belongs to the Verdant League?"

"Actually, this area was Paiute and Shoshone. At least it was in the last century. But even before that, this part of Nevada was the site of the Sacred Caves going back thousands of years, and we're loyal to that."

"Where are they?"

"Below us, around us. Huge underground caverns, aquifers. There are long lava tubes and subterranean rivers redirected to build that damned waterway for the reservation. The Indian spirits probably blocked the drain for despoiling their holy place. There are documents that go back a hundred years foreseeing this area as the final reservation of the world's many scattered tribes."

"Who documented it?"

"A Paiute mystic who was raised by whites. He talked

about a dung-filled meadow where herds of buffalo could graze while the albino man destroyed himself."

"Was it Black Elk?" Uli asked, as they continued paddling over the shit-filled basin.

"No. Wovoka. But the whites gave him a Christian name, Jack Wilson." Uli remembered that as the alternative name of Flatbush Avenue. "He came back repeatedly, pretending to be one of the refugees, swearing he was from Manhattan."

"What do you mean he *came back*?"

"Actually, he was always here," Tim corrected. "Jackie Wilson was alone here for over a hundred years, waiting without aging, knowing without saying, being without hoping."

"And this is the guy who summoned me?"

"Yes."

"By name?"

"Yes, and he also gave me your face."

"So what's my name?" Uli asked, trying to get his mind off the smell.

"Ew-el-la-lee."

It sounded biblically similar to the other name he had heard two days earlier in Brooklyn—Huey. "Did he tell you why I'm here?"

"He doesn't answer questions. He shows."

After ten more minutes of being paddled through an ever-narrowing creek, Uli asked, "Where exactly are we heading?"

"This is the canal that Rafique made that drained most of the water covering Staten Island," Tim replied calmly. "It leads to an old lake bed, and at the end of that is what was called the Goethals Bridge. Actually, the rock formation that once arched over the Goethals Basin collapsed, so it's really now just an overhang . . ." As the chieftain talked, it was obvious that the odors didn't bother him. Just as Mallory had said, everyone he had seen since arriving at the terminal had evidently sacrificed some of their senses for surviving in Staten Island—any indication of their having an olfactory system was gone.

"So what is all that white stuff on your face?" Uli asked the chief, still trying to get his mind off the stink.

"I'm Irish. It's sunscreen. This place is a melanoma nightmare," the man replied as Uli pulled out the nose pin he had bought on the bus. "You okay?"

"My nose is dying a cruel and unusual death." Tears were streaming down Uli's face. Although his sinuses were as blocked as the sewage river, the toxic vapor seemed to infiltrate every pore of his body.

"Oh! I brought this for you," Tim said, and casually pulled something out of his waistband. He handed Uli a tiny tin. "We should start preparing for your meeting with Wovoka. Lie back in the canoe, remove your nose pin, put some of this on your top lip, close your eyes, and just listen to my voice."

Opening the tin, Uli found a clear ointment and smeared some under his nose. The long and skinny claw of E. coli that had hooked up into his intestines suddenly withdrew. A strong mentholated aroma liberated his sinuses. Lying back in the rear of the boat, Uli closed his eyes and listened to the chieftain, who said, "When we get to our destination, what you're going to be doing is commonly called *bilocation*. With Wovoka's help, you're going to travel out of here."

"Where?"

"You two will decide that," Tim said. "All I want you to do is try to relax, and when the time comes I want you to just let go. Do you understand?"

"Not really."

"We'll practice. I'm going to put you in a scene, and I want you to try to just lose yourself."

"Okay."

"Envision a cool November day. You are walking

upon the spongy floor of soft pine needles, among rolling hills of a New England forest. I want you to think of this as you inhale and exhale. Imagine your breath is like the spirit of some bird; look and try to find your bird guide, and it will take you over the trees and gentle pastures. Just inhale, exhale, and stay focused on your guide."

6:53 p.m.

After roughly half an hour of contemplation, imagining himself as a pigeon flying through some pastoral scene, Uli's cool inner reality came to an abrupt halt. The canoe started tipping from side to side. The woman warrior said, "Come on. We walk from here."

Nearly naked now except for scanty articles of cloth and homemade moccasins, his three companions were waiting for him.

When Uli got out, Bea and the silent paddler pulled the canoe up on the shore and flipped it over, draining the putrid water that had leaked inside. The man unknotted the long thick rope from the front of the boat and wrapped it around his bulging chest.

"I'm surprised the sewage flows this far," Uli commented.

"This was all the backed-up water that covered Staten Island," the chieftain said. He led the three others up along a series of stony plateaus rising like a row of massive steps. Although the copper rays of the setting sun illuminated everything, clouds blocked Uli's view of the summit. Looking back, he could see Staten Island spread out below. The black lines of sewage water snaked over it like veins and arteries on an old person's hands. Manhattan and Brooklyn were barely visible in the distance.

"What is this place?"

"It's a very big, very old volcano," Tim replied. "There

are only a few of them left in the world. Some are thought to be a thousand times larger than a regular volcano. And they are devastating. In fact, thousands of years ago, one of them in Africa was responsible for the near extinction of mankind. They believe that after it blew, only about seven thousand people remained."

"And this is one of those?"

"The entire reservation is built on a super volcano. The sacred caves are its lava vents and fumaroles, and someday when it blows the entire country as we know it will come to an end." Tim paused. "Strange things don't happen here simply because we pray for them or because old Indians say they do. They happen because this is a portal. It's literally the beginning of the end. In a few minutes, when you are lowered into the Goethals, you're going to be closer than anyone else alive to that awesome power."

"I'm not going to be bitten by snakes or anything, am I? Cause I'm terrified of snakes."

"No, you'll just sweat a bit."

They continued climbing upward several hundred feet until, winded, they reached the last step, a long flat plateau. Just when Uli thought the hike would get easier, the terrain started buckling into layers. He felt as though he were on the surface of a hostile planet. Trenches and precipices began appearing along with endless steam-filled ponds and geysers.

They finally reached a massive rock formation that rose like a stone rampway and jutted out over a large bubbling gorge. They walked out onto the rocky overhang about a hundred feet, until it nearly vanished into the mist.

The muscular paddler took the thick rope he was holding and began making complex knots.

"Once we lower you, I want you to close your eyes and concentrate like you did in the canoe," Tim instructed.

The muscle man told Uli to lie flat on the hot rocks as he slowly fit the knots around Uli's limbs, then wove the rope into a harness.

"What was your bird guide?" Tim asked.

"I imagined I was a pigeon."

"The flying rat of New York, perfect! Now, instead of green fields, let your winged rodent take you over a special place somewhere in New York."

"Can't we just do this here?" Uli asked, referring to the terra firma of the ridge.

"The visions over the Goethals are the strongest."

"My memories of the Big Apple aren't too good."

"Do you remember 42nd Street?"

"I think so," Uli said, and closing his eyes he was able to recall a postcard image of Times Square.

"Just focus on that," Tim said.

Wrapping the loose ends of the thick rope around their waists, Bea and the paddler lowered Uli off the narrow overhang of rock and into the foggy breach below. Laying flat like a static superman, Uli saw steamy plumes rising from the crater, shrouding the surface of a deep and bubbly cauldron. To push away all fear, he closed his eyes and tried to recollect the group of old buildings squeezed together by intersecting avenues around the palpitating heart of 42nd Street.

He simply couldn't remember a lot: Moderately sized buildings and low-level theaters with all the flourishes of the last century were pressed up against the cracked New York sidewalks. The strangely futuristic white structure— the Allied Chemical Building—with its lightbulbed news ticker sat in the middle of the Square.

A backfiring truck sent a flutter of pigeons high in the air. Uli watched as they descended in a dense yet complex pattern like little gray-feathered bombs flying onto the sill of a grungy office building. He now realized that he was one of them. But he wasn't in Times Square, he was in a residential community in one of the outer boroughs, he didn't know which. The backfiring wasn't a truck. It was the subdued explosion of dynamite under a steel blanket.

A freeway was being built right through some neighborhood. Then, as though seeing old photographs from his past, he remembered attending an Ivy League school and traveling down to Mexico. Uli had no idea why he was seeing this, but pushing it out of his head, he directed his thoughts back to the unharmonious buildings around Times Square.

Time seemed to slow down. The artful manner in which the body harness gently looped around his shoulders, waist, and thighs made him feel as if he was flying.

His blurry images of 42nd Street crystallized. The buildings in the Times Square tableau began moving like chess pieces being played. As though a great lens were being brought into sharp focus, vivid details came to him. He saw the faces of people that he couldn't possibly have imagined. Cornices, friezes, and intricate designs appeared on the façades of each of the old buildings. He could faintly make out neon signs and illuminated billboards. Blockbuster movies and musical theater were shamelessly advertised around the vast urban canyon. Rings of steam rose out of a billboard of a giant cowboy's mouth simulating cigarette smoke.

The minutia of cracks and potholes came into view along with litter on the pavement: Cigarette butts, broken ice-cream sticks, and ripped bus transfers washed around the dirt-encrusted gutter. Drug dealers, prostitutes, pimps, and cops all played out their fleeting routines. It was as though another bigger brain had climbed into Uli's cranium and usurped his feeble memory.

As darkness came, so did more people. Theaters and movies let out. People slowly evacuated until there were only a few homeless ones lodged in vacant doorways. Soon a new sun arose on Times Square.

Dawn—at 42nd and Seventh Avenue. Before rush hour could commence, Uli watched a tall, older figure wheeling a shopping cart. The man took an object out of his cart, left it on the curb, and waited for the light to turn green. Once a few cars passed, he walked out into the middle of the empty street with the object and lobbed it high in the air. He missed whatever he was aiming at but carefully caught the object as it fell. It resembled a large bola—two weights connected by a long string. He repeated this exercise until the light turned red, then retreated back to the corner and again waited for the light.

Uli tried flying down to see what the bola-like object was, but he couldn't budge. After ten minutes of tossing, Uli finally moved closer. The object appeared to be an old pair of sneakers tied together. Again the man dashed into the middle of the street, aiming for the arching bar holding the yellow metal casing around the three circular lights. Finally, the dirty laces of the two sneakers, which were knotted together, wound several times around the end of the narrow metal bar.

The old man returned to the corner, grabbed his shopping cart, and slowly wheeled it away. All that remained was the street and the sneakers dangling from the pole.

By the rising and setting of the sun, Uli could tell that time was speeding up. Yet life seemed to stop. The zebra flashes of day and night brought no more people or cars or trash or anything. Nothing but the wind and strobes of days and nights.

Eventually people started returning to the streets. One by one, the many cheap hotels and little porn theaters were renovated and improved. New chain stores replaced small businesses. The decrepit and isolated men and women were transformed into pudgy jolly families from out of town. Even the sidewalks were pulled tight and clean like new gray sheets.

As though someone had changed a TV channel, a flash of a family seated around a table interrupted his vision. It was the turn of the century now. Not in America. Strange soldiers burst into a dining room where a young husband, his beautiful wife, and their two children were eating from a platter of pilaf and lamb. He recognized the woman somehow.

Although he couldn't hear anything, Uli saw the family being forced outside. There they were joined by other members of their village. Something more than the rolling hills told him that they were in Asia Minor.

Again he tried to remember 42nd Street, and he was now back in midtown Manhattan. A nearly transparent force rippled and rushed like a surge of water down flooded avenues and streets. Uli realized he was literally seeing time. Instead of rushing steadily forward, time pushed forth and pulled back out: A fluttering of architectural corrections and stylistic revisions built up and receded in each of the many buildings. Then, one by one, the buildings shuddered, flaked, and collapsed as though suffering heart attacks. Newer, sleeker, taller buildings quickly rose in their places. Finally, time stopped and the city of buildings seemed to present itself across the ages all at once. Small, ancient wooden shacks mingled with towering futuristic skyscrapers.

The walkways came alive, trembling and broadening from dirt paths into stone slabs and cement sidewalks. They carried the interplay of varied city dwellers: occasional Native Americans from hundreds of years earlier, Dutch settlers from the early seventeenth century, subjects of the Crown in tricornered hats, bearded pioneers of the mid-nineteenth century, top hats and waistcoats from the Gilded Age, a pageantry of turn-of-the-century immigrants. They weren't merely walking side by side, but overlayed like transparencies, occupying the same space as the Depression-era downtrodden and happy-go-lucky hippies. Like shadows breaking off from darkness, sleek figures appeared who had to be citizens from the future. The entire city was becoming one giant shimmering termite hill. Communities with different races gave way to a single group of homogenized Americans.

8:47 p.m.

The rope suddenly snapped. No longer some god-damned bird, Uli was just a man falling to his death. Throwing his arms down to block the fall, he hit something wet. The pungent reek of shit filled his sinuses. He realized he was shivering in the bottom of the canoe. The others were sitting upright, gliding in the bright moonlight back over the flooded airfield. He could make out the dark figure of a rusting aerial tower overhead.

A massive front-lobe headache pushed away all thoughts. His entire body felt like a single aching board. At the same time, utterly exhausted, he couldn't stop shivering. He couldn't remember ever feeling so cold.

"He's freezing," Tim said, rubbing Uli's hands.

"We're almost there," replied Bea.

In another minute the muscle man jumped onto the muddy banks of Staten Island and pulled the narrow boat ashore. Bea and Tim tried lifting Uli, but the older man had trouble holding his legs, so Bea carried him in her arms like a child. She took him inside a small army surplus tent, where she dropped him into a pile of blankets and skins and started tearing off his clothes. In another moment, semi-delirious, he became aware that she was pressing against him naked, rubbing and tumbling her slick hard body against his quivering flesh.

"Thank . . . you . . ." he shivered out the words, then passed out.

10/31/80

1:22 a.m.

Uli woke to the sound of drumbeats and distant chants. Though a great deal of time seemed to have passed, it was still the same night. Bea was lying naked, bracing him tightly in her arms. He felt so grateful to her, he wanted to kiss her, but be also knew she hadn't done anything for romantic reasons.

"You okay?" she asked.

"I don't know what happened. I thought I was going to die."

"You were down too long. Do you remember anything?"

"Yeah, but . . . it was wild."

"Do you remember anything about New York?"

"Yeah, I thought I was a goddamned pigeon. I felt as though I were gliding above Times Square, just hovering."

"Nothing else?"

"Actually, I remember seeing this strange old man doing something, I'm not sure what . . . and then I saw New York over time . . ."

"Did you find out anything about your reason for being here?"

"No, not really. But I don't know, I saw a lot of things." Sitting up, he yawned. "God, I'm starving."

"Me too," she replied. "Let's get some chow."

A distant bonfire produced enough light for Uli to inspect her long lean body as she rose to dress. He watched her muscles ripple when she pulled on her shirt and shorts.

After helping him dress, Bea led Uli outside to their large communal space, a dry patch on the former rec field, where the tribe of roughly a hundred had pitched tents behind the old terminal. For some reason the smell here wasn't as bad as the rest of Staten Island.

It was a moonlit night and several circles of Indian-fusion types were celebrating on large homemade drums, all to a single beat. A bigger group was chanting. Among them were several large topless women swaying with their hands up in a trancelike state. In the middle, a small group of oddly dressed men and women were dancing in a circle.

"What's all this? Are they on the war path?"

"No, it's just a powwow," she explained. "They do it for purification, friendship, the wiping of tears, all that stuff."

"They have great costumes," Uli said.

"They really strive for authenticity here. That thing is called the bustle." She pointed out the colorful items sticking out of some of their backs: feathers and pointy quills that looked like they had been plucked from porcupines. "On their heads are war bonnets—those are optional."

"What about that guy wearing the German shepherd?" Uli asked.

"That's a coyote skin for animal medicine," she replied. "Some of them are shapeshifters, but no one here is actually Native American, so in a way it's all just an homage."

"And how about the topless ladies?"

"They work for tips," Bea kidded. The only person not dressed like a Native American was the blind, deaf old man who was now seated next to the drums.

Bea led Uli to another fire pit off to one side, where a collection of large cast-iron pots simmered from tripoded bars of steel over bright embers. She collected spoons and a pair of large wooden bowls and handed them to Uli, who held them out as she used a stick to remove a kettle top.

With a large ladle, Bea filled the two bowls. From a small metal container, she took out a loaf of black bread, then the two of them walked over to the outer circle and sat down to watch the evening's festivities.

"What's with the blind old guy?"

"He just showed up one day. Someone said he came from across the desert, but who knows."

"He doesn't seem to be one of the tribe."

"No, we feed him and look after him, but he's locked in his own world."

Inspecting the soup in the moonlight, Uli was surprised to see that it was purple. He nervously took a sip from his spoon and was delighted to find that it was a bowl of Russian borscht. "This is wonderful," he said between slurps, ignoring the dancing and festivities before him.

"The cook still has her sinuses and taste buds," Bea explained. "She also made some kind of stew in the big pot."

The two returned to the tripods of crockery, where Bea served them several racks of what looked like lamb chops.

"This is the best food I've eaten since I got here," Uli said with a full mouth. "What the hell is it?"

"Feral pigs. They're all over the place out here."

"You're kidding."

"Nope. Sometimes they grow as large as eight hundred pounds. It's one reason I won't leave."

"What did you do before you came here? Back in New York."

"Before coming here I had been unemployed for quite a while, which was one of the reasons I moved."

"What did you do before you were unemployed?"

"A lot of freelance gigs."

"Did you ever have a steady job?"

"Once, and I held it for about five years."

"What was it?" he asked with genuine curiosity.

"I was the general secretary for the J.C.S.L.E.S.E.," she said, as though it was universally known.

"What's that?"

"That was the Joint Committee to Stop the Lower East Side Expressway. I had to quit because I got arrested and then we ended up disbanding after we won."

"What was the Lower East Side Expressway?"

"Something that bastard named Robert Moses tried to build."

"Why does that name sound so familiar?"

"He was a big New York politician for years."

"I bet your parents didn't like you taking a job that would put you in jail."

"Actually, I ended up taking it because of them. See, I was born in the East Tremont section of the Bronx. When Moses constructed the Cross Bronx Expressway, it destroyed my neighborhood."

"So you moved to the Lower East Side?"

"The Bronx turned into a ghetto. My father vanished, my mother got killed, and I ended up being raised by a foster family."

"I guess things hadn't really improved when New York got hit . . ."

"My life here is actually better, a lot better than in New York," she said. "I'm pro-life, and if we were told we could return to New York tomorrow, I think I'd stay here. I really do. I mean, I've never felt so equal, or so powerful."

"But don't you feel cut off from civilization? Don't you miss the technological advances? Men walking on the moon and all the electronic gadgetry?"

"You have no clue how much that stuff has taken from us."

"Like what?"

"Like that," she said, pointing up. The brilliant glow of a million constellations burned brightly in the sky. "If you stare up there for ten seconds, you'll count more shooting stars than you've seen in a lifetime. It's more amazing than any TV show could ever be. And it makes you think more about God and man than all the college classes put together."

An owl hooted nearby.

"And listening to nature is far more rewarding than most phone calls."

"I've always been a city boy myself," Uli replied.

"The price of all this technology is that people aren't evolving spiritually anymore."

Uli yawned, then apologized and explained that the day had knocked him out.

"Me too," she replied. "Do you want to sleep in your own tent or would you like to come back with me?"

"I was very comfortable with you."

She brought Uli to the line of latrines placed at the edge of the encampment so that all waste flowed into the polluted basin. While Bea was in the bathroom, Uli heard some rustling behind a clump of nearby bushes. Expecting to see an animal, he was surprised to come face-to-face with a naked old man scurrying around on all fours. The guy hissed at Uli, then ran into the distance. Uli watched him as he sniffed a large rock and then urinated.

"What the hell is he doing?" he asked Bea upon her return.

"Oh, that's Sam. He's just prowling."

"Prowling?"

"You'd probably regard it as flaky," she said with a smile. "He's trying to become a badger."

"A badger? Have you ever seen anyone turn into an animal?"

"I don't know all the jargon, but there is worldwide documentation of shapeshifting. In Europe there are ample cases of werewolves, weredogs, werebirds . . . there are even claims of weredolphins."

When they got back to Bea's tent, she dropped to her

fours and crawled in through the flaps. As she pulled her shirt and pants off, Uli dropped his line of questioning. He turned around, took a deep breath, and removed his own clothes. Together they got in under the thick quilt. Uli began gently stroking Bea's back, amazed by how muscular she was.

"What are you doing?" she asked.

"I was wondering if you wanted to . . ."

"Not until the third date," she said tiredly.

"Huh?"

"It's my one rule: If I date anyone three times, I'll sleep with them. And though this isn't technically a date, I'll let it count as the first."

Exhausted after the long day, both were fast asleep within minutes.

 7:20 a.m.

The large cougar was asleep on their legs.

"Bea," Uli softly prodded her, attempting not to panic.

Still asleep, she reached out and swatted the animal's flanks. It hopped to its feet and bound out of the tent.

"We could've been killed," he complained with a sigh.

"We can always get killed," she sleepily replied, and pulled him closer.

When he kissed her she didn't stop him, but she didn't kiss back. A bright sun was just peaking up over the hills. In a moment, they both started dressing.

"This place is really beautiful," he commented.

"Want to go on a hike?"

"Sure."

Before the camp could become busy with activity, Bea filled a bag with shipped-in oranges, apples, homemade biscuits, and some leftover racks of pork from the night before. She offered him a nose pin, but he still had the one he'd bought on the bus. Together they went out to the basin, where she grabbed one of the four handcarved canoes. They got in and paddled over the basin for roughly half an hour until they came to land on the far side. Bea pulled the canoe up on an isolated landing and led him on a walk through the sparse landscape. The region wasn't all desert, and the two hiked over parched salt flats with strange mineral formations until they came to a steep hill. With sweat trickling down his face, peering back over the vast skyline and rolling hills, Uli felt raw, endless beauty in the soaring expanse. It was as if no other humans had ever set foot here.

Upon reaching the top of a hill, Uli spotted a seemingly perfect curve in the wild—a long, bending concrete wall in the distance.

"That was the original end of the retaining wall where the sewage river once flowed."

"Where was it blocked?" he asked.

"A ways north of here. Want to see it?"

"Sure."

"We won't be back in Tottenville till later this afternoon."

"My appointment book is wide open."

Over the next few hours, as they hiked, Uli recounted how he'd found himself walking along a road near JFK without knowing who he was or how he got there. He had been programmed to kill Dropt, who was then murdered yesterday.

"Did your trip to the Goethals answer any questions?"

"Nothing clearly. At one point, I saw this family and I think they might have been Armenians during the genocide."

"Maybe you're Armenian."

"Did Tim tell you anything about me?"

"He only said that an important person in deep trouble would be passing through."

"I have this awful feeling that he's mistaken me for someone else. It's happened before."

"The vision you told me about . . ." she started.

"I'd call it a dream."

"Well, I've never heard of anyone being able to move through time."

"A dream's a dream," he opined.

"Unless, of course, you learned something in that dream that you didn't previously know."

"Since my memory is missing, I'm not sure what I knew, and I have to confess right now that I think this entire Wovoka thing is a load of bullshit."

"Consider this: If it's *not* bullshit, he might've been showing you something."

As they walked, Uli contemplated his dream sequence. He remembered the tall old man tossing the pair of sneakers over the Times Square sign pole. What significance could this have?

"So, what do you want out of life?" he eventually asked.

She shrugged.

"Do you want children?"

"Not anymore. Now that no one else can have them, it doesn't really bother me."

"Have you ever committed any terrorist acts?"

"Would it bother you if I did?"

"Nothing you can do would bother me."

"Just for that, I'm gonna count this as a second date," she kidded.

By 11 o'clock, the sulfuric odor had intensified as the land turned to marsh. After another hour, Bea pointed at a hill to their right. Large craggy rocks surrounded its top like a crown.

"Up there somewhere is the hole Jackie Wilson supposedly bore into the old sewer system when he was trying to fix the drain."

Uli felt a dull pain in his lower back and the arches of his feet. He sighed, wiping the sweat off his forehead.

Bea knew she should've brought a canteen, and sensed that he was tuckered out but too proud to say so. "Would you mind if we returned now?" she asked.

"Really?"

"It's going to get a lot hotter and we still have a long walk back."

"Good point."

Turning around, they hiked back up the hill they had just descended. At the first clearing, the stench diminished and they sat down to eat the remainder of their food.

When they were nearing the canoe, moving through a bog of tall grass, they heard something rushing toward them from several hundred feet away. Bea sniffed in the direction of the rustling.

"It's probably one of those feral pigs," Uli speculated.

"No, they run off when they hear people." Stepping backwards, she asked him, "Do you remember where we left the canoe?"

"Yeah, why?"

"Take it and paddle back across the airfield," she said, then suddenly dashed off in the direction of the sounds they'd just heard.

"Wait a sec!" he called out.

"Go, I'll catch up!" she yelled back. "Just do as I say!"

"Wait a second!"

He tried to follow her, but in a moment she had vanished. He continued heading where he thought she had gone, but soon the landscape was totally silent. Feeling vulnerable in the maze of tall grass, he rounded back toward the Bay of Death before him. As he approached the canoe, he heard a galloping sound from several directions at once. Climbing up onto the limb of a dead tree, he could see the top of the grass rustling from a couple hundred feet away. Then he spotted it in a small clearing: The large brown razorback of a wild boar, complete with a sharp pair of dark gray tusks, was charging toward him. Before he could react, he heard a second boar coming at him from the opposite direction. Dashing through the tall grass, it moved like a wave, passing right alongside of him and intercepting the first boar. The sound of insane squealing filled the air. He watched as the first boar, which had to be at least a couple hundred pounds, was tossed up above the grass before slamming back to the wet earth.

Uli used the opportunity to race to the clump of bushes where they had left the canoe. He pulled it across the muddy bank, into the water, and floated out. Looking back to the shore, he wondered what to do about Bea. Suddenly, something very large plopped right into the front half of the canoe, almost catapulting him into the toxic sludge.

Uli leaned back instinctively to keep from tipping over and quickly realized it was Bea who had jumped in.

"Where the hell were you?" he gasped.

She was winded and covered in sweat. He carefully climbed over to her and found that she was freezing.

"You okay?" He put his hand to her face, causing her to flinch. She seemed to be elsewhere.

"Give me a minute," she said, still panting. Her shirt was nearly torn off.

"Where did you go? Why did you run off!" He hugged her tightly to him, trying to get her core temperature up.

"A minute," she said, pushing him away, still trying to catch her breath.

Uli picked up a paddle and started rowing them across the large basin.

3:23 p.m.

As they neared Tottenville, Uli noticed someone on the far shore staring out at them. It was an older, slightly hunched man, and though Uli wasn't certain, he thought it might be Rafique. Then he saw the figure limp away. When the canoe glided onto shore, Tim and a small entourage walked stiffly over to the river's edge.

"Uh oh, I think we're in trouble," he said.

"I can't imagine why," Bea responded.

Tim asked if he could speak to Uli alone. Getting out of the canoe, Uli watched as two of the chief's sidekicks led Bea away.

"You just missed the afternoon bus," Tim said sternly.

"I wasn't planning on catching it."

"Well, you can't stay here."

"Why not?"

"Look, the curfew has been lifted, so unless you have further business with Rafique . . ."

"I don't understand."

"There is a limit to the amount of people we can feed and house here. Hell, there's a list of applicants waiting to join us. We simply can't let anyone just live here."

"I was only hoping to spend a few more days here."

"There's another bus at 6. Please get on it."

"Where did they take Bea?"

"This place doesn't run itself, she has chores to do like everyone else," Tim said, then walked away.

When Uli called out to Bea, a group of large men who looked like security staff walked over in tight formation.

"I just want to talk to Bea."

"Well, she doesn't want to see you," said the biggest of them. "Now please go."

"I'm not leaving until I'm convinced that she's safe," he declared.

"Then you're going to make us remove you by force," the man responded, and reached out to grab Uli. Without thinking, Uli pulled the man forward, sending him to the ground. When a second man lurched at him, Uli swooped low and flipped the guy over his back.

"Don't touch him!" Tim shouted in the background.

Everyone took a step back. "I'll tell her to speak to you when she's done with her chores."

Although Uli offered to help one of the men to his feet, the guy got up on his own.

Realizing that he couldn't fight the entire tribe, Uli walked over to the main road. The security team followed at a distance. Uli sat up against the only tree and waited. The guards finally walked away.

Over the next two hours, Uli tried to figure out what could have offended the tribe. Eventually he dozed.

5:38 p.m.

*B*y *the arid and hilly landscape, Uli instantly knew he was back in Asia Minor and felt a palpable sense of dread. He noticed the young family he had seen dining earlier—minus the father. It seemed that a few days had passed. The beautiful mother, now filthy and exhausted, was clinging to the hands of her two toddlers. The three of them were standing at the rear of a long bedraggled line of a hundred or so women and children—all dressed in heavy turn-of-the-century garb, covered in the dust and dirt of the unpaved road—moving tiredly in the burning noonday sun.*

He watched them all shuffling along like sleepwalkers. Some in slippers, clothing torn. Others in long, heavy dresses that were frayed at the hems. Hair matted, caked in dirt and grime. White powder crusted around the sides of their chapped lips. From the scabbed wounds and bruises along their arms and faces, it was clear they had survived some sort of attack.

Uli sensed that their men had already been slaughtered. The slow line was being led by two short, fat soldiers. A third soldier was bringing up the distant rear. It appeared that they had already walked miles through the dust.

As he shifted positions for a better view, Uli could see a gang of beefy men hidden up ahead behind a mound of large rocks. As the refugees approached, some of the younger men in the gang bolted out to grab them.

An older man with an eyepatch and walking stick took off after the younger marauders. Amidst screaming and shouting, a fight broke out. Uli realized they were battling each other for the prettiest girls in the group—though none of the women were much younger than twenty-five. All the teenage girls must have already been taken.

When a young attacker tried to grab one of the women, she kicked him. The youth punched her hard in the face, then tried dragging her away. Before he could get very far, however, a large older woman, perhaps the young woman's mother, raced up and gouged her fingers into his eyes. She knocked him backwards, but another man approached, pulled out a dagger, and calmly slashed her throat. As she fell to the ground gagging, the teenage attacker took out his penis and started urinating on the dying woman.

The daughter was too tired to even rise from the dirt. When one of the other soldiers yelled at the throat-slitter, the teenager stopped pissing on the dying woman and instead kicked the daughter in the ribs, stomping her midsection until she started to cough blood.

Uli noticed that none of the men actually had guns—they didn't need them. As a mother and her two children tried to march past the small band of now-retreating attackers, one of the men grabbed her daughter. The little girl let out a high-pitched shriek and her brother froze in terror. The mother tried to hold her daughter around the waist. Uli watched as one of the men tore off the back of the young mother's lace shirt, then ripped her corset down, exposing her breasts, before knocking her to the ground. Another older man lifted the screaming girl over his shoulder and walked off up a hill. Realizing that the man had abducted the little girl, the first attacker raced after him to recover his prize. The terrified boy ran over to his weeping mother, who struggled to her feet, half-naked and bloody. Without even glancing at her screaming daughter being carried away, the mother pressed on with her son.

The other men let them pass, as they were busy clubbing some of the other prisoners. Once hit, the victims either stumbled onward or simply collapsed to the ground, too exhausted to do anything else. None of the attackers finished them off. Apparently, there was no point in humiliating people who were nearly dead.

He awoke to the sensation of something trickling down his neck. At first he thought it was just sweat, but when the delicate sensation moved upward, he flinched, fearing it was a spider. Bea was kneeling before him, stroking his head with one hand and holding a brown paper bag in the other.

"Sorry," she said. "You looked so much at peace, I didn't want to wake you."

"I was having some weird dream," he replied as he rose to his feet. "It was almost a continuation of something I saw at the Goethals."

"It might not be a dream," she said. "You know how sometimes you get really good TV reception if you place the antenna in a certain place?"

"Yeah."

"This place has another kind of reception. Dreams here are far more vivid. Some think it's a form of communication."

"Tim seemed really pissed off," Uli said, changing the subject. He didn't care for all her hocus-pocus. "Maybe we weren't supposed to talk about that thing at the Goethals."

"Actually, he asked me to help you think about it."

"Oh?"

"You have to understand. He's never had a vision about some mysterious stranger coming, and he's never taken a stranger out to the Goethals," she said softly. "You're here for a reason."

"What reason could that possibly be?"

"I don't know. Neither does he. But he does know that whatever your purpose is, it's not going to be achieved hanging around here."

"Do *you* want me to remain here?" he asked.

"Look, I'm sure we'll meet again, but for now I actually agree with him."

"What am I supposed to do?"

"What were you going to do twenty-four hours ago when you walked out of your meeting with Rafique?"

"Frankly, I haven't given it much thought. I don't have a home or job, I don't even know who I am."

"I promised not to counsel you. All I can say is trust your instincts," she said, "and be very careful. Rescue City is as divisive and deadly as any prison yard."

"At least tell me why you ran off when we were on the other side of the basin today."

"It's a little embarrassing," she said. "I'd rather not go into it."

"I really need to know."

"I thought that animal was stalking us because of me, and I was trying to lead it away."

"It was a wild boar," he said.

"Yeah, well, I just began menstruating. I figured he caught my scent and I was trying to draw him away from you. In case you didn't notice, I'm very fast."

"I did notice. I couldn't keep up with you."

"I went back to where we had come from, but after a while, when I realized it wasn't following me, I ran back to you."

"How did you get into the boat? I had already left the shore."

"I jumped from a big rock," she replied. Uli decided not to ask any more questions, since she obviously didn't want to talk about it.

They chatted idly a bit more, until the 6 o'clock bus finally appeared in the distance. She kissed Uli gently on the lips as the vehicle came to a halt in front of them.

"Oh, this is for you," she said, handing him the paper bag she had been holding. "It's just some fruit for your trip."

He thanked her. "The next time we meet, will it count as our third date?"

"You bet," she said with a smile.

"Then I'll definitely see you later." Uli kissed her again and stepped inside the bus. The little door folded shut and the vehicle sped off.

"Well, looky here, it's my old traveling buddy."

It was the one-armed driver he had been hijacked with in Borough Park three days before. Uli greeted him and took a seat.

"I hate to tell you this, but the fare is still a sixteenth-stamp."

"Of course." Uli rummaged through his pockets and discovered that the few stamps he'd had yesterday were mysteriously missing. "Can I owe you?"

"Nothing personal, but I don't even let my mother ride for free. What you got in there?"

Uli opened the brown bag that Bea had given him. "Apples, carrots, and bananas."

"With these old teeth, all I can eat are the nanas." Uli handed them over and took a seat across from the driver. "So, what happened to that lady and the retarded guy?"

"Both were killed."

"Shame," the driver replied, not particularly surprised.

"Let me ask you something," Uli said. "Where would you go if you didn't have any money or a place to sleep?"

"Well, seeing how you're educated and all, there's only one place out here where you can just walk in and get an instant job and a home, but I don't particularly recommend it."

"What is it?"

"P.P.," the driver said. "Last stop."

"Why wouldn't you recommend it?"

"Everyone calls it *Pud Pullers*, cause they don't really fuck you, but they don't get you off either."

In a way it made complete sense. The dubious philanthropic organization, Pure-ile Plurality, seemed to be the hidden citadel of power behind the Piggers. Uli remembered what the girl on the bus had said—that if someone could get evidence that the organization was controlled by the Piggers, the City Council would be forced to stop funding them.

"How long is the trip?"

"Long. Several hours. You're lucky cause we bypass Manhattan, going directly over the Zano on the way back to Brooklyn. I'll wind through Park Slope, then over toward JFK."

Uli was glad to hear it. The thought of seeing the decimated Crapper headquarters again was just too much for him.

The bus slowly headed north. No one got on at either Charleston or Rossville.

After another half hour, as the setting sun shot blood-red rays across the desert landscape, the driver switched from fuel cells to the battery, and the bus pulled into a neighborhood called Bull's Head, where a few others boarded. They drove along the eastern side of Staten Island, where a delta of shitty creeks and inlets broke off from the primary river.

Despite the cool evening air, the toxic smell intensified again, making Uli's eyes tear. The bus lumbered across another of the many long flat riverbanks where the backed-up sewage swelled out over the highway. Uli tried to snooze but the smell was too much, even with his nose pin.

As they drove up onto the Zano Bridge, they passed over a small barge heading south along the shoals of Staten Island. Since the water under the bridge was significantly less polluted and a gentle breeze was blowing down from the north, the odor virtually vanished as they crossed into Brooklyn. As soon as they arrived in the borough—around 8:30—the bus hit traffic. It took fifteen minutes for them to get through Bay Ridge.

Wanting to avoid traffic coming in over the Brooklyn Bridge as they progressed up the western side of the borough, the driver detoured east, cutting out a few stops in Cobble Hill. The speed dropped dramatically as the vehicle labored up the steep slant of Park Slope.

When the bus reached the plateau, Uli realized they

were near Flatbush Avenue/Jackie Wilson Way. He began to smell something burning.

"Shit!" the driver muttered, seeing a column of thick black smoke rising in front of them. "Everyone take a deep breath, we're going in."

Throughout the next several blocks, smoke shot out of windows and doorways of buildings on both sides of the street. Uli spotted some guy throwing a Molotov cocktail into the window of a sixteenth-stamp store. Men in blue shirts were running up the street.

"Get that fucker!" Uli heard one of them yell. "He stabbed Barnes!"

Red-shirted figures were slowly retreating. As the bus proceeded, Uli saw two lines of men fighting side by side with pipes, spears, and chains—a gang war was raging.

"It's retaliation for the Manhattan bombing," the driver said. "The guys in blue are Crappers, the red shirts are Piggers."

"Actually, it's retaliation *for* the retaliation," some old voice behind Uli chimed in.

"They probably blew up the building themselves. The Crappers are always provoking things," another rider opined.

The further east the bus proceeded toward the Brooklyn-Queens border, the hotter the conflagration grew. Soon, burning debris thrown from a partially collapsed building blocked the street.

Uli watched as two red shirts grabbed one of the overweight blue shirts. While one spun him to his knees, the other shoved a knife into the man's neck. Not content to simply let him die, more red shirts joined in, stabbing and kicking him.

Others on the bus looked away, but Uli found himself transfixed. Something new inside of him, some deep animalistic power, like an erection in his heart, made him yearn to join the red shirts.

In another moment, the driver zoomed through the inferno, rolling right over burned pieces of wood. Once clear, the bus sped along for several more blocks until screeching to a halt before a man sitting on a tiny traffic island with a single metal pole. A sign on the pole said: *Grand Army Plaza*. As the man rose, Uli saw he had a shirt that was half red and half blue. For a moment he wondered if it was a statement of bipartisan unity. Then he realized the guy had incurred a serious stomach wound and was bleeding badly. Mercifully, the driver let him stagger on board without paying. The wounded Crapper soldier struggled down the aisle holding his stomach. He limped to the back and dropped into a double seat. Perhaps fearing gang reprisals, no one helped.

When the bus hit a huge pothole, Uli whacked his head against the seat in front of him. The ensuing headache compelled him to sprawl out over two seats and before long he was asleep. Immediately he returned to his interrupted dream.

The mother and son had almost escaped when the last of the marauders, the older man with an eyepatch and walking stick, noticed them passing by. As though inspecting a farm animal, he cupped one of the young mother's exposed breasts in his hand. She kept moving as though nothing had happened. He grabbed her thick black hair, twisted it tightly around his large hand, and yanked her away from the group. Her crying son clutched her dress, refusing to let go. An older woman protested forlornly, but when the eyepatched man cursed at her, she just looked down and kept walking. The young boy started furiously kicking and slapping the old man with the eyepatch. Without any indication of anger, the guy released the mother and stepped away as though to let them pass. Then, as the two proceeded onwards, he lifted his heavy walking stick and brought it squarely down on the top of the boy's skull. The child flopped forward, convulsing and gushing blood, and his mother slumped next to his small body. The man with the eyepatch calmly coiled the woman's long beautiful hair in his hand like rope and led her back up to join the rest of his band behind the pile of boulders.

The last soldier, an older man whose fat head swelled out of his tight helmet, brought up the rear of the prisoners and cursed. As he stepped around the fallen elderly bodies—still alive, yet too injured to keep walking—he shouted angrily at the attackers. For a moment, Uli thought he was condemning the violent assault, but quickly realized why the soldier was outraged: Since the marauders hadn't slaughtered or taken all the women, he now had to march them into the endless expanse of burning desert.

Suddenly Uli's vision changed. Someone was holding his arms and legs down. A slender pair of hands were unzipping his pants, reaching into his underwear. Far from erotic, the hands were stabbing a sharp needle into his groin.

An intense pain shot through his body, causing him to leap to his feet and scream. Covered in sweat, still on the bus, Uli felt embarrassed. Yet something was indeed pressing into his groin. Reaching into his pants, Uli found that his missing roll of food stamps had somehow slipped through a hole in his pocket and gotten caught in his underwear.

"Sorry," he said to no one in particular.

Aside from the weak bus headlights, the streets were pitch black. It had to be at least an hour later. The bus was nearly empty. The working streetlights were far and few. The sporadic buildings in this section of the reservation were mostly industrial warehouses with hurricane fences. There were no other cars or people around. Uli figured they were somewhere in outer Queens. As they rolled past blocks of darkness, haphazard piles of garbage and vandalized solarcars littered the streets.

Soon the road narrowed into a tight single lane as it hugged a concrete retaining wall that went on for at least a mile. When the road lifted above the height of the wall, Uli saw a large enclosed reservoir with a sign that read, *Jamaica Bay.*

Slowly, vaguely, through the darkness, Uli recognized this moonlit basin from a few days earlier. He had come full circle. He heard a large cargo plane overhead, which reminded him that he was near JFK Airport. At a lonely intersection in a neighborhood that the driver identified as Rosedale, Queens, the bus came to a tired halt, the last stop.

The driver threw open the door and called out, "Pud Pullers. Time for everyone to get rubbed off!"

Looking out the window, Uli saw the four large brownish buildings before him. He remembered seeing them from the far end of Jamaica Bay on the first day he had arrived.

"Hey, this guy's not moving," an elderly passenger said, referring to the wounded blue shirt. The guy had flopped sideways and was dripping and drooling into a pool of blood below him. Uli helped the driver carry the street fighter's body off the bus.

Some strange girl who was waiting outside came over as they laid the dead Crapper's body on the sidewalk. She took rosary beads from around her neck, dropped to her knees, and started praying: "Jesus, son of Yahweh! This man hath fought in the army of Satan. For him it is too late. Please burn his body for all eternity like the many fetuses he aborted and the countless children and virgins he doubtlessly sodomized. Amen."

Uli realized immediately that it was the zealous Shub campaigner who had threatened him when Oric was detained. Everyone walked away from the dead man on the sidewalk.

"You're just going to leave him here?" asked Uli.

"Someone will find him before the dogs do," the driver assured him. "The local gangcops get a reward every time they bring in a body."

The driver walked around to the rear of the bus, where he pulled out a lengthy orange extension cord and plugged it into an outlet at the base of a streetlight. It was time for a recharge. He returned to his seat and pulled the visor of his hat over his eyes, instantly falling asleep. Uli followed the small crowd heading toward the complex of buildings.

At the doorway, a plaque read, *Pure-ile Plurality: How the Other Half Should Live.* A broad walkway led into a narrow courtyard in front of a large well-lit lobby. Only through this central building could one gain access to the overpasses leading to the three neighboring warehouses.

Roughly a dozen women holding infants or pushing strollers dashed past Uli, presumably to catch the bus. Uli thought perhaps he had been misinformed about the EGGS epidemic.

One straggling mother, noticing his eagerness to glance at her child's face, smiled proudly. She pulled back a small comforter, revealing a shivering Chihuahua dressed in swaddling clothes. Its moist eyes blinked delicately.

"Dat's mi bebe," she cooed.

"But it's—"

"I think I might owe you an apology," he heard from behind. It was the self-righteous campaigner who had just condemned the lost soul of the dead soldier.

"Sorry?"

"It wasn't very Christian of me, scalding your poor feeble-minded friend," she said. "I know I should be more forgiving, but you have to understand that decent people have suffered so much." Turning to the mother, who was patiently waiting for her dog baby to be adored, the young zealot said, "You better hurry, Consuela. The bus back to Manhattan is almost recharged."

"Much gracias," she said, then dashed off with her pup to the bus.

"May I ask what it is you're doing here?" the zealot said to Uli.

"Actually, I was hoping to volunteer."

"Great, where you coming from?"

"I just arrived from Staten Island."

"Let's go, I'll show you the way."

The young campaigner introduced herself as Deer Flare. As she led Uli inside, she softly explained, "These ladies are here for treatment. You've got to be very careful."

"Careful how?"

"Since the EGGS epidemic, many women have been traumatized about being reproductively challenged. The man in charge here, Rolland Siftwelt, has set up a variety of workshops to help them cope with their infertility. He's also established these furry surrogates."

A security guard at the central building asked Uli to pass through a metal detector and then took his fingerprints. When Uli turned up without any kind of record at all, the guard stopped him.

"It's okay," Deer assured the man. "I'll vouch for him. Mr. Siftwelt wants to see him."

On the second floor, she silently led him down a linoleum-tiled hallway, up a short stack of steps, and through a large outer reception area with a middle-aged secretary stationed in front of a tall set of cloudy glass double doors.

"Joane, could you tell Mr. Siftwelt that a new arrival is here?" Deer said politely. Looking at her watch, she added, "Oh gosh, I'm late for a strategy meeting. I'll see you later." She abruptly ran off.

"Name?" the frumpy secretary asked Uli.

"Huey, I think."

The secretary suggested he take a seat. Looking over at a magazine rack, Uli saw a number of illustrated pamphlets printed on cheap grainy paper. One with a large yellow oval on it was entitled, *Making Lemons out of Lemonade*. Another pleaded, *Join the Gang o' God!* Inside was a cartoon of a robust, happy creature and a puny, gloomy figure. The big fellow was pointing to a multilayered cake. Underneath, in a small font, it said, *When Unhappy—EAT!*

The intercom buzzed. The secretary smiled and nodded for Uli to go inside—Rolland Siftwelt was ready for him. Uli entered his office, but the chairman of P.P. was nowhere to be seen. A wide variety of trinkets and snow globes filled his shelves. Posted behind Siftwelt's big desk was a large map of New York, Nevada, divided up by red and blue borders.

Uli heard a flush, then a red-faced man with a muscular chest and huge biceps burst through a small side door that had to be his private bathroom.

"The name's Rolland Siftwelt." He gave Uli a powerful handshake and talked in a low, confiding voice: "Remember what New York City was like before we were attacked?"

"I'm suffering from acute memory loss, so . . . no."

"It was very, very dangerous. Divided by gangs and drug dealers, the homeless roamed the streets and the average inner-city resident was incarcerated at least once before the age of twenty-five. Teen pregnancies boomed and life-expectancy dropped."

"Don't all those things still exist here?"

"We do have some drugs and two gangs, but there are fewer bullets and teens with every passing day."

Siftwelt's phone rang and he pardoned himself to answer it. He listened for a moment with a pinched expression on his face, then shouted, "There's a big difference between a three-foot prototype and one designed to carry people! I've got someone in my office." He slammed the phone down, took a moment to recompose himself, and asked, "Ever heard of Jack Wilson?"

"Yeah, they renamed Flatbush Avenue after him," Uli said.

"He vanished a number of years ago. Rumor has it he was killed by one of his lieutenants and his body was dumped in the desert. But lately a crazy new rumor has been surfacing—that he learned to fly."

"He could fly?"

"A plane."

"You mean . . . an airplane? He built an airplane?"

"It's absolutely ludicrous, but the rumor has all these kite flyers thinking they can be the next Wilbur and Orville Wright."

"How'd the rumor get started?" Uli asked hopefully.

"Someone supposedly found a miniature prototype. But guess what: I can make a prototype by folding a sheet of paper." Instantly changing the topic, Siftwelt leaned forward in his chair. "Before we go any further, let me fill you in a bit on what we're about. We started out as a religious mission that went door to door in many of the inner cities of this great country."

"Does that mean—"

"If you let me just make my pitch, I think it'll answer all your questions." Uli smiled and Siftwelt resumed. "For starters, we have a big dorm that most workers live in. Novices usually start with outreach. We pair them up and send them into tough neighborhoods, where they try to spread the word of a good, healthy, violence-free, community-building lifestyle. As well as the value of getting educated."

"You know, there's a rumor that the Piggers run P.P."

"Yes, and one that P.P. runs the Piggers."

"So it's false?"

"Let me put it this way: Even when the Crappers were in power, I was friends with Mayor Will just as I am with Shub. Could I get either man to do as I say? No."

"Are you a religious organization?"

"Everything's religious," the man replied.

Before Uli could ask any further questions, a cute thin woman with a box-shaped head and a crisp brown tan entered.

"This is Ernestina Eric," Siftwelt introduced. "And this is our newest member, Huey. Ernestina is the supervisor for Brooklyn South." Turning to her, he added, "Huey is going to be working with you. Would you mind giving him a tour and bringing him up to speed?"

"Sure." Instead of taking a seat, she led him out the door. Uli thanked Siftwelt as he exited the office.

"This job is mainly old-fashioned street-corner work," Ernestina said. "We have to try to energize a listless people. It's late. Why don't you get settled? We'll talk more over dinner."

Joane, the executive secretary, instructed Uli to fill out a batch of forms. While he did so, she typed him a temporary ID and mentioned other perks such as a free haircut and suit, both available in the basement. She concluded by giving him a dorm key to a room in Building 4.

He thanked her and headed downstairs, where he tried to see the tailor. A sign on the door indicated he had missed his chance for the day. In the next room over, a bald man was sitting in an empty barber's chair reading a copy of *The Godfather* by Mario Puzo. Uli approached him and asked if he could get a quick haircut. "I'd like a little taken off the sides, but leave the top and sideburns intact."

"Sure," the barber replied. Uli took a seat and had a large white bib buttoned around his shirt collar. Looking straight ahead, Uli noticed a photo of Vice President Spiro Agnew staring back at him in place of a mirror. He sat for ten nervous minutes as the barber snipped away. Then, without asking, the man applied hot lather to his face and gave Uli an extremely close shave with a straight edge razor. He padded him down with talcum powder and brushed off all the snipped hair.

"Thanks," Uli said.

The guy nodded. When Uli caught a glimpse of himself in a passing window, he realized why the barber had no mirrors. The old bastard had given him a crew cut. Uli ran his hand over his quarter-inch of bristle and sighed. For an instant, he remembered being in boot camp.

Uli got directions to the cafeteria, which was located in Building 3. It was a large, harshly illuminated area lined with low tables and fold-out benches. The cashier at the entrance asked to see his ID and slowly copied the name *Huey* onto her clipboard.

Dinner that night was a choice of smoked hocks or meatloaf. There was also a selection of green vegetables, yellow vegetables, and white starches. He moved his tray along a shiny metal counter and inspected the various steamer pans through a glass case. He picked the hocks, potatoes, broccoli, soda water, and a bun. Most of those present were men missing at least one limb. They seemed to have either just completed their day shifts or were coming on for the night shift. By the time Uli took a seat, he was starving.

The vegetables were mush that seemed to undergo a cellular breakdown as soon as they were taken out of their watery solvent. The hocks, which Uli strongly suspected to be reshaped Spam, retained some kind of stringy texture, perhaps protected by the grease, but they only tasted like the salt and pepper he shook on them. The stale bun and flat soda water were the highlights of the meal.

After downing what he could, Uli sat with his eyes closed and tried not to throw up. When he heard footsteps approaching, he glanced up to find Ernestina Eric standing before him with a few battered books.

"You're literate, aren't you?" He nodded yes. "I located some material about this place that might be helpful."

"Thanks." Uli noticed a film of dust on the cover of the top volume.

"Most people here are nonliterate," she said, taking a seat across from him. She flipped through one book entitled, *T.R.C.N.Y.* Inside the title was spelled out: *Temporary Rescue City of New York. Copyright 1971 by the U.S. Army.*

"This book is just about the New York contingent. It doesn't really include other protectees who wound up here over the years."

"Which other protectees?"

"Earthquake and hurricane victims. Some time ago, for

instance, three people from the Love Canal area arrived. People who couldn't find perma-temp shelter anywhere else."

As Uli flipped through the pages, he glimpsed facts, figures, pie charts, and graphs on the New Yorkers shipped here ten years earlier. Nearly a million people had initially been brought in from the city. They comprised a little less than one-eighth of all New Yorkers, mostly from the poorest rung of the city.

Judging by a shorter document entitled, S.D.P., or *Supplemental Detainee Profile*—which had been issued by the Department of the Interior, copyright 1975—over the course of the next three years the core purpose of the place seemed to have shifted from a rescue location to a detention center. A hundred and fifty thousand people from around the country with questionable criminal or political backgrounds had been relocated here. Most of them had higher levels of education.

"How many doctors are there on the reservation?" Uli asked, flipping through the pages.

"Alternate Service was responsible for bringing in all the trained professionals, but they were only able to enlist about twenty-five doctors. That was ten years ago, and ten have been killed or died, so now only fifteen are still active. The good news is that a lot of residents died as well. If you're unfortunate enough to wind up in the hospital and you don't die while waiting for treatment, you'll probably be seen to by a nurse or P.A. They do most of the work."

"And what exactly will I be doing here?"

"We have a budding educational system. All literates are automatically assigned to go through various parts of south Brooklyn and try to register people in our new school. We'll give you cartoon brochures for the nonliterates."

"What's the attendance now?"

"We have about fifty people currently enrolled."

"Sounds easy enough."

"If you can register one person per week, you'll be way ahead of the curve."

Ernestina gave him other supporting materials to review, which dealt with how to approach and treat reservation residents.

"We meet at 9 a.m. out front at the bus stop. You'll be introduced to Patricia Itt, your new outreach partner," she chirped.

"Great," Uli said, as he accidentally belched out the fumes of his meal.

After Ernestina left, Uli returned his food tray and tiredly crossed an overpass searching for his assigned dorm room. He paused by a window midway and looked out. Past the back half of an empty warehouse built along a pier he could see the crystal clear waters of Jamaica Bay and the desert beyond. Scanning the building he had just exited, now across from him, he caught sight of something strange a few flights down.

A muscular Siftwelt was standing forward at his desk. His shirt appeared unbuttoned and untucked. His tie was pulled loose. He was bumping repeatedly against the edge of the blotter, then he collapsed forward on his desktop. Uli noticed a slim, almost ghostly shape behind him. He tried to make out who this erect form was, but the person reached over and pulled a cord, dropping the blinds.

Uli walked on to a large room filled with quiet men and women seated in old cloth sofas and armchairs bordered by end tables with ugly brass lamps. There were islands of small cubicles, each with its own portable black-and-white television. In the middle was an open area with a large color TV for group viewing. Another room had a series of small tables where several men sat busily writing. Two older gentlemen discreetly played cards. Another duet was focused on some board game. Upon one table was an abandoned copy of *The Clarion Call*, which appeared to be the official P.P. newspaper. Uli mindlessly scooped it up.

Following the numbers stenciled on the doors, Uli walked down an ever-narrowing corridor, then up a stairway, until he came to the top floor in the rear of Building 4. There he found his door. He opened it and flipped on a light to see a boxy room, seven feet by seven feet. His new home consisted of a slot of a window, a single bed, a chest of drawers, and, like in the recreation room, an end table with an ugly lamp. Lifting the little window, he wondered if it was deliberately narrow to prevent suicide.

He gazed out at the courtyard and over a bordering wall to the pier that jutted out into the bay. Another large warehouse stood along the pier. He hung up his jacket, took off his shoes, and lay down on a squeaky bed with a flattened mattress. How many other bodies had passed over it? he wondered.

He cracked open the U.S. Army–authored, Xeroxed book that Ernestina had loaned him and skimmed facts and figures about the reservation as recorded ten years earlier. The introduction explained what Lucas, the bucket-passer at the Crapper headquarters wreckage, had told him—that the place had been created by a presidential act prompted by a class-action suit following a coordinated terrorist attack in Manhattan. Before he was able to even turn the first page, Uli fell fast asleep.

11:32 p.m.

A distant canine howl woke him some time later. He could faintly hear a bongo drum, broken by occasional barks. In the large windows of the deserted warehouse on the pier, he thought he saw a figure moving along the upper floor.

The sky was a silky shade of blue. Reading *The Clarion Call*, he learned that a suspect had already been apprehended in the bombing of the Crapper headquarters.

DROPT'S ASSASSIN ARRESTED
by Christen Soll

Daniel Ellsberg, a suspected terrorist with CIA ties, was arrested for bombing the Manhattan Crapper headquarters and killing nearly two dozen people including the Crapper mayoral candidate, James Dropt.

Tom Di Hammer, an up-and-coming District Gangcop Lieutenant from Jackson Heights, Queens, arrested the man who masterminded the bombing. Ellsberg, a former Pentagon employee according to an unnamed source, has clear connections to the notorious Weather Underground. He was apprehended early yesterday on Ditmas Boulevard and charged with twenty-two counts of murder along with a host of related charges that included stealing four road repair trucks. According to confidential sources, Ellsberg has not revealed the identity of his coconspirators. He was sent into detention here eight years ago for allegedly stealing military secrets from the Pentagon and trying to smuggle them to his contact in Hanoi . . .

The story definitely had the stink of conspiracy theory. Another article also caught Uli's eye:

TERRORIST TRUCK BOMB KILLS 2 NEAR ST. PAT'S
by Harold Steward

A truck was blown up today in front of Rock & Filler Center killing two people and wounding three others. Sources claim that Crapper guerrillas intent on blowing up the Midtown Crapper Administration at 30 Rock & Filler Center accidentally detonated their bomb before they were able to remove it from the truck. Mike Mulligatawny, 53, and Sam Reynolds, 62, both registered Crappers, were killed. Four others were wounded. Pray for their eternal punishment.

Instead of blaming random terrorists, as had the paper he found on the bus, this publication only fingered Crappers. What bothered Uli most was that the article about Rock & Filler Center had greatly undercounted the dead and injured. The dozen or so who had been killed and the countless wounded were victims again—this time to propaganda.

Depressed by the news, Uli pulled his shoes on and walked back to the television area which was now empty. He followed the sound of deep chuckles to a small chubby man sitting alone in front of the large community TV.

"What's up?" he asked the merry viewer.

"Jack Gleason in *The Honeymooners*," the man said, trembling with laughter. When he caught his breath, he shook his fist and said, "To the moon, Alice!"

"They broadcast this?"

"No, we get to watch the tapes." Pointing to a broom closet, the viewer added, "We have an archive next door."

In a little room lined with bookshelves, a clipboard listed all the videotapes in the library. The collection consisted of top-rated television shows, including *The Twilight Zone, The Outer Limits, The Prisoner, Naked City, Gilligan's Island, Wanted Dead or Alive, Gunsmoke, Hogan's Heroes, The Andy Griffith Show, Ben Casey, The Tonight Show,* and *Bewitched*. Uli felt too exhausted to watch anything, so he went to the communal bathroom and took a hot shower. Utilizing the free supplies, he brushed his teeth and gargled, then returned to his little cubicle. Glancing out the skinny window, he spotted a lone figure coming from the empty warehouse on the pier.

As soon as Uli lay down, he heard the distinct clicking of high-heeled shoes. Peering out the window again, he saw a woman exiting the warehouse as well. Uli was fairly certain it was Ernestina Eric. Her eyes were open wide and there was a strangely vacant smile on her face.

He watched her vanish around a corner, then he went back to bed.

11/1/80

The next morning Uli woke to a strange synchronized chant: *"We're right, cause we're right, cause we're right, cause we're right . . ."*

Looking out the window into the courtyard, he saw a group of roughly two hundred men and women donning gray sweats in tight formation, doing jumping jacks to the beat of the word, "Right!" Uli figured this was why all the workers here looked so trim and fit.

He shaved and showered, then slipped on his filthy clothes and jammed two food stamps into his pocket. In a corner of the room where the carpet was coming up, he hid the balance of stamps that Mallory had given him two days earlier.

Down in the cafeteria, people were gathering for breakfast. Grabbing an orange tray, he moved down the food line.

"Name?" asked a large curly haired woman who monitored everyone entering.

"Huey."

The monitor checked under the letter *H* and told him to proceed. Uli was given a plate of reddish scrambled eggs and yellow mashed potatoes; both appeared to be made from a mix. He took two pieces of black bread, a cup of watery coffee, and an unripened apple. He found that if he ate quickly without inhaling, the food didn't taste so bad. Since he needed energy, he had two more helpings of everything. His dirty clothes made him feel self-conscious, so after stacking his tray in the dishwasher's window, he raced downstairs to the tailor. He found a short line of men and women already gathered. After twenty minutes, it was his turn. He was given a baggy suit to try on and a stool to stand upon. A woman with a mouthful of needles and a piece of chalk made notations on the cloth.

"How soon will the suit be ready?" Uli asked eagerly.

"Every morning I get the same number of people waiting for me that you saw today," she said laboriously. "There's a one-month backlog."

"A month? My clothes are literally falling off my body."

"I'm sorry, but unless you want to pay something extra . . ."

"How much to get it done right now?"

"Four stamps for right now."

"I've got two stamps." He held them out and she snatched them.

He waited in the hallway until five minutes to 9, an hour and a half later, when she waved to him. His suit was done. He immediately put it on. Although the polyester blend abraded his inner thighs and the fabric felt carcinogenic, it was a perfect fit. He walked proudly to the bus stop. In the half an hour or so that it took for the bus to arrive, about two dozen others joined him. The men all wore the same style and color suit as he, while the women had on long, dark blue dresses with matching jackets.

Ernestina Eric, the Brooklyn South supervisor for educational outreach, was the last of the group to appear. "I've been waiting eight weeks for a new suit," she said to him. "How'd you get one so quickly?"

Uli shrugged innocently, then asked, "Did I see you outside last night?"

"Outside where?"

"You were coming from the abandoned building on the pier." He pointed over to it.

"No way, it's dangerous out there."

"What the heck is that place anyway?"

"They were going to convert it to a school, but then they decided to turn it into a giant church instead."

Ernestina introduced him to his new team of coworkers: Lionel, Eileen, Harvey, Linda, Derek, and Sam. Uli knew he'd never remember their names, he wasn't even sure of his own. After a flurry of handshakes, the little group returned to their conversation about the upcoming mayoral election and how if Shub lost, it would mark the advent of godlessness in Rescue City.

"And this is your new partner, Patricia Itt," Ernestina said, leading him to a woman with goofy curls shooting out of her head like mattress springs.

His new partner didn't so much as look at him. Instead, she walked over to the bus as it pulled up and kicked its dented fender. Then she screamed up to the driver about being late. Uli looked at their supervisor with concern.

"She's a Taurus," Ernestina explained. "That's what they do. They're impulsive."

"Okeydoke."

Ernestina joined others boarding the bus. His new coworker, however, stood before the vehicle and continued to berate the driver as everyone got on. Regarding her as a kind of angry female Oric, Uli gently took Patricia by her arm and led her onto the bus.

When the two sat down in the rear, his new partner finally seemed to notice him: "I heard you're from old New York City."

"I don't really remember."

"What's it like there now?" Patricia asked. "They were supposed to clean it up."

Uli repeated what he had just said.

"They told us that once it was cleaned up they were bringing back the evacuees and releasing most of the detainees, and I was told I was only a suspect, so I would probably be released."

"Good." Even Oric had been easier to deal with.

"I heard they elected some guy named Koch as mayor." Something shifted in Uli's memory, confirming the name. "So why hasn't he done anything to help us?"

Uli replied that he had no idea what was keeping them from containing the microscopic traces of radioactive particles from each tiny crack on the endless streets and buildings that made up lower Manhattan. Impatient with his answer, Patricia turned around and started making barking sounds at someone behind her.

Uli noticed early-morning nomads canvassing the garbage piles in that tricky zone between Brooklyn and Queens. Billboards along the roadway had pictures of Mayor Shub squinting earnestly, along with the slogan, *Vote Shub & Don't Look Back!*

He ain't lyin or flirtin, another campaign poster rhymed, *reelect him or you'll be hurtin!*

As the minibus bounced and skidded along King's Highway, it stopped every once in a while to pick up passengers.

Unlike that nightmarish bus trip on the first day, this one remained packed with P.P. people. It passed through east Brooklyn, where Uli realized that he preferred the traditional Japanese architecture over the dreary Soviet designs.

About an hour later, when they reached the southern end of Brooklyn, teams of missionaries started bailing out two at a time at each stop.

"You and Patricia are going to be at the western end of Coney Island," Ernestina said, giving Uli a small stack of leaflets and two full paper bags. "Hand out the pictograph flyers and these are your lunches. I'll come at the end of the day to collect you." Uli felt like a child whose mother was depositing him at school.

The bus slowed down as they approached a miniature amusement park. The supervisor signaled to him that it was their stop.

Once on the sidewalk, Patricia raced up ahead of Uli, past the food concessions and the half-dozen or so rides that made up Astroland.

"Slow down!" he shouted as she bounded over the sparsely populated walkway. Uli now felt like a geriatric father in pursuit of some hyperactive child. He stared out over the narrow manmade river to see the results of a strange catastrophe. The wreckage of four rusty roller coasters were coupled together—it was the old Cyclone ride. Two of the cars were half buried in the sand on a little beach. The rest were submerged in the bluish-green waters of the long winding canal.

"Wow!" Uli uttered. It appeared that at the zenith of the ride, the roller coaster had come off its track and flown out over the desert, crashing into the river.

Apparently having seen it all before, Patricia just pulled out her stack of brochures and raced over to passersby: "Hey, you! Get an education! Right here, right now—*pow!*"

Uli spent the day trying to hand out the educational pamphlets. But by lunch he had only gotten rid of three and he saw all three people toss them to the ground. Patricia kept up her effective rhyming system, and by 4 o'clock, when some youth walked by Uli, he tried to make a similarly upbeat plea: "Get an education—it's better than Claymation!"

"You fucked that up big time," Patricia said to him.

"What are you talking about?"

"You ain't suppose to tell folks to get no cremation."

"No, I said it's better than *Claymation!*"

"Well, you ain't suppose to throw big words at folks trying to make 'em feel small an' all," she said in a sing-song beat.

"I was trying to convince him—"

"If you do it again, see if I don't report you to Ernestina," Patricia said and dashed off.

Uli waited a moment longer, then sunk down on a

bench and tried to imagine the ocean lazily lapping at the shores of old Coney Island. Eventually, he leaned over, pulled his legs up, and nodded off to sleep.

"Lazy Jehovah's Witnesses!"

The words jolted him awake. Some old-timer, a pale giant of a man, was sitting next to him on the bench and staring at his stack of brochures. The ancient fellow had deeply sunken eyes, floppy ears, a long narrow nose, and he lacked a single strand of hair. "This ain't South Ferry, but it'll have to do," the guy said as he pulled a large Danish from a brown paper bag. "That's where I used to live in the old town."

"Would you be interested in getting an education?" Uli asked, offering him a brochure.

"I have a graduate degree from Yale, hotshot." The hairless man took a bite out of his pastry and continued talking: "I just couldn't get a job, that's how I wound up in the Bronx way back when. But that wasn't why I had to change my name. That was something else entirely . . ."

Uli still felt exhausted and decided to take advantage of the situation. To dupe Patricia, he acted as though he was listening, pretending to attempt a recruitment. While the old man's voice droned on, Uli closed his eyes.

There was something familiar about the guy's high voice—as though he were speaking at a frequency only Uli could pick up—but it didn't make complete sense: ". . . *indguessoonlytonenofeusecouldoprevail* . . ." Slowly screening out the static, Uli was eventually able to decipher what the man was saying: "The other had to eat crow and that was me . . . We were a redundancy of sorts. What he did was amazing, the great pyramid of parks, beaches, highways, bridges . . ."

Uli's awareness seemed to click off, yet he could feel his brain digesting information like a stomach filling inside his head. When he awoke again, he could still hear the old man's words flowing almost magnetically into his ears, and yet he hadn't really grasped any of it.

"I'm truly sorry, Millie! Sorry about the failed revolution! Sorry about then leaving you in New York . . . Sorry, Elise, for using you to compete with Mr. Robert . . . Sorry to Teresa and the kids for all our hopes that drowned in the goddamn pool . . . Sorry, Lucretia, for not putting it all behind me and abandoning you . . . Most of all, Bela and Beatrice, I'm sorry to both of you, letting one die without knowing what she meant to me, and not feeling worthy enough to claim the other when she had been abandoned . . ."

"I'm sorry too," Uli finally joined in, yawning. "But at least it sounds like you had more than your share of women." He looked over to the million-year-old man, only to see he was fast asleep. Apparently, Uli's own brain had devised and unspooled this bizarre "sorry" soliloquy. He quietly rose to his feet and left the strange elderly man snoozing on the bench.

At 6 p.m., supervisor Ernestina waved over from the street entrance to the boardwalk. Uli signaled to Patricia Itt and together the three of them returned to the minibus, which collected all the outreach workers as it headed back to the P.P. compound.

Patricia ratted him out on the bus ride back: "He was just a lazybones! Spent the whole day with some old liver spot, not doing nothing." Uli didn't respond.

Back in his dorm, he washed his face. Finding a pair of abandoned slippers in the communal bathroom, he put them on and came down to dinner in his former shirt and pants, not wanting to get his new suit dirty.

"So, how'd you like your first day?" Ernestina asked as Uli sat staring at his inedible dinner of something brown floating in something green.

"Maybe a good night's sleep will make a difference," he replied.

"Actually, I wanted to invite you to a prayer meeting we're having downstairs."

Uli said he was experiencing indigestion, which was partly true, and he politely declined.

As he headed out of the cafeteria and up to Building 4 after the meal, his limbs felt increasingly heavy. He was simply tapped out.

Lumbering up to his distant room, he barely heard the sultry whisper: "Blowjob?"

He turned to see Deer Flare, the girl with the abrupt forehead who he'd met yesterday getting off the bus. She was wearing a white shirt, a tight plaid skirt, dark nylon stockings, and seductive black heels.

"Did you say something?"

"Sleeping on a bench with some old mummy when you should be trying to educate the masses. Tsk, tsk," she said, walking toward him.

"Huh?"

"I spotted you today out in Coney Island, hon," she replied, then smiling she added, "I guess I'm not the only one who's seen something I oughtn't."

"I think you've confused me with someone else."

"You saw us last night," she accused. "Did you take a photo? Is that it?"

"What are you talking about?" But Uli knew exactly what she was talking about. Now he was sure he had seen Siftwelt in the middle of some vague sexual misconduct the night before.

"Why are you here, pal? Trying to dredge up the dirt, is that it?"

"I'm stuck here," Uli replied. "I'm just trying to do a little good."

"Give me the film or you'll regret it."

"Give me a break."

Deer Flare turned and walked away, sternly snapping her high heels against the hard tile floor. Uli returned to his little room and found that someone had gone through his meager belongings. The little stash of money that he had hidden under the fold of his carpet was sitting on top of his chest of drawers. He was actually glad they'd searched his room. He didn't have anything to hide.

Uli was about to lay down, but thought he heard something in the distance once again. He looked out the window at the long building on the pier that Ernestina had said was about to be converted into a church. Although he didn't see anyone enter or exit, a lone person passed by one of the darkened windows.

He found himself thinking about the macabre fantasy or vision he'd had about the tragic Armenian woman and her children, and wondered if it could have been real. Then he thought about Mallory and Oric's painful deaths and soon felt wide awake. He headed downstairs and tried to exit the building. The guard on duty asked him where he thought he was going.

"Just hoping to catch some air."

"Doors close after 10 p.m.," said the older man.

Uli thanked the guard and figured there had to be at least one unmanned exit in this four-block complex. Heading down to the basement cafeteria, he saw two workers silently piling a mountain of black plastic garbage bags into the back of a pickup truck in an adjacent garage. When the workers walked off, Uli casually grabbed two of the bags and carried them out. After loading them in the rear of the pickup, he continued down the empty street along the old brick wall. He headed to the abandoned warehouse—a two-story structure on the water.

P.P. had torn down all the other buildings in the immediate area. Uli figured they could easily erect yet another connecting overpass to this one. Reaching the doorway, he found it cinder-blocked shut. The windows on the ground floor were covered by worn sheets of plywood, but he was able to easily slip one board aside and climb in. Within the dark, cavernous warehouse, he felt a chilly wind.

The ground floor was alive with the sounds of scam-

pering and flapping. Small desert animals and birds had
taken shelter in the empty structure. Above, he could hear
footsteps. Uli proceeded up the stairs to the second floor,
where the windows allowed moonlight to pass through. To
his surprise, he came to a long corridor filled with silent
people, like a party of spirits, buzzing to or from one of
three massive rooms. Inside the first large area, Uli made
out sweaty and interlocked forms in tight and repetitive
motion.

As his eyes adjusted, he saw that though most of the
copulators simply lowered their garments, some were
completely naked. He recognized one woman, a fellow
neophyte, who was orally enveloping a much older man.
Despite the fact that some of the couples appeared to be
of the same gender, they were all having muted sex. No
sooner did he realize this than a lean, bald man dropped to
his knees before him.

Uli jumped back in shock. Until that moment, he had
felt as though he were invisible. He quickly retreated to
the last room of the warehouse. Roughly ten couples were
engaged in heated states of intimacy. Near one corner,
he spotted her. Ernestina Eric was gratifying two men simultaneously. Uli walked over as one of the men shot his
ample emission onto the floor, then stumbled away. A moment later, the second man also disengaged from her and
ejaculated.

"Ernestina," he whispered, acutely aware that he hadn't
heard anyone speak. "I knew I saw you."

Without responding, she reached up and started un-
clasping his belt.

"Wait," he whispered. Lowering his face to hers, he
asked, "What are you doing?"

She wore a lusty smile, an expression uncharacteristic
of the cautious person he had briefly come to know. Her
eyes appeared glossy as though she were in some far off
place. At that moment another man, skinny with an alarm-

ingly large erection, walked right up and simply entered her without making a peep.

"Hey!" Uli said.

The guy didn't respond. As the newcomer had feverish sex with Ernestina, Uli stared at the man's face. He was a member of the same outreach group—Lionel. Though they all acted as if they were sleepwalking, Uli guessed that the men were actually faking it.

After watching Ernestina have intercourse with three more males, he saw her silently rise, fix her blouse, and leave the building. The smile never left her face.

Uli followed her down the steps and across the street. She headed to a service door in the rear of Building 2 that had no knob. With the tips of her fingers, she was able to pry it open. Uli caught the door before it closed and trailed her up the steps. She walked across an overpass, finally turning off at the women's dorm.

Uli continued on to Building 4 and his own room, where he laid on his bed and stared upward. As the darkness was gradually replaced by the morning light, he tried to figure out what the hell was going on. Finally, without sleep, he rose, dressed, skipped breakfast, and went back to the bus stop out front—a new work day had begun.

11/2/80

When Ernestina joined the group outside, she looked thoroughly rested. Uli asked her how she had slept. She didn't bat an eyelash. "Fine, how about you?"

"I had a weird dream."

"What kind of dream?" she asked politely.

"That a lot of people were in a large warehouse silently making love to each other."

Ernestina looked away nervously and said, "I don't want to sound like a prude, but I feel really uncomfortable hearing things like that."

"I'm sorry, but you asked."

"I won't make that mistake again," she replied, then boarded the bus. Slightly embarrassed, Uli got on last, pulling Patricia Itt in with him. Some of the men he'd seen having sex with Ernestina and one another were seated calmly in the back of the vehicle as it rolled out to south Brooklyn. Like the previous day, Uli and Patricia Itt were the last to be dropped off.

Arriving on the mini-boardwalk of Coney Island with the thick-headed Patricia, Uli immediately felt tired. If these people haven't wised up while stuck in this awful Rescue City, he thought, a brochure filled with dumb cartoons and morbid statistics wasn't going to do it.

He glumly watched Patricia as she moved excitedly from person to person like a hummingbird on amphetamines. She appeared truly happy. Slowly he distilled her secrets: Reject the big picture. Be lower-brained. Stay small and vibrant. Ernestina's lessons weren't bad either: Follow your base urges and simply deny.

"Hey Jehovah, want some rugelach?" It was the tall hairless Lazarus from the previous day, splayed out on the same bench, again eating a pastry out of a brown paper bag. Uli politely declined the man's offer and told the guy he was busy.

Uli tried to purge his own cynicism as he occasionally flung flyers toward those walking past. After a few hours, and as people grew more scarce, he looked over and saw Patricia trying to hand a flyer to a stray mutt. The dog sniffed the piece of paper and dashed off.

When Uli sat down again, the old man muttered, "At my age, everybody is just five things."

"What five things?"

"Five fingers on the hand," the guy said, holding his large palm open. "Five appendages on the body. Five books of the Torah. Five boroughs of this city—"

"So what five things are you?" Uli cut him short.

"I used to be a father, a son, a husband, a brother, and an uncle."

"Aren't you still?"

"Now I'm a terrorist, a traitor, a coward, a monster, and a fraud."

This is going to be a long day, Uli told himself as the old man droned on. Just as before, Uli began dozing. He found himself thrust into a complex dream in which he was someone else, trapped in some dark subterranean system along with a filthy tribe of bewildered half-wits fighting for leadership and a way out.

He abruptly awoke with the hideous thought that the creepy Deer girl was somewhere nearby watching him. The old man was sleeping again as Uli stood back up and headed over toward the amusement park. He noticed Patricia staring at him.

"There are people down there," Uli said to her, spotting a clump of youths who had just exited the park.

"I'll come along," she said.

"No, stay here." He pointed to a dilapidated building nearby. "The seniors in that home are going to come out for an afternoon stroll. I saw them do it yesterday and we missed them."

By the time he made it to the amusement park entrance, the youths had vanished. Between the evenly spaced slats of wood that made up the promenade, something red caught his eye—someone had dropped a string of tickets, still unripped on the sand below. He was about to return to Patricia, but he became transfixed by more youths getting spun around a ride as though in a huge blender. Another ride looked like a flying cup and saucer. Participants had to stand up against the inner rim of the giant cup as it whipped around at gravity-defying angles, the centrifugal force holding them in place. Uli watched a lone bumper car driver, a middle-aged man with a joyous expression, smashing into a group of vacant bumper cars over and over. Without thinking, Uli found himself smiling. Catching sight of the large roller coaster that had crashed into the river, he thought that in one sense the doomed ride must've been a godsend. After all, where these newer ones merely teased people with a spectacular body-hurdling thrill, that one had actually delivered.

Peering down the boardwalk, he saw Patricia standing alone, holding a flyer out to the empty space. She waved from the distance, and he wondered if her perkiness somehow fed off of his despair. He pointed angrily to the old age home. When a single lone figure exited the building, Patricia rushed over and Uli made his move. Scrambling underneath the boardwalk, he grabbed what turned out to be three unused tickets.

Sneaking inside so that Patricia wouldn't see him, Uli

first rode the Loop-the-Loop, then the bumper cars, and finally the mini–roller coaster.

Roughly twenty-five minutes later, feeling refreshed, he ran back out to the boardwalk, but there was no sign of of his coworker. In the old age home, he asked if anyone had seen a woman with a bad haircut—they hadn't.

He spent the remaining three hours searching for her. He began to suspect that the despicable young woman with the prominent forehead was somehow behind this disappearance. Deer Flare thought he had taken blackmailing photos of her with Siftwelt and had probably sworn revenge. Would she actually kidnap his partner just to make him look bad?

At 6 o'clock there was still no sign of the Itt girl. In a slight panic, Uli took half of the remaining brochures and shoved them into a garbage can. Then he returned to their original spot to find his supervisor waiting for him.

"Where's Patricia?"

"I don't know. I went into the amusement park to hand out some flyers." He held up the remaining stack. "When I came back, she was gone."

"You're supposed to look out for each other," Ernestina said. "That's why we have partners."

"She was handing out flyers to the seniors at the home. I went away for just a moment and she was gone."

"Did you check the home?"

"Yeah," Uli responded absently. "Maybe she returned to P.P. alone."

"I just hope she didn't drown," Ernestina said and sighed.

Uli thought she was kidding, but looking out at the narrow band of greenish water he realized she was serious. She said she'd have to notify the local Crapper gangcops as well as the City Council police.

"She probably went home early," he said. "It was a pretty slow day."

"Let's hope."

Together the two boarded the bus back to the compound, where they found that Patricia had not returned. No one had heard from her. Uli offered to go out tomorrow and hand out flyers alone.

"That's not my primary concern right now," Ernestina said, clearly agitated.

She reported Patricia Itt's disappearance to Rolland Siftwelt, who checked in with the authorities.

To keep from worrying, Uli spent the evening in the P.P. library reviewing audio-visual and tape recordings of inspirational speeches by religious and secular leaders of the last forty years. In addition to stirring oratories by the Kennedy brothers and Martin Luther King Jr., he listened to George Meany, Jimmy Hoffa, and Albert Shanker all rallying their labor forces.

After several hours, he started to feel a tingling in his conscience. He wasn't sure if it was a result of the speeches or guilt for losing his partner. All he knew was that social change seemed possible. As he walked past the cafeteria, he spotted Ernestina talking to another outreach worker.

"Excuse me," he said, "have you found out anything about Patricia's disappearance?"

"I think the correct word is *recidivism*."

"What do you mean?"

"Patricia was a recovering drug addict and prostitute. A healthy percentage of the P.P. labor force are former addicts. This is a rescue mission."

"Patricia is a—"

"From the first day, her pimp started sniffing around, trying to win her back. She probably went back to him. It's amazing that we even got her in the first place. She had only been sober for about two months."

"She was really a prostitute?"

"And a drug addict. Many of us were," Ernestina replied flatly.

"You too?" That might've explained her nocturnal conduct.

"Didn't you have any problems with crime or addiction?" Ernestina asked earnestly.

Uli looked off sadly and nodded yes. But as far as he knew, he had never taken drugs or had a criminal record. Then again, large parts of his memory were missing, so maybe he had.

"Are you okay?"

"I just feel awful about all this," Uli said. "I should've kept a closer eye on her."

"Here at P.P. we're great believers in forgiveness," she replied gently, placing her hand on his shoulder. "Everyone screws up—frequently the hardest part is forgiving ourselves."

Uli smiled weakly.

"I'm sorry for judging you earlier," she said, "when you shared your strange dream."

"I should probably keep certain things to myself."

"No, you were right. It's probably healthier to let it all out." Looking down, she added, "All we really have is each other."

Uli took her hand in his, gave it a soft shake, and returned to his room.

He lay on his bed feeling sad, until he heard something in the darkness, a kind of ecstatic bark. He got dressed and headed down the stairs to the kitchen door he had left through the night before. He walked across to the future house of worship and again climbed in through the ground floor window. Inside, he scurried up the steps to the last room in the front. A number of people were copulating, yet he was glad that he didn't find Ernestina among them. Although he felt sexual stirrings, he kept reminding himself that he was in enemy territory. This could be some kind of trap, he thought, though it was intriguing to watch. As long as he didn't participate, he couldn't be accused of anything. He waited an hour, waving off a number of offers. He felt like a zoologist watching as more people came, copulated, and left.

Finally, to his thrilled disappointment, she arrived. He watched as one man made love to her, then a second man, then a third and fourth simultaneously. Before a fifth one could grab her, Uli put his arm around Ernestina's slim back and led her to an isolated corner. Spinning her around against a wall, he made her spread her arms and legs apart as though he were about to search her. She offered no resistance. Reaching underneath her wet dress, he gently stroked along her curly hairs and moistened lips. Then he unzipped his pants, but stopped before he fully succumbed to his burgeoning desire.

Turning Ernestina back around so that she was facing him, he looked deep into her eyes. She smiled mindlessly. Her pupils didn't seem focused. He could've been anyone. He kissed her hard on the lips, but she didn't kiss back. Unbuttoning her shirt, he was surprised to find that she was wearing a bra. He unclasped it and suckled her until she started gently moaning. She whimpered softly as he left a deep crimson hickey on it. Then he did the same to her other breast, leaving a matching mark. She tried thrusting her hips into his, and though he was thoroughly aroused, he abruptly left the warehouse.

11/3/80

Bright and early the next morning at the bus stop, Ernestina announced to everyone that it was going to be a short day. They had to return to the complex no later than 6 p.m.

"Forecasts show a storm brewing tonight. And I don't want anyone getting stuck outside."

As all boarded the bus, Ernestina took Uli aside and suggested that he join another outreach group that was looking for new workers to rescue prostitutes in Brighton Beach.

Instead of responding, Uli posed his own question: "Did you find marks on your breasts?"

"I beg your pardon—"

"I made them," he interrupted, "but I'm sure you must've found other strange things on your body as well."

"You're crazy!"

"Late at night you go to the abandoned warehouse on the pier and you have sex with multiple partners. None of you seem conscious."

She didn't say anything, just stared at him vacantly.

"I'd like to go back to Coney Island one last time," he resumed. "I think I was getting through to some of the locals and was hoping to win them over. I guess I'm also half hoping to catch sight of Patricia."

"If you do see her with someone," she finally replied, unable to make eye contact, "don't fight. Just try to find out where they're going and notify the authorities."

On the rest of the ride out to Brooklyn, Ernestina didn't so much as look at Uli.

When the bus arrived at Coney Island, Uli headed toward the boardwalk. Only the tall hairless senior was there, sitting on his usual bench, muttering to the boundless emptiness surrounding him.

"Remember me from yesterday?" Uli greeted.

"Sure," the old man replied with a smile, "you're the parasite who crawled into my ear and got lost in my brain."

Though the man seemed somewhat senile, Uli couldn't resist asking, "Do you remember the girl who was with me yesterday? She vanished. You didn't see her, did you?"

"You know what I know," the old bird replied, then closed his eyes.

Stay on course, Uli reminded himself. *Patricia will be found. You're here to try to bring people a purpose in life.* He decided to try a different technique and looked for a crowd.

Walking a few blocks away, he spotted a group of men in the distance. There was an open-air court bracketed by ten-foot-high basketball hoops. A number of guys roughly his age were in the middle of a fierce competition. Uli waited, but the game wouldn't end.

Compelled by the urgency of his mission, he walked over to the edge of their court and shouted: "Your only way out of here is through *education!*"

Some of the men running back and forth under the hot sun glanced at him, but they continued playing. Uli attempted to be a little more confrontational, muttering, "Don't be apathetic *dolts!*" When they raced by him toward the opposite end of the court once more, Uli yelled, "You're all a bunch of stupid *motherfuckers!*"

The shooter stopped mid-jump, still holding the ball.

Uli took to his heels with the entire basketball team running behind. The river was three blocks away. He passed the first block without a problem. By the end of the second block, the most athletic pursuer was right on his tail. A punch slid along his kidney, giving him a second wind.

A row of carbonized buildings lined his escape route. At the end of the street was a hurricane fence that had been clipped and rolled back. A retaining wall separated him from the waterway. Dodging singed furniture abandoned on the street, Uli jumped the wall, inhaled to the bottoms of his lungs, and speared hard into the blue-green waters.

Moments later, when his head broke the river's surface, he gasped for breath and looked back. Twenty feet behind, their heads were bobbing over the crumbling concrete wall. Not one of them cared to join him in the slow-moving river. Something whizzed by, then a host of other items kerplunked about him. Stones and sundry salvos were being thrown as he splashed away. Fortunately, he discovered that he swam well in a suit. The water was as warm as a bathtub. But just as he was taking comfort in his lead—*bang!* Something big crowned him hard. Dazed, Uli unintentionally gulped the acrid water.

Flailing, he knocked into a long rectangular object drifting past him. It was an eight-foot-long wooden sign that read, *Water Hazardous—Do Not Swim.*

"Don't let us catch y'ass," one of the basketball players shouted from the distance. "Cause when we do, you're fuckin dead!"

Uli kicked off his shoes and climbed up onto the wooden sign. Though he could've headed over to the desert side of the river on the far shore, there was nowhere for him to go from there, so he just kept floating downstream. He realized he never should've interrupted their game, let alone insulted them. He was simply trying to get their attention—to *help* them.

Soon he could see an even spacing of sewage pipes

jutting out below the retaining wall of Brooklyn. Liquid refuse from the borough was intermittently plopping into the river. Still, the water here was nothing like the toxic muck drowning Staten Island. Before floating under the distant span of the Zano Bridge, he spotted some kind of ragtag community on the desert's edge.

Staten Island—or rather a slice of desert dividing it from Brooklyn—was on the far side, but the water was moving too rapidly to cross. The angle of land shooting out from the desert turned out to be a sharp bend in the river, sending the waters north. Drifting closer, he saw that near the bend, along the banks dead ahead, there was a row of faux skyscrapers, similar to those he had seen from midtown. Like everything else here, these panels were an homage—an unintentional modern art installation mimicking the Wall Street skyline.

Moving along, he saw that the bend gave rise to a long wall extending all the way toward Manhattan. On the opposite side of the bend there appeared another waterway. In fact, a long concrete dam separated the northward-flowing river of Brooklyn from the southward-oozing sewage. The waste of all five boroughs was draining somewhere south along the eastern edge of Staten Island.

Uli floated alongside the base of the pseudo-skyline and finally located a small walkway next to the concrete wall where he was able to climb up onto the narrow shore between the two waterways.

Examining the lower panels of the walkway, Uli saw that each one was a diaphanous fiberglass sheet, ten feet square. They were locked into rusty steel frames and held up by scaffolding. Sand had accumulated along the steel grid, and an array of intricate cableworks were anchored into the earth with large spikes.

In the distance, Uli could see cars rising and dipping over the creaky two-lane causeway that joined Manhattan to Richmond County—the Staten Island Ferry Bridge.

"What the fuck you think you doin?" The voice came before the pain. A long chain whipped around his neck and pulled him backwards to the ground. Three paunchy middle-aged men moved close around him. The leader was short and balding with a close-cropped beard and wire-frame glasses. He held a thick lead pipe that looked perfect for breaking bones. The second man was stretching a black leather bullwhip before his huge beer belly. The last man, younger with a bushy mustache, sported an old machete with black electrical tape clumsily spooled around its handle.

"I'm sorry," Uli said exhausted, "I was chased into the river."

"Who chase you?" asked the leader, glancing around.

"A gang upstream in Coney Island."

The guy with the pipe switched to Spanish: "Faggot thinks we're idiots."

"I think no such thing," Uli replied in his own tortured Spanish.

"Look at his bullshit suit," the one with the bullwhip said.

"I'm from Pure-ile Plurality," Uli explained.

"Anyone can steal a suit," said the man with the pipe. "You a Pigger runt?"

"No," he replied, and buttoning up his shirt, he added, "I'm an outreach worker for Pure-ile Plurality. I was trying to get students to join our new educational program."

"Hey," the one with the bullwhip said, "you think you smart cause you speak a little Spanish? What are you doing on our monument?"

"Just admiring it, I assure you."

"He's scoping it out," the man wielding the machete opined to the others.

"Look, he's bleeding," observed the guy with the whip. Uli touched his head and found blood on his fingers.

"Prove to me you're from Pud Pullers," the man with

the heavy pipe said, giving him the benefit of the doubt.

"Call Rolland Siftwelt. He'll vouch for me."

"We're in the desert, asshole, do you see a phone any-where?" the whipper snapper said, then kicked Uli behind his knees, sending him back to the ground in pain. The fat man snapped his whip in the air.

"Let's do the motherfucker," snorted the machete man.

"Not here. Remember the last time. We got to get him to dig his own hole."

"Oh yeah. Get up," the pipe swinger commanded.

With his knee throbbing, Uli slowly rose to his feet and was pointed to the left of the faux monstrosity. For ten minutes they hiked him back south down the broadening isthmus between Staten Island and Brooklyn. *If the son of a bitch hadn't injured my knee, I could outrun them,* he thought as he limped onward.

When they moved back under the Zano Bridge, Uli got a better look at the cluster of shanties he had passed—a suburban encampment. Older women and disfigured men sat in the doorways of small earthen-floored structures.

The pipe wielder pulled a short-handled shovel out of a desert shrub and slung it over his shoulder. "Keep walk-ing!" he ordered as they trailed behind Uli.

Staring into the empty horizon, thoughts of the blond stranger from Green-wood Cemetery flashed through Uli's head. He was the only person Uli had recognized in Res-cue City. At that moment, he deduced that this must be the reason he came to this place—to rescue this man. But why?

As the trio marched him forward, Uli confirmed that he couldn't run. *I might be able to take out one, even two of them, if lucky,* he thought, *but not all three.* Suddenly, a pack of minia-ture dogs descended upon him, snapping at his heels.

"Conchita!" a shrill female voice cried out. "Conchita! You come back here, you bad baby!"

He turned around to see the reproductively crippled woman he had met briefly yesterday at Pure-ile Plurality. She was chasing after her surrogate baby, the big-eyed Chihuahua.

"Hold it!" Uli shouted. The three men froze beneath their raised weapons. "She can speak for me!" Her name popped into his head. "Consuela! Remember me from Pure-ile Plurality?"

"Oh yeah, I *always* see you there. You're *always* so sweet," Consuela replied. Fortunately, her mental fuzziness went well beyond the trauma of child deprivation. She ran up to Uli and started petting his sweaty head like he was a tall dog. "He's *so* good, he's *so* right."

When Uli hugged her, she hugged back, reluctant to let him go.

"All right," the leader said, pulling Consuela off him. Picking up her dog-child and handing it back to her, the man directed her to her shack, then he just stood there staring fiercely upward.

"Man, you not gonna let him go, are you?" the fat man with the whip asked, obviously disappointed.

"You wanna know why? I tell you why," the leader answered. "Cause we kill him and Pure-ile Plurality gonna investigate. Then iz gonna be a matter of time before Consuela starts yapping about the nice man who was here, and they add one plus one, and we each lose our right hand, and I tell you right now, I don't mind losing a hand, but I ain't ready to give up sex."

"Shit!" the bullwhipper said.

"No hard feeling, man," the leader said to Uli, and as an offer of reconciliation, he held out his hand and said, "Slap me five, dude." Tiredly, Uli slapped the man's palm. "You tell 'em. Tell 'em. We didn't mess you up or nothing, right?"

"Absolutely."

"So that's got to be worth a little something," the leader suggested.

Uli reached into his pocket and handed the man a soggy stamp. He started to ask the guy how he could navigate around the waterway to get back to Brooklyn, but the mustached leader simply shoved him backwards, plunging him back into the swiftly flowing current. With his knee still in pain, Uli thrashed about helplessly in the water.

"*Vaya con dios!*" the leader called out, laughing.

Uli fought to keep his head above water. The strong current and his exhausted body did not allow for a clean swim. The best he could do was drift along on his back for what felt like miles.

Paddling to the river's edge back on the Brooklyn side once the powerful flow subsided, Uli grabbed at a narrow ledge that couldn't have been more than five inches wide. He tried climbing onto it but slipped back into the water three times before he was able to edge up slowly. Reaching over a filthy drain pipe to the top of the retaining wall, he carefully hoisted himself up, flopping onto the paved shores of Brooklyn. Eventually catching his breath, he rose to his feet and stumbled sopping wet down a wide street until he came to a hand-painted signpost that read, *Atlantic Avenue*.

Shoeless, he hobbled up the boulevard for roughly twenty minutes, dripping a trail of water behind him, until he spotted the familiar dome of the Williamsburgh Savings Bank.

After another fifteen minutes of trekking, which somewhat dried his suit out, he reached Jackie Wilson Way, then turned left toward the grand bazaar of downtown Brooklyn. He moved amid the slow schools of bargain hunters who, like aquatic bottom-feeders, scavenged back and forth amid endless purchases. In stockinged feet and feeling clammy all over, Uli shoved his way through the market crowd. He angled along sidewalks covered with food vendors toward the Fulton Street bus stop. Nervously locked in the crush-and-pull of urban shoppers, he momentarily forgot that he was trapped on a small isolated colony in the middle of a desert and simply thought, *I got to move out of here.*

Irregular shoes and shoe parts, most of them with laces knotted together into asymmetrical pairs, were heaped in large orange bins. Sorting through the tumble of footwear while being elbowed by other consumers, he located a pair of shoes that was approximately his size. The fact that they were blue suede and loose in the toes didn't matter. He paid a wet half-stamp and laced them on.

As Uli continued through the packed downtown streets, he realized they were actually narrower than even the sidewalks in other parts of Rescue City. The lanes squeezed people into tight spaces, where odors, chants, and a million little conversations were exchanged amid cacophonous music and blasting business bulletins.

We're safe, the entire environment seemed to hum. *How can anyone hurt so many of us?*

Shoving through the crowd, Uli thoughtlessly counted the maimed and blind people he passed, both men and women. Perhaps they had been injured during the endless turf wars. Even if they had only suffered slight wounds, however, he figured their conditions must have been exacerbated by the poor medical care.

"Your fly's down!" some youth barked at him. Uli checked his zipper, only to find that it was secure.

"He's just snagging you," a female called through the crowd. Looking up, he saw it was Deer Flare, the sanctimonious campaigner. She was surrounded by others from Pure-ile Plurality, but instead of their official charcoal suits they were wearing *PRO-LIFE!* T-shirts. He listened as they shouted angry political slogans through bullhorns while handing out *Reelect Shub* brochures.

Noticing his bruises and scuffs, Deer asked, "What the fuck happened to you?"

"I did something stupid and was chased. So I jumped into the river and they threw things at me."

"That was smart," she retorted. "These animals don't know how to swim or even want to know. Where did you go?"

"Near that Staten Island isthmus where the Wall Street skyscrapers are. Then some Spanish-speaking gang grabbed me, but they didn't hurt me, they just tossed me back in."

"You're a regular Huck Finn. You didn't swallow the water, did you?"

"A little, why?"

"Did you go in the Brooklyn or Manhattan side?"

"Brooklyn."

"That's still not great, but if you had gone in by Manhattan, you'd probably be dead by now," she said. "When the water loops around Manhattan, it's so backed up and polluted that people immediately come down with dysentery and cholera."

"I heard," Uli said, nervous about the strange taste in his mouth.

"I'm sorry about the other day. It was wrong of me to make an insane accusation like that."

"It's all right." Nodding toward the campaign brochures, he said, "I thought P.P. wasn't allowed to perform religious or political acts."

"We're not P.P., we're D.T."

"What's that?"

"Domination Theocracy. You'd like us, we're actually against the Piggers and feel that the party should be taken over by Pure-ile Plurality." She paused, then added, "The only reason I'm telling you this is cause someone said you share our values."

"Sure," he said in a daze.

"If you want to join us, we're having a strategy luncheon at the Queens Pigger headquarters in about half an hour. In fact, I've got to get going right now."

"Fine, where's the bus?"

"Bus?" she laughed, letting out an unintentional snort. "Buses are for Crappers."

12:24 p.m.

While speeding north in a sporty new solarcar driven by Deer Flare, Uli knew something was off. For starters, she had interrogated him the night before about what he'd seen at the warehouse on the pier. Now she was being utterly charming.

"Why are we heading north?"

"Because we're going to Rikers Island—the political action center," she said reasonably enough.

Uli hoped that seeing him bloodied and vulnerable, perhaps she had found a tender spot in her heart and changed her mind about him.

She drove along what seemed to be the Brooklyn-Queens Expressway through Williamsburg and Greenpoint. As they approached Long Island City, Uli noticed men on ladders with binoculars sitting along the side of the road, inspecting cars as they slowly entered Queens. He imagined it was some kind of Pigger border patrol. When they exited the freeway and passed through the northeastern end of Astoria, Uli saw a distinct change. Unlike the slums and abandoned stretches of Brooklyn or the overcrowded streets of Manhattan, this place was cleaner and well-zoned. People looked better-dressed. Instead of retro-supported structures originally built for target practice, the houses here appeared to be new single-family dwellings. Likewise, there were fewer projects and tenement buildings. Each home had either a red Pigger flag on the porch or the statue of a saint on the front lawn, or both.

"You see it immediately, don't you?" Flare said. "The streets here are safer, cleaner."

"What about it?"

"This is the difference between pro-life and pro-choice. Piggers aren't trying to cut and run like Crappers. They've accepted that this is their life and they're going to make the best of it."

"All politics just comes down to housing assignments," Uli joked.

"What do you mean?"

"Somebody should do a study and see if everyone who got a nice place became a Pigger and everyone who wound up in one of the dumps in Brooklyn became a Crapper."

"A healthy percentage of folks originally assigned to places up here moved down there, and vice versa," Deer countered, shooting down his theory.

They turned left on Steinway Street and sped north onto a narrow causeway over a swamp and entered a small fortified island. Remembering suddenly that this site was a jail in the old city, Uli felt a strange chill. He recalled lying on a table in a small room in JFK Airport here in Nevada, the sounds of cargo planes whirring in the background. A man with a shaggy head of white hair who looked like a schoolyard bully (Underwood?) was holding a small dog while staring down at him as two men wearing doctor masks did some kind of work on his cranium.

Walk to Sutphin, catch the Q28 to Fulton Street, change to the B17 and take it to the East Village in Manhattan, wait outside Cooper Union until Dropt arrives, shoot him once in the head, then grab a cab back to the airport . . . He remembered the strange phrase being played over and over.

"Wait a fucking second!" Uli exclaimed as they sped past a sentry before the only entranceway.

"We're here," Deer announced, as a large goon dashed to Uli's side of the car, blocking his possible escape. Two familiar faces approached. One was the shaggy-haired bastard, still holding the small brown dog in his dainty little hands. The other was Chain, the murderous thug with the telescopic eye. The goon who helped Uli out of the car was one of the gangcops he had encountered with Chain the other day in Borough Park.

"What's going on?" Uli asked calmly.

"This is the D.T. welcome committee," Deer said, getting out of the car, "and we're initiating you as a new member."

"Remember me?" the white-haired man asked in a high-pitched voice.

"You were the one who programmed me."

"But we were friends long before that."

"You're Underwood, aren't you?"

"Yeah, and for the record, sorry about the whole brain-programming thing. Apparently we were supposed to take you as close to the target as possible before releasing you. Live and learn." He pet his little dog and added, "Now, Cirrus and I just want to talk to you about a certain missing person."

"Did you put something in my head?" Uli asked uncertainly.

"Just a plan to get you out of here."

"Come on inside," said the gangcop he recognized. "Let's talk about the missing girl."

Uli figured they were referring to the disappearance of Patricia Itt. Since they didn't even bother handcuffing him, Uli wasn't too worried. They walked him into the large gothic building that looked like a small medieval castle, past a guard and down a flight of steps to the basement.

"How many teams do we have on Fulton Street?" Underwood asked.

"About ten," Deer replied. "Where we really need more campaigners is Greenpoint. Polls show we're only about twenty points behind there. If we assemble some ground forces for a door-to-door, we should be able to close the gap."

"I'm not worried about Greenpoint," Chain said to her calmly. "J.J. Weltblack is the head of the polling center there."

"It don't matter," Underwood said.

"To hell with their big announcement!" Flare declared. "Shub will win this one just like all the others!"

"No, he won't," Underwood said to both of them, "and we don't want him to. We got a brand new plan and it's a beaut."

"What's their big announcement?" Uli asked as they reached the bottom landing. Chain and Deer glanced at each other, as though surprised that Uli understood English.

"Just that your old bus buddy is running," Chain said. "She fooled me in Borough Park, but she won't fool me again."

"Running from who?"

"Running *for* mayor."

"Who's my bus buddy?" Uli pressed.

"Former Councilwoman Mallory is running in Dropt's place," Deer spelled out. "She's got exactly one day to campaign. The election is tomorrow."

"Good news is she's way ahead in the polls," Underwood added, handing his little dog off to an assistant.

They all packed into a small, stuffy windowless room in the basement. Uli felt strangely at ease in this tight space and focused on Underwood's Brussels griffon, specifically on a small wire running from the back of its neck to a tiny bulb on its collar. He recalled seeing it before.

"They say dogs can pick up on earthquakes and stuff before they happen," Underwood said in a friendly voice. "Some pointy-head figured that if they can tap into that part of the brain, they might be able to sense other dangers before they occur. So far, knock on wood, Cirrus's light-bulb hasn't gone off."

At that point, Chain switched on his prosthetic polygraphic eye. "Does it surprise you that Mallory's ahead in the polls?"

"No, I'm just amused."

"Why?"

"Cause it's a lie. She was crushed to death."

"Which means that you know that *we* know that you were trying to locate her body," Chain said.

"I was trying to find *anyone*," Uli replied.

"Are you glad Mallory is running?" Deer asked with a smile.

"If she really is alive and running, sure, why not?"

"Cause that's only half the news," Deer answered, and chuckled. "The half they broadcast." She looked at Chain and Underwood with a glorious grin.

"What's the other half?" Uli asked.

"Telling him won't make a difference," Chain said smugly.

"She mysteriously vanished from St. Vinny's Hospital this morning," Deer relished in telling.

"So I guess the Crappers will run someone else," Uli speculated.

"They got no one else with the same numbers in the polls," Underwood said. "Mallory was their only real shot."

"They're still running her even though she's missing?" Uli asked.

"That's right, only they haven't reported her as missing," Newt Underwood explained. "Which brings us to who *you* abducted."

"I turned my back for five minutes in the amusement park and she was gone. I looked all over for her."

"In the amusement park?" Underwood said.

"Oh, he's talking about our little Patsy Nitwit," Deer chimed in.

"What did you do to Dianne Colder?" Chain asked.

"The blond lobbyist?"

"That's the one."

"Nothing, why?"

"We found her head hanging in East New York. Her hair was knotted around a street post."

"Oh god!" Uli gasped, trying to sound sincere.

"Tell us everything from the meeting I set up—when you first met her in downtown Brooklyn—until you last saw her," Underwood said, taking a seat directly in front of Uli. Before he could respond, Chain muttered something and everyone abruptly exited, leaving Uli alone in the interrogation room.

He vaguely remembered going through difficult interrogations in the past—when *he* was the interrogator. There were all kinds of prisoners: whites, blacks, Latinos. He remembered hot lights and sweat. He remembered interrogating Asians—those grillings were tougher. Cruel, not always effective. It must've been when he served in Vietnam. From the point of view of the prisoner, interrogations involved giving a single story that checked out, and then sticking to it under constant pressure and terror and finally torture. But eventually everyone cracked, and everything spilled out—lies, truth, piss, shit, everything.

Ultimately it all depended on how they wanted to handle him. If they were simply trying to force out a confession, it was just a matter of torture. If they were looking for the truth, though, they would have to be more crafty, meaning he had half a chance.

The three soon reentered. Underwood took a seat facing Uli and once again asked him to start talking about the Colder woman upon first meeting her.

"She offered to help me assassinate Dropt in the Lower East Side, but she got sidetracked," he recounted.

"By what?" Deer asked.

"She saw a retarded man named Oric who she felt was some kind of agent."

"The half-wit in the bus?" Chain said.

"Yeah."

"And I saw you with him at the Shub rally," Deer interjected.

"I got to know him on the ride from JFK and we were

heading in the same direction, but we weren't together."

"Go on."

"Colder thought the guy could be a possible asset," Uli said.

"Why?"

"I'm not sure."

"Why do you think?" Chain asked, thrusting his polygraph scope in Uli's face.

"She heard him say something that made her think he knew something about something, but I don't know what."

"Think you might remember if I remind you?" Chain said, almost tenderly.

"I might."

"Did she say anything about the mission being in jeopardy?"

"You mean my mission to kill Dropt?" Uli asked.

"Any mission."

"As you probably remember, since you caused it, I have a memory problem."

"What exactly do you remember?"

Uli was convinced that if Underwood knew he and Oric had eluded Colder by jumping out the bus window upon reaching Manhattan, they would be torturing him right now. So he proceeded with the assumption that they didn't know.

"I told her that I thought we should stay on track with the assassination," Uli said. "But Colder insisted that we had to abduct the retarded man."

"How?"

"We said we were going to take him to get some cake."

"Where?"

"Some pastry shop in the East Village. He had the mind of a child."

"Then what?"

"I sat with him while she called someone."

"Who?"

"I don't know."

"What was the name of the pastry shop?" Chain asked.

"I don't remember, some Italian name. He had a slice of chocolate cake."

"Then what?"

"Roughly an hour later, some guy showed up. We put the retarded man in a car and drove him down to some pig farm in Staten Island."

"What happened there?"

"I didn't think what was going to happen would happen."

"What happened?"

"She tortured that poor retard for hours."

"If you didn't want to help her, why did you?"

"Cause of you," Uli said, talking directly to Underwood.

"What about me?"

"She said you worked for her and were a liar, that you had no way out of this hellhole or you would've taken it long ago. But she said if I did as she told me, she'd help me eliminate Dropt and then get me out of here herself."

"That sounds like Dianne," Chain grinned. "If she needed someone, she'd snap him right up."

"What exactly did she get out of the retard?" Underwood asked.

"No clue," Uli replied stiffly. To his surprise, Underwood whipped him across the face with some kind of hard plastic cord. When Uli jumped forward, Chain grabbed his hands.

"What did the retard say?"

"Conversation's over."

"Hell it is," said Underwood.

"You people are government officials and I have rights."

"All rights were suspended long ago. Now what'd the retard say?"

"I don't fucking know!" Uli shouted.

"Cuff his hands," Underwood said. Chain and the other gangcop each pulled an arm behind the chair and slipped his wrists through a hard plastic loop connected by a narrow band. He heard the clicking of notches as it closed into the catch lock. When Uli struggled to get to his feet, they fastened white bands of plastic around each of his ankles, connecting them to the front legs of his chair.

"Get the fuck off of me!"

Deer took a rag and wrapped it over his mouth. She pulled his head back, jerking his neck against the top of the chair. The weapon in Underwood's hand turned out to be an extension cord with a plug on one side and the two copper wires on the other.

"You're smart," Underwood said, as he plugged the cord into a socket and held the two wires apart. "There was a reason she was torturing the retard and I want to know what it was!"

Deer ripped open his shirt and Chain splashed a small paper cup of water on him. Underwood pressed the wires to his bare chest. The shock of electricity running through his body felt like a mashing and burning around his lungs and heart. Underwood quickly withdrew the wires.

"Okay!" Uli groaned. "I know! I know what it was!" He took a deep breath, but before he could say anything, Underwood pressed the two wire ends to his cheeks, causing him to writhe in anguish. "A *seer*!" he shrieked. Underwood removed the wires. "A Crapper seer, she called him."

All gasped.

"What else!"

"She intercepted him before he could get to the Crapper headquarters."

"If he was a seer, why was he traveling alone?" Deer asked.

"He wasn't alone!" Uli shouted to Chain. "He belonged to that couple you hung in Borough Park."

"What's this?" Underwood asked Chain.

"The two Crappers I caught on the bus. One of them who called himself Chad had a rifle lodged inside a metal detector and a bucket of old bullets. I left Chad and his wife hanging out there."

"How the fuck did two know-nothing Crappers acquire a goddamned seer?" Underwood asked Uli.

"How the hell would I know?"

Again Underwood jabbed the charged copper wires against Uli's bare chest. The muscles in his body cramped all at once. The electricity seemed to reshape time itself, turning it into a vortex of excruciating pain. When the man pulled the wires back, Uli gasped for air. Every cell in his body hurt. Before the sadistic son of a bitch could re-electrocute him, Uli blurted, "He had a metal cross sticking out the back of his skull."

"A brain cuff," Chain said.

"That explains his retardation," Deer added, "but it doesn't explain his gifts."

As though Uli were a broken information machine, Chain grabbed the wires to fix him with another jolt.

"He was a twin! His twin was chasing us!"

"A twin?" Underwood said. "Sounds like our Crappers were able to secure an experiment. What happened to this twin?"

"He got blown up at Rock & Filler Center," Uli said, trying to catch his breath.

"So much for grabbing any assets," Deer muttered.

"Okay, now listen up," Underwood commanded, bringing his own sweaty face within inches of Uli's. "You're going to tell me exactly what that retard said. What predictions did he make?"

"Gibberish," Uli replied sternly. "He talked gibberish."

"I will fry your balls until smoke is coming out of your asshole."

"I really don't know!" Staring terrified at the copper

wires, Uli tried to maintain steady breaths. "He kept saying *big bang boom* or some shit. I think he knew that the Manhattan Crapper headquarters was going to get blown up."

"What else?"

"That was it."

"We both know he said something else," Underwood seethed. "And you're going to fucking tell me what it is!"

Deer reached down and started undoing the buckle of Uli's belt. She tore his pants open, ripping the zipper down the middle. As the young sadist fumbled in his underpants, Uli yanked forward, trying to rise out of the chair. "Karove! They're going to shoot someone named Karove!" he screamed.

"I knew it!" Underwood shot back. Apparently, Uli's fabrication was exactly what he had been hoping to hear. Turning to Chain, he ordered, "Call them! Tell them it's high alert. Move him to the Bronx. Stick him under Yankee Stadium."

Chain dashed out of the little room.

"What else?" Deer asked, visibly disappointed.

"That's all I remember, I swear it. He died after that."

"You done good, son," Underwood said. "What happened to Dianne after she killed retardo?"

"We drove to Manhattan to finish the primary mission."

"Okay, now a trick question. What was the name of the Pigger worker who picked you up at the pastry shop and drove you down to Staten Island?"

"Don't remember." He started hyperventilating.

"What kind of car did he drive?"

"Some sporty car."

"What did he do then?"

"He drove us down to the pig farm and left."

"He drove away?"

"I guess." Uli felt utterly frazzled.

"If he drove away, how the fuck did you and Colder get to the Lower East Side?"

"I told you, in his sports car."

"But you just said he drove away!"

"I meant he *went* away. I don't know where. For all I know, he lived within walking distance," Uli said. "What does it matter?"

"We found him dead in the Calypso pig farm where you just said he left you!" Underwood shouted spittingly.

"That had to have happened after we left," Uli replied.

Underwood and Chain stormed out of the small interrogation room, leaving Uli alone with the cruel campaigner.

"Who killed him?" Deer asked, eager to take charge of the interview.

"No clue," Uli answered, collapsing back in his chair.

Deer grabbed the electrical wires. "I owe you this for Siftwelt."

"What are you talking about? HELP!"

She slipped the needle-sharp wires through his underwear and jabbed them into the soft base of his testicles. An unbelievably searing pain coursed through the most sensitive part of his body, shooting up his thighs and midsection. Uli tried struggling back. With a fixed grin, Deer held the wires pressed to his gonads, sending more volts through him. He attempted to focus on some tiny point deep inside himself, but he couldn't get a fix. He found himself silently, manically counting to ten over and over, as though he were forcing time to move faster. But the pain intensified beyond levels he thought humanly possible. He could actually feel his flesh cooking, frying from pink to brown.

As soon as he blacked out, his eyes popped open elsewhere. He seemed to be in some large barren field surrounded by sandy hills. At first he thought he spotted the young Armenian mother, but then realized he was mistaken. Strangers were standing around. His heart was beating frantically; something exciting had just happened, but he didn't know what. He couldn't hear a thing. Suddenly, coming down a sandy slope before him was Bea in all her muscular beauty. She was smiling at him. He saw blood on her shirt, but he knew it wasn't hers. As she approached, he watched in slow motion as the front of her skull erupted, spraying her blood, bone, and brains into his face.

"No!!" he cried.

Someone tossed a cup of water on his face, waking him to the smell of his own sizzled skin. He was still strapped to the wooden chair, but Underwood and Chain had returned and pulled Deer off of him.

"Where exactly is Colder's apartment located?" The Pigger leader had to ask the question several times before it sunk in.

"Fourth . . . and . . . First." Uli was barely able to get the words out. The pain was perfectly balanced with exhaustion.

"That's right. She liked the Class-A Lady on First," said Chain dolefully.

The third-degree burns on his scrotum and mesoderm felt like red-hot nails had been driven up through his peritoneum. He sensed the worst was over.

"What happened there?" Underwood pressed.

Though Uli's mouth moved, nothing came out. He had pissed his pants. The surging agony made it difficult for him to breath, let alone speak.

"Croak him up," Chain said.

A few minutes passed before a gangcop assistant produced a syringe and injected the drug into Uli's bound arm. As the glowing numbness spread, Uli passed out in joy. Another moment and he was wide awake again.

"What happened when you got to her place?" Underwood repeated.

"She went upstairs and came back down a few minutes later. Then I left her to use her bathroom and she waited in the car. When I came out, she and the car were gone."

"How long were you up there?"

"Five minutes tops."

"Why didn't you report it?" Chain asked.

"I did. I called 911 and got a recording."

"It's true," Deer chuckled. "The Crapper gangcops have a recorded announcement for 911 now."

"So the hotel clerk saw both of you together?"

"Yeah, but the guy who stole the car and kidnapped Colder killed him. You can confirm that."

"Bullshit, you killed him and you killed her!" Underwood shouted back viciously. "You killed her and chopped off her head."

"All I've ever wanted since I got into this toilet was to leave. And she offered me a way out. I sure as hell wouldn't have killed her until after I got out of here. Keeping her safe was more important to *me* than to any of you." A moment of silence convinced Uli that his attempt at sincerity had stuck.

"So what'd you do next?" Chain asked.

"I thought maybe she had gone to the Manhattan headquarters to do the job herself, so I headed over there."

"But—"

"Just as I got there, the place was blown up."

"So why didn't you return to me?" Underwood asked innocently.

"Because I had a hunch that you might do to me then what you're doing to me now."

"What'd you say to Adolphus Rafique?" Underwood asked, surprising Uli. They seemed to know almost all his movements.

"Where would I have seen Rafique?'"

"In Staten Island," Underwood replied. "You went down there after the Crapper headquarters was blown to smithereens."

"Says who?" Uli shot back, sensing they had simply gotten lucky.

"Says me!" yelled Deer, who had been silently basking in the sight and fumes of her work.

"She's crazy," Uli replied.

"You caught me and you didn't even know it," Deer countered.

"What are you talking about?"

"I saw you sticking around afterwards, digging clams out of that Crapper mud pile. When you were done, you got on the bus to Staten Island. The next day, when you got to P.P., I greeted you. If you really were who you're suppose to be—" Deer went dead silent. A moment later she resumed, "Hell, we talked to each other when you arrived at P.P."

"So what happened?" Underwood asked. "What turned you around and made you head down there?"

Uli realized he had to switch course. "After seeing that couple get strung up out in Borough Park and their retarded son eaten alive, only to show up at the Crapper headquarters just as it was blown to bits, do you know how much carnage I've seen? I spent hours digging bodies out of that wreck. Then I heard that there was an alternative to living between two warring gangs—a third group that just wanted to be left alone down in Staten Island—so I went down there and discovered that they are a bunch of delusional savages who think they're Indians and elected a pig as their leader." He took a deep breath. "You're all too stupid to realize that you're captives here, and instead of joining together to escape, you fight each other and you are all going to die here."

"Pal," Chain replied sternly, "the reason we don't leave is because *we* are men of honor. And men of honor honor their contract."

When Uli rolled his eyes, Underwood let out a big guffaw. Chain did as well.

"This guy's right," Chain remarked. "If I could get out of here, I'd have left on day one."

"Speak for yourself," Underwood responded. "Reigning in hell is better than serving in heaven. Anyway, people have definitely escaped from here, but no one knows how."

"Why don't you just drive out?"

"If you haven't noticed, we're in the middle of a mountainous desert. There's no vehicle in this place that could possibly handle the terrain. Driving out of here would be suicide."

"Can't you just let me go?" Uli asked, changing the subject and trying to warm up his Piggers captors. "After all, I'm minding my own business just working at P.P."

"And we'd be content to leave you there," Underwood said. "The only problem is, we have an informant who claims that you ditched Colder and were trying to bring the retard to Crapper headquarters yourself."

"That's completely absurd." This was the piece of the puzzle Uli feared would come out.

"Here's what we're going to do," Underwood said. "We're going to hold you until our informant gets here. If the informant says they've never seen you before, we'll let you go."

"Fair enough," Uli replied, unable to imagine who this person could be.

"Before leaving you alone, though, we're going to need your personal effects so you don't kill yourself," Deer said.

"You mean like my deep-fried balls?"

"Your belt," she said, pulling it off his pants. And staring at his hands cuffed behind his back, she added, "I'll need that ring as well."

"Come on, that's all I have to remind me of my wife," Uli pleaded, having no true memory of a wife.

"We once had someone in lock-up who choked to death on a ring," Chain explained.

"I'm not going to kill myself with my wedding band."

"Look, it's your choice." Chain pulled out a bulky pocket knife. "You can hand it over peacefully or we'll take it ourselves along with your finger."

Uli slid the ring off with his hands still cuffed together.

Deer grabbed it like a shiny new toy. They clipped off his leg restraints and helped him to his feet.

"It'll be returned after you've been vindicated."

They led Uli out of the interrogation room, down a hallway, and into a dark concrete holding cell. Chain kicked Uli hard behind the knees, sending him to the ground, then locked the large metallic door behind him.

While lying on the cold stone floor, Uli had a strange sense of déjà vu. His memory released another tidbit: He had been incarcerated before. *If they simply wanted to execute me,* he thought, *they would've taken me out by now.*

With his wrists still cuffed together behind his back, Uli could barely move. The croak was thinning in his system and the pain from the electrocution and other injuries was returning with a vengeance. Once again, he passed out.

He was at some great monument that looked like the Lincoln Memorial, but Lincoln was missing. Another man was sitting in his chair. With an arrow face and highlighted hair, the man looked like Charlton Heston as Moses. Another man was hiding in the shadows of the surrounding pillars, watching Moses, but Uli couldn't see who it was. Somehow he knew that this man was sad. Heston rose from Lincoln's marble chair and the real Moses stepped out from Heston's body, then a third, taller man stepped out from Moses. The person hiding in the shadows turned out to be Richard M. Nixon, but instead of being sad, Nixon was happy; in fact, he was laughing. Uli watched him sit in Lincoln's marble chair.

He awoke from his dream to see the heavy door swinging open. A short girlish figure stepped forward from behind a wall of lights. He squinted and made out the cute rock-and-roll deejay he had met on the bus—the hurricane evacuee, Kennesy.

"They got you too?"

"No, silly, I got *you.*" She closed the door and walked off before he could struggle to his feet.

Ten minutes later, he heard the bolt slide to one side

and the heavy door swung open once again. Chain, Newton Underwood, and three other goons were there to collect him.

"Good news, your appeal just came through." Underwood held a form in one hand and his little dog in the other. "You're going back to New York."

Chain, who now had a large pistol in a holster, reached down, grabbed Uli by his cuffed elbows, and lifted him to his feet. As they led him upstairs, every muscle and bone in his body ached. He could barely walk.

"Can I get more of that painkiller?"

"You're going to get the ultimate painkiller soon," Chain replied.

Once he got outside, though, Uli felt heartened just seeing the sun. It was difficult to believe that there was only one sun and that this exact same fiery ball was shining upon the real New York City.

"This is it, isn't it?" Uli asked, squinting. "You're going to kill me."

"Well, Officer Who-wee, life is just too intelligently designed for me to believe that this is all," Underwood waxed philosophically. "I like to think that the great engineer in the sky finally brings us home for a much greater purpose."

"Or, if you prefer," Chain added softly, "you're the great-grandson of a chimp and you're about to go from being to nothingness." One of the other goons chuckled.

The narrow bands of the plastic cuff dug into Uli's wrists, cutting off his circulation, as they walked him to a nearby car. Chain and his giant assistant got in the back and Underwood sat in the driver's seat, setting his little dog in his lap. Uli was deposited next to them, with his hands still cuffed tightly behind him.

To relieve his pain he kept jerking forward in his seat. While they sped along, he noticed something flickering in the distance. It was a relatively thin building that couldn't've been more than four stories high, but it was strangely shimmering and had a sharp point at the top. A portrait of a tall armless man in a diaper adorned the front of the structure.

"What the hell?" Uli whispered as if seeing something divine.

"The Jesus Chrystler Building," Chain said. "Loosely based on the old Chrysler Building."

"How'd they get Jesus on it?" Uli asked, referring to the image. The savior looked elegantly deco.

"They can put Jesus on anything nowadays."

"Shouldn't that building be in Manhattan?"

"Yeah, but they already had this pointy little thing out here," Underwood said, almost kindly. "It was actually a radio tower that was partially destroyed during a gang fight, so some Christian developer took it over."

"Oh god, looky!" Underwood observed, despite the fact that he was driving, "The little red light bulb on Cirrus's collar just flipped on—"

A heavy, older-model truck cut them off, forcing their vehicle off the road. Chain pulled a huge pistol out of his holster. As Underwood fumbled to get the car started again, the first arrow shattered through the side window, just missing Underwood's thick neck.

"Shit! We're under attack!"

Chain and his assistant popped open their doors. A three-pronged frog spear was immediately thrust into the younger gangcop's face. He seized the weapon, but before he could turn it back on his attacker, Chain accidentally squeezed the trigger of his pistol and blew off the back of the young cop's skull.

"Shit!" Chain groaned.

"Back in the car!" Underwood shouted, finally getting his vehicle into reverse.

Pulling his door shut, Chain accidentally squeezed off a second round. It tore through the seat in front of him, lodging firmly into the former City Council president's back.

"You . . . moron!" Underwood gurgled out, grabbing his chest.

"Shit!" Chain groaned again. He opened the driver's door and tugged Underwood out of his seat, dropping him to the ground.

Uli took a deep gulp of air and swung his legs over the stick shift. As Chain flopped himself into the driver's seat, Uli kicked the man right in his telescopic eye. The cyberhorn cracked off, and Chain fell to the ground onto Underwood. Before the gangcop leader could rise, a shaggy-haired assassin stabbed him in the back, then again in the side. Chain tried to crawl away on all fours, but the assassin continued jabbing the knife into him.

"WAIT! Don't kill him!" Uli shouted. "He knows where they're holding Mallory!"

Underwood's little dog huddled next to his dead master, cowering in fear. The assassin placed his bloody blade against Uli's throat and was joined by a second man, at which point Uli recognized who they were. It was Bernstein and Woodward, the two men he had pulled from the wreckage of the Manhattan Crapper headquarters.

"Hold on!" he begged. "I was the one who rescued you guys."

"Let's see the hands."

"I can't!" Uli bent forward.

"He's handcuffed," Woodward confirmed.

"What the hell are you doing with these Domination monsters?" Woodward asked.

"They kidnapped me. They were going to kill me."

Bernstein pulled out a knife and cut off Uli's plastic handcuffs.

"My heart!" Chain screamed, rolling around in a growing pool of blood. He grabbed his chest, which, ironically, seemed to be the only part of his body not stabbed.

"Where are they holding Mallory?" Uli asked him. No response.

Bernstein grabbed the long sharpened chain dangling around the gangcop's neck and wrapped it twice about his thick throat. Then, flipping the sadist onto his belly, Woodward yanked the chain around his knees and ankles.

"She's . . . in Manhattan." He gasped for breath as the chain dug into the soft turkey gobbler of his neck. "Please, let me go—"

"Where in Manhattan?" Woodward demanded.

"Evil! Evil—" He gagged and soon throttled himself with his own chain.

The three men jumped into the old truck and pulled away. Bernstein explained, "Someone in Rikers informed us that they were holding an important Crapper prisoner. We were hoping it might be Mallory."

"Who told you that?"

"We don't reveal our sources," Woodward said, slipping on a visored hat so that he looked like an employee of a trucking company.

Wincing in agony from his recent torture, Uli asked if either of them had any painkillers.

"Actually, I just got a great bag of choke," Bernstein said, pulling out a cellophane baggie. He also produced a small pipe, and soon Uli was deeply inhaling as much of the narcotic as he could. Within minutes, the pain became manageable.

As they drove through the clean streets of Queens, there was no sign of warfare. They could've been in Queens, New York.

"It's difficult to believe a place like this exists in America," Uli blurted.

"It started out as a wonderful thing, truly compassionate, with the very best of intentions, and then . . ." Woodward reasoned.

"So Nixon did this?"

"When things started going sour here, he supposedly said that he didn't know why the people weren't grateful. And you can't really blame him. Hell, Washington, Adams, and Jefferson all violated civil rights in their day believing they were saving our great republic."

"Abe Lincoln suspended habeas corpus and arrested judges and other government members just for their dissenting views," Bernstein added.

"Don't forget Woodrow Wilson, who arrested Eugene Debs and countless others for speaking out against America's involvement in World War I, which we entered without any provocation."

"Or Roosevelt, who interred thousands of Japanese-Americans for absolutely no reason," Bernstein countered.

"Not to forget the systematic genocide of the American Indians," Woodward shot back.

"Screw the Indians, how about the slaves?" Bernstein said, clearly winning the round.

"How did you two end up here?" Uli asked, trying to get his mind off his stinging genitals.

"Back in '72 we were covering a hot story," Woodward explained. "A burglary at the Watergate complex in Washington. Some of the criminals had ties to the CIA."

Uli thought he remembered the incident.

"It wasn't until we started reporting on an unnamed source inside the White House that we got in trouble. Attorney General John Mitchell wanted a name," Bernstein said.

"Did Mitchell threaten to arrest you?" Uli had this strange sense that he had met this attorney general. In fact, he felt he had known the man quite well.

"No. In fact, he invited us to dinner with Martha. We consulted our editor and publisher, who backed us a hundred percent," Woodward said. "We thought we were safe cause Edgar Hoover had just died."

"But in the middle of the night we were awakened by knocks on our doors."

"Then what?"

"We were told that we were going to be questioned. They gave us some coffee, and the next thing I know I'm passing out," Woodward said.

"Me too," added his partner. "We woke up on one of those goddamned supply drones landing here. That was eight years ago."

"Why didn't you just stay on the plane?"

"They don't take off until they're empty. Besides, we had no idea what was going on. This entire country is in a state of denial," concluded Bernstein sadly. "To this day, I still wonder if my wife knows what happened. I have this awful fear that she thinks I ran off with another woman."

"Maybe that's what happened to me," Uli said.

"They put the whole counterculture here."

"Were you investigating the war in some way?"

"I don't really know, I've been having memory problems." Uli didn't think he had been a reporter, or even opposed the government. "When exactly did the war start?"

"The Democrats started it slowly under Kennedy. Johnson escalated it. Then the antiwar movement kicked in and Nixon claimed the peaceniks were preventing the U.S. from winning, so after New York got hit, they tied the movement to domestic terrorists and a lot of the leaders were rounded up and sent here."

"When did the war end?" Uli asked.

"It hasn't," Bernstein said. "As of two months ago, based on radio reports we've managed to pick up, over a quarter-million Americans have been killed—"

"You know what just occurred to me?" Woodward interrupted. "She could be in the East Village."

"Who?" Bernstein asked.

"Mallory."

"Why do you say that?" Uli asked.

"That Chain guy's last words."

"He called us evil," Woodward remembered.

"No, we asked him where they were holding Mallory and he said *Evil*, which is an old Pigger term for the East Village."

8:07 p.m.

After the sun had set, their old truck finally rolled into downtown Brooklyn, where it immediately got stuck in bumper-to-bumper traffic.

The crowd of pathological shoppers were fumbling through the latest tawdry products piled in the blue sales troughs along the sidewalk: plastic belts, unmatched flip-flops, rubbery wallets, broken flashlights, hazardous children's toys, board games' missing pieces, carcinogenic paint sets, lenseless reading glasses, dented cans of unlabeled food, half-crushed boxes of pasta, aerosol cans without spray tops, nonbiodegradable cleansing solutions, and so on. All selling for peanuts.

"What you're seeing is one of the greatest feats of Pigger ingenuity," Woodward said. "This place started out as a fully subsidized pantry of free items. By referendum, the Piggers were able to convince the majority of people here to auction off these supplies, thereby switching the place over from a charitable service to a free-market economy."

"Why?"

"They claim it's all taxed to operate the city government," Bernstein replied. "But now the Pigger Party and the city government are essentially one and the same."

"Subsequently, the Piggers always have the largest war chests during election times."

"Ninety-four percent of the time the candidates with the bigger budgets win."

The engine of their truck suddenly stopped humming, and they came to a silent halt in downtown traffic.

"Shit!" Bernstein muttered. "We're out."

"Out of what?" Uli asked. Horns behind them instantly blared.

"Electricity," the driver said. "The sun set an hour ago. We've got to run a cord to an outlet and recharge for the night."

"You better scat," Woodward said to Uli as they got out to push.

Bernstein steered, as the other two pushed.

"We still have to find Mallory," Uli said.

"We're reporters. We're not trained to go running around fighting," Bernstein replied.

"He's right. We'll tell our people to look into it," Woodward said, "but poor Mallory's probably dead. And all those Piggers at Rikers Island know your face. You can bet that before this day is through you're going to be public enemy number one."

"Your best bet is to head down to Stink Island if you can," Bernstein added. "You can camp out in the desert. Bring a warm sleeping bag. Cause if you light a fire, they'll spot you."

The two men gave Uli ten stamps, all they could spare. Uli thanked them for the money and advice and helped push their truck down a side street to a small clothing shop. A proprietor they knew allowed them to plug in their extension cord for a recharge at the discounted price of two stamps.

The reporters headed south toward Park Slope and Uli turned west to where Deer Flare had been politicking earlier, near the corner of Jackie Wilson Way and Jay Street.

Her coven of campaigners were gone. As Uli passed through the late-night throngs of consumers at the grand bazaar, he saw trucks unloading a wealth of new items. The Piggers had obviously privatized the economy for more than just the revenue to run the city. When an economy was doing well, constituents usually elected the incumbent party. By dumping cheap items on the eve of an election, the government could simulate boom conditions and get itself reelected.

Uli's only chance of not getting caught, he realized, was by radically altering his appearance. Goin Outa Biznez, a popular clothing franchise that he had seen scattered throughout Rescue City, had a line of green army surplus jackets hanging from a drop gate. Uli picked one that fit loosely and selected a flannel shirt with a flower pattern, along with a tight pair of canary-yellow bell-bottoms.

About a block away, he passed a young woman wearing a T-shirt with the apt remark, *Quit Honking—You Ain't Gettin' There No Faster*. She was selling a large box of curly black wigs. Uli pulled one over his P.P. crew cut and paid her.

He spotted a colorful diner near Jay Street called JR's. Inside, the food line was shorter than the line for the bathroom. Pushing to the rear, he calculated that at the ambitious rate of two minutes per person, it would take twenty minutes to get to a toilet stall.

Forty-five minutes later, Uli found himself in the filthiest, smelliest restroom he had encountered in Rescue City. With little arm and leg room, he stripped off his torn and wrinkled Pure-ile Plurality suit, shoved it in the garbage can, and pulled on his new floral shirt and flared yellow pants. The fact that he hadn't shaved in a few days accented his hippie look.

Someone started banging on the flimsy plywood door. "Hey! We gotta shit too!"

When he opened the door, he saw that the line of bowel-laden, bladder-heavy people had practically doubled. Some burly fellow screamed at him about getting high in the john, which convinced him that the hippie disguise was working.

Uli walked the few blocks to the Fulton Street bus depot. Strangely, the only person there was an older man in an official uniform, precariously balanced on a wooden milk carton, snoring loudly. Uli noticed the insignia on his visored cap, *Transcouncil Bus Service*.

"Do you know what time the Lower East Side bus comes?" Uli asked softly.

"Bus service had been suspended for the rest of the evening due to the coming storm."

"How the hell am I supposed to get home?"

"Shoulda thought of that before you came out, freakin hippie."

Uli sighed aloud.

"Take a freakin cab," the scheduler suggested.

"I don't have enough."

"Where you going, Crazy Fag Island?"

"No, Manhattan."

"Oh, that dumb-ass hippie festival," the guy replied.

"What dumb-ass festival?"

"That Foul Festival celebrating the Day of the Dead. I'd shake my LSD if I were you, boy. When the sky breaks, it's going to come down like the Hoover Dam and wash you hippies clean."

Despite the foreboding clouds and the empty bus stop, the streets were still filled with people. Uli heard a bull-horn shouting deals: *Big storm a-coming, folks, and we got no-where to put it all, so these are end-of-the-world sales . . .*

Feeling irritable as the choke began wearing off and the stinging in his seared scrotum worsened, Uli glanced up and observed the clouds and sky growing phosphorus one moment and mustard-colored the next. People were shopping frantically. The winds began rising. That was when he spotted the first *MALLORY FOR MAYOR* poster. It looked like it had just been put up and the storm had already pulled it partially loose. He lumbered over to a soda vendor that advertised a greenish drink called Bolt! that looked like antifreeze.

"How much?"

"A sixteenth," the vendor said. Uli handed him the denomination and got a tiny chilled bottle. It tasted pleasantly minty, so Uli gulped it down and bought a second bottle.

"Don't drink too much of the root or you'll get the jitters," the merchant cautioned.

As Uli gulped it down, some rude bastard deliberately knocked into him, causing him to spill half the bottle on the ground. It was a member of a gang walking in tight formation through the crowd. People quickly parted for them.

Pigger gangcops must be out looking for me, he thought tensely. *Shit! They must've discovered the bodies of Underwood and Chain!*

Not aware that Bolt! was a carbonated antihistamine, Uli broke out into a feverish sweat and decided it was entirely up to him to warn the masses that the gang from the northern boroughs—who had just assassinated their candidate—had also grabbed their replacement candidate.

"The Piggers kidnapped Mallory!" he shouted into the wind. "They are stealing your election and we must fight them! Fight them in the streets, fight them in the river, fight them in the desert!" He borrowed liberally and unknowingly from Churchill, but no one reacted. He opened his arms and grabbed a passerby. "Don't you see? The terrorist attack on Manhattan was just part of their plan! That's how they were able to put us here and gain control in the first place!" He started trembling. In a moment he fainted.

Uli woke moments later gagging, unable to breathe or see a thing. The rain hadn't commenced, but a violent sandstorm was in full force. Leaflets were scattered everywhere. The world was a brown snow globe being shaken by a madman.

Through granular waves, Uli stumbled along with outstretched arms and fingers. A random sequence of metal gates slammed down far and near. Unable to keep his eyes open, he pulled his shirt up over his mouth so he could breathe and hobbled forth . . . Bumping into something, he fell down . . . Crawling on his knees, he was able to feel cheap merchandise that had been cast off . . . toys, appliances, clothing . . . He felt a pair of glasses, which he slipped into his pocket. Rising slowly, tripping again, bumping blindly into others bumping into him . . . The entire time hearing the sounds of negotiation . . . Voices still making low-ball offers . . . *"Take it for whatever's in yer pocket"* . . . Counteroffers were ping-ponged back, storm-proof haggling . . . Others frantically crisscrossed like beetles, knocking over sales bins and each other . . .

A tremendous explosion blasted a hundred feet before him . . . An orange fire ball under an amber veil of sand, then blackness. *"All sales are final."* Gagging, coughing through the thick burning smoke. Screams. Shouts . . . *"A car bomb sale!"* . . . Sirens. People dashing around him in panic . . . Crying for others . . . *"Final sale before dying"* . . . *"Oh my god! Help me! . . . My leg! I don't have no leg!"* . . . *"Cynthia! Cynthia! Where the fuck are you?"* . . . *"Sixteen for a sixteenth-stamp!"* . . . He could hear objects crunching under endless feet . . .

Uli moved away from the blast site and sales . . . downhill into the grainy darkness . . . Looking up through the black smoke and sand, he made out the geometric rooftops of mini-warehouses . . . north of Brooklyn Heights . . . The storm simmered down just long enough for him to make out one of the narrow suspension towers . . . The overpass to Manhattan was several blocks away . . . much smaller than the original Brooklyn Bridge. Faux webbing connected to a thick cable reached upward to the top of the two stone towers. The wind kicked up again, forcing Uli to close his eyes . . . Breathing through the thin fabric of his new floral shirt, he moved blindly toward Manhattan while grazing his open palm along the railing.

When Uli was roughly halfway across the waterway, the wind tapered again and he found himself facing a blockade in the center of the bridge. A group of blue-uniformed men were stopping cars going in both directions, checking their trunks.

"Hands up," a uniformed guard wearing swimming goggles ordered. "We have to frisk you."

"Why?" Uli asked, as they patted him down. Without explanation, they allowed him to continue into Manhattan.

Unlike the vehicular exit he had taken with Oric, the Brooklyn Bridge walkway descended onto 14th Street further east, at Avenue B. Uli proceeded westward, the howling winds deafening once again. The sand was now so thick he couldn't see his hand in front of his face.

Ten minutes after getting off the bridge, Uli walked smack into a building. Groping around blindly, he located a door and tried the knob—no luck. With his eyes tightly shut, he continued down the sidewalk. Feeling for other doors, grabbing and turning knobs, one after the next, to no avail. After moving a couple of blocks south, he stumbled several long blocks west. He finally found his way into a courtyard, where he tried the knob of a large majestic door. It opened and Uli toppled in, quickly shoving the door shut behind him. He was in the rear of a large church. At least a hundred young people sitting quietly in rows of pews turned around to see him—reminding him that he was a fugitive.

"Sorry," he said, pulling his wig on straight. The glasses he had grabbed off the ground in Brooklyn turned out to be sunglasses, so he slipped them on too. A young redhaired man standing at a podium in the front of the room returned to a poem he was in the middle of reading: "Having just won the nomination of his fringe party / the well-meaning candidate celebrated over an unpopular brand of herbal tea . . ."

"Quarter-stamp admission," whispered a striking young woman with bells on her wrists and a reindeer tattoo on her shoulder. She pointed to a handmade sign that said, *Quarter-Stamp Admission.*

"What exactly is this?"

"Karl Marx Brothers Church of Political Poetical Potency."

"Is it a funeral?"

"No, the Foul Festival poetry reading."

"Is this really a celebration of the Day of the Dead?" He thought maybe the cynical bus dispatcher in Brooklyn had been kidding.

"We used to celebrate Halloween, but the Piggers accused us of Satan worship, so we moved it to All Soul's Day, which is both a Catholic and pagan holiday."

"Wasn't that two days ago?"

"Yeah, but the celebration permit just came through today."

The belled beauty handed Uli a mimeographed map of the area, complete with dots showing where various artistic, theatrical, and musical happenings were taking place.

"Zoning madness, irrational parking regulations / unscheduled bulk trash collections," he heard the poet rant. "Do pigs roll in crap, or the other way around? / Soon he, she height, brings us all way, down, down . . ."

"Do you have anything to drink or eat?" Uli asked softly, surrendering his quarter-stamp. The bell-jiggling lady meekly inked the back of his hand with a chicken-foot peace sign.

"You're in luck," the woman said, pointing to a table several feet away "There's a cactus soufflé that, like the poet who made it, was unfairly neglected."

"What time does this end?" he asked, hungrily inspecting various dishes sitting on the tabletop.

"It's an all-night marathon," she replied, as another poet moved to the podium.

While the new poet read more civic-minded verses, Uli gobbled up the last squares of casserole. He gulped down several cups of bitter cactus tea until he felt bloated. Almost immediately, though, he started feeling queasy and needed to sit down. The only available seat was in the front row.

"I'm sure our next reader requires no introduction," the woman with the tiny bells introduced. "Along with Gregory Corso and Jack Kerouac, he is one of the founders of the Beat movement. When he came here, he felt bumped out of life, so he now refers to himself as founder of a new movement—the Bump poets. I have the privilege of introducing Allen Ginsberg."

In a show of appreciation, everyone in the audience bumped their feet against the wooden floor.

"Happy belated Day of the Dead, I hope you all remember to vote tomorrow." The poet commenced reading his latest work, "Foul": "I smelled the worst farts of my age and wondered, what do these pigs eat? / But then I remember that crap smells like perfume to none but the Crapper . . ."

Uli brought his hands to his face. The cactus was returning with a vengeance. "Where's the bathroom?" he nervously asked the poetry aficionado sitting next to him.

"There." The youth pointed to a door behind the podium.

Uli rose to his feet and staggered three short steps down the center aisle before he felt his entire midsection clench up. A projectile of bright green vomit shot out of him onto the poet's beard and chest.

"Oh my god!" yelled the emcee. A neo-Victorian free-associator who thought she was witnessing a violent act tackled Uli as he was still heaving.

"Leave him alone!" Ginsberg shouted sympathetically. "The poor bastard's sick."

After a minute of regurgitating tremors, Uli finally regained gastrointestinal control. He rose, wiped his chin, and explained that he had just filled himself up at the food table.

"Take it easy, son," Ginsberg said, wiping the vomit off his own shirt. "That cactus dish was sitting in the sun way too long."

"I'll be glad to pay for the dry cleaning," Uli offered.

"It's okay," Ginsberg said, and added, "I was meaning to buy a second shirt anyway."

Most of the people had returned to their seats but were still chattering anxiously as two volunteers hastily mopped up the greenish puke.

After a few more minutes of fidgeting from the crowd,

the bell-wristed woman approached Uli with her middle and index fingers V-ing upward. "Peace, bro."

"I'm really embarrassed about all this."

"Listen, I know this sounds really uncool," she said in a whisper, "but if I refund your admission, would you mind leaving quietly?"

"But—"

"The thing is, until you're gone, it's going to be difficult for us to regain our peaceful poetical center."

Uli saw her point, but he explained that he too was in a bind. A fierce storm was raging and he simply had nowhere else to go.

"Down the block is Post Script 123, a gallery that's having a humongous art exhibit. I bet you can crash there for a couple of hours."

Passing on the admission refund, Uli left quietly. Outside, the sandstorm had turned into a thick, windy rain, which at least served to rinse off his filthy clothes. In a doorway, he took out the event map that the woman had given him. Sure enough, the group art show of the Foul Festival was taking place just a few blocks away. Through the wet darkness, Uli navigated a couple blocks east to First Avenue and 9th Street.

He spotted it in the distance—Post Script 123 was located in a former municipal building. He walked past a group of men unloading five coffin-like boxes into the rear of the large structure.

In the alcove of the gallery entrance, Uli dried off as best as he could, then stepped in and began inspecting the art. Few artists had more than two pieces on the wall. What was lacking in technical skill was generously made up for in daring conception. Stick figures sheepishly performed deviant sexual acts and other base biological functions. Childishly drawn gang members wearing red and blue shirts were locked in mortal combat, complete with chopped-off limbs and eviscerated intestines. Seeing a portrait of a Pigger warrior murdered in his sleep, Uli realized that all he really wanted was a place to rest until morning.

In order to avoid drawing attention to himself, he kept looking at the art. Drawn in crayon, packs of dogs with ferocious yellow teeth were barking at blue and red people on yellow bus platforms. In acrylic, unmanned supply planes circled overhead. One series of paintings really captured the spirit of the place: water color renditions of points at which the city bordered the limitless expanse of desert. Six vibrant silk-screened posters of Pigger and Crapper politicians were mounted side by side.

With no more artwork to peruse, most art lovers gone, and the snack bowl of pretzel crumbs empty, Uli decided to make his move and snuck out into the end corridor. There, he tried turning the knobs of four doors before he finally caught one that was unlocked—a custodian's closet with a large marble sink. Pushing aside an old mop bucket, he created just enough space to lie down in a fetal position. He removed the wiry wet wig that had become itchy and cold on his head and hung it on a hot overhead pipe to dry. With a dry mop as a pillow, he rested his head.

11/4/80

"What the fuck?" was the phrase that woke him the next morning. An old man with a stubby cigar—the janitor—had just opened the door and caught him sleeping under the sink. Exhausted, Uli lay perfectly still. The back of his head where he had been hit the night before felt a bit less swollen. His seared groin was in slightly less pain.

"Get the fuck out before I drag you out!" the mop jockey barked.

Uli slowly rose, yawned leisurely, and grabbed his now dried-out, shrunken wig. He heard it rip when he yanked it over his scalp.

As the custodian led him back through the large gallery toward the front doors, Uli saw that the art had been removed from the walls and the spacious room had been transformed into a local bastion of gangocracy. Five large accordion-like outhouses—antiquated voting booths—were stationed at equal intervals around the space. Uli realized that this was what the men had been unloading the previous night. Next to each one was a small registration table. It all served to remind Uli that even though his candidate of choice was missing, this was the big day of both the mayoral and the national presidential elections.

He stepped outside to find a line of roughly fifty young people waiting for the polling place to open.

"Anyone heard anything about Mallory?" Uli called

out. No one responded. "Anyone know where the Manhattan Pigger headquarters is?"

"Go back to Queens, asshole," one shabbily dressed rebel yelled.

To the east, Uli caught sight of a single-humped Arabian camel rolling across Avenue A. He headed in that direction and came to an empty lot stretching three blocks south and one block east. A handmade sign strung to a gate said, *THOMPSON SQUARE PARK.*

The dromedary camel was grazing on one of the few trees in the north end of the park. Uli figured it was one of the desert animals Jim Carnival had said Feedmore set loose on the reservation to mellow out the inhabitants. Peering south, he saw a line of ragged kids. As he drew closer, he discovered they were waiting for food being doled out from the back of a stylish gray minivan. The small Styrofoam bowls of steaming lentil beans on white rice with a side of shredded Spam looked surprisingly appetizing. Jumping to the back of the long line, Uli could hear the thumping of music coming from inside the little gravel park. Some band was performing from a wooden makeshift platform. A kid with bright orange hair got in line behind him. As the music poured from the loud speakers, Uli thoughtlessly rocked back and forth.

"Can you believe this sell-out shit?"

"Sell-out shit?" Uli thought the youth was talking about the free food.

"Yeah, bunch of faggots think they're the Beatles."

Behind the orange-haired kid stood a green-haired kid. In another minute, blue-haired and yellow-haired kids also beaded the line.

"You want a glimpse into the future of rock music, come see us perform this afternoon," the orange-headed youth suggested.

"Who exactly are you?"

"We're Fuck the Rainbow. I don't suppose you're important or nothing?"

"Important, how?"

"Like the music critic for *Rolling Bone* magazine?" said the green head.

Instead of pointing out that he was waiting in a free food line because he was impoverished, Uli just smiled.

"We'll put you on the guest list anyway. One o'clock at CoBs&GoBs over on Bowery."

The line was inching forward and Uli found himself at the minivan's side window. It wasn't until he was being served that he realized this was a Pure-ile Plurality service. He didn't recognize the woman handing him the plastic spoon, napkin, and carton of milk. But the fellow who gave him a bowl of rice with shredded Spam and lentils was the same one who had been laughing to *The Honeymooners* in the TV room. Uli's hippie disguise seemed to do its job as he took the steaming food, thanked the guy, and walked solemnly into Thompson Square Park. He slipped down the long walkway toward the center of the lot. Joining the youthful audience, he squatted on a rocky field dotted with camel dung.

Uli ate his food while an ugly man in a skimpy dress with pancake makeup sang "The Tracks of My Tears" by Smokey Robinson & the Miracles. The cross-dressing crooner covered another four songs before being forced off the stage by an emcee with a blond halo-cut named Jonathan Sexual.

"Folks, as you know, today is erection day, so when you go into those little booths, be sure you pull the right lever. And just remember that Mallory is the only candidate who came out against the war. Now please join me in welcoming our next performer, Taboo!"

Another female impersonator came on stage and began singing a string of campy folk songs in a tinny falsetto. People kept flooding into the little field of stones, forcing those sitting in the rear to stand in order to see.

Suddenly, *boom!* A car bomb exploded on the east end

of the park. Wild screams and black smoke, thick as wool, rose from the site. Most of the crowd hurried over to see the carnage.

"Folks, please clear the area so we can get an ambulance in there!" the emcee shouted, to little avail.

More people on Avenue A rushed forward until *boom!* This time Uli actually saw bodies flying through the air. An even bigger car bomb went off twenty feet in front of the first one. The dense crowd crushed along the east end of the park broke out in pandemonium.

From the painful shrieks and panicky shouts that rose up a block away, it was evident that people were getting knocked down in the stampede. Out of nowhere, scores of balloonishly overweight men in tight blue button-up shirts converged on all surrounding corners—Pigger Council cops.

A new voice came over the P.A.: "Stay calm, folks. I'm Council Officer Gonzalez. Please help us." It was a chubby Pigger who had just mounted the stage. "There's a terrorist in the crowd detonating the bombs. We got three clearing stations. One on 7th Street, another on 8th Street, and the last is on 9th Street. Please get in one of the three lines for a quick ID check, and we'll try to find the bastards who just brutally killed your neighbors."

They're using the explosions to screen the crowd, Uli thought. He discreetly blended into the frantic rush of hippies streaming southwest. Pigger agents were corralling everyone into a line at the clearing station on 7th Street.

As Uli moved toward the rear of the line, he passed an older man holding a bag of groceries. He was the sole person walking against the crowd eastward. Uli hung slowly behind him until he spotted the man entering an apartment building on 7th Street within the confined zone. Uli caught the door just before it locked shut. He waited until the old man had climbed the first flight of steps, then slipped inside. Walking to the rear of the building, he found a door to the backyard. He climbed over the rear fence and was able to open another door to a run-down apartment building on 6th Street.

Once out on Avenue A and just south of the sealed perimeter, Uli looked over at the 7th Street checkpoint and saw the Piggers fingerprinting everyone. *That was close*, he thought. He had to get out of the open. Then he remembered the invitation from Fuck the Rainbow. Rubbing his hand through his mop-headed wig, he headed a few blocks southwest to the venue on lower Bowery.

A dirty white canopy announced *CoBs&GoBs* in black letters. Inside the dark alcove, a large guy on a stool pointed to a sign: *Quarter-Stamp.*

"I'm on the guest list," Uli said.

"Name?"

Uli realized he hadn't given the band his name and let out a frustrated sigh.

"Oh, wait," said the doorman, "this must be you."

Seeing the guest list upside down, Uli read, *Old hippie dude in army jacket and yellow pants.* He thanked the doorman and heard lite muzak playing as he walked down the corridor to the rear of the venue where the stage was located. In addition to the scent of choke, which seemed to be ubiquitous in the East Village, he also inhaled a far more pleasant aroma—a hairy guy was operating a small concession stand selling steaming cobs of buttered corn, thus explaining the name of the venue.

When Uli reached the small dark auditorium at the end of the corridor, he realized that the lite muzak he had been listening to was none other than the rebellious sounds of Fuck the Rainbow. He also saw why they had taken pains to put him on their guest list. The only other person in the place was some elderly lady who looked to be the mother of one of the band members.

The green-haired kid was the group's high-pitched vocalist. Orange-head was on the drums and blue-hair strummed the guitar. Uli noticed that the floor of the stage was covered with corncobs and figured that patrons used them to show their appreciation. The good news was that Fuck the Rainbow's gentle tunes were perfect for repose. Taking one of the empty booths in the back, Uli found himself lullabied back to a soothing sleep.

6:02 p.m.

A sudden crashing of cymbals and drums pulled him back up. A loud new power had seized control of the littered stage.

"Hey! Dude! Pull out of my bush . . ." he heard shouted over the microphone. A group of lean hard bodies were shoving and spinning around on the darkened floor.

Upon a deep yawn and good stretch, Uli rose and headed back toward the entrance, where he bought a warm corncob, well-lubricated in a cup of butter. He salted it and asked the concessionaire for the time.

"Six o'clock."

Fuck the Rainbow had finished performing hours earlier. The new group of young men who had taken up the stage announced between tunes that they were playing covers of a different group called the Rolling Stones. He listened to two more songs before grasping that the band was probably bastardizing the lyrics.

"I have a pussy and I want it to gro-o-ow out," the singer ranted. "Pound it, bang it, slap it, slam it hard, hard as rocks, make my balls two big orbs in the sky . . ."

Squinting through the darkness, Uli saw that all the boyish band members—just like everyone in the audience watching them—were actually young ladies. Evidently, the lyrics had been revised to suit the strange female subculture. The band's name, emblazoned on the biggest drum, was Girls Beat Boys.

Uli slipped out to the men's room. As soon as he locked the door of the smelly corner stall, he heard a couple enter.

"Someone spotted him in the park, so *blam!* Then the Council came in, but . . ."

"Technically, I'm supposed to keep campaigning until the polls close. But what's the point, the whore's going to win anyway."

Uli recognized the voices immediately, but he didn't know from where.

"At least she's *our* whore now," the first voice spoke clearly. "Just pisses me off that Shub is getting his ass kicked even up in Queens. I mean, where's the loyalty?"

It was that monstrous Pigger Deer Flare. It took a moment longer to place the second voice—Kennesy, the curly haired deejay who ID'd him at Rikers.

"Come on," Flare said sensually, "I know where we can get a little R-and-R before getting back to P.P."

Through the hinge space in the stall door, Uli watched the two women kissing. When one pulled back, Uli caught a glimmer of something shiny in the long bathroom mirror. The wedding band that Deer had stolen from him was now dangling from Kennesy's neck. A flush later and they were gone.

Uli decided to take a chance in his hippie disguise and follow the couple. He pulled on the cheap sunglasses he'd found during the windstorm and left. Outside CoBs&GoBs, he trailed them up Bowery.

From a block away, he saw the pair, arm-in-arm, enter a dilapidated building at the corner of 4th Street. A sign over the door said, *Mamasita's Blah Blah Theater.*

If anyone knew where the Piggers were holding Mallory, it would be Deer. Fearful of getting ambushed, he knew he had to play this carefully. He waited roughly ten minutes before another couple exited the establishment, then slipped inside. A tall fold-out signboard listed three plays being performed that night as part of the Foul Festival.

An elderly ticket seller sitting in a closet behind a Dutch door said, "Welcome to the festival, how many?"

"Just one."

"Two of the plays began at 5," he said, "but you really didn't miss much."

"How much for a ticket?"

"A sixty-fourth stamp." It was the smallest denomination he had heard of in Rescue City. He gave the man a sixteenth-stamp, told him to keep the change, then walked into the lobby.

Uli examined the titles of the three plays concurrently in progress. They were civic-mindedly enigmatic: *The Assassination of Councilman David James* by Jessica Exhausto, *Downzoned: A Battle of Building beyond Local Ordinance Limits* by Wilson Roberts, and *The Meteoric Rise and Mediocre Decline of A. Clayton Powell* by Chichi Chekovsky.

"Doesn't look like there's a comedy in the group," Uli said to the old man who had climbed out of the ticket booth and moved behind the narrow candy counter.

"They're the nexus of where Soviet proletarian social realism meets the French theater of the absurd," the man replied with a blank goose-eyed expression. Uli noticed that this was the tag line written at the bottom of the sandwich board and nodded.

"Why are they all local politics?"

"We only get grant money if we write something government-related."

Uli thanked him for the insight and entered the first theater. Far from a political thriller, *The Assassination of Councilman David James* revealed a politician taking a sad inventory of his political life. The only other person in the theater was a somnolent woman; Uli figured it was Ms. Exhausto, the playwright.

Next, *The Meteoric Rise and Mediocre Decline of A. Clayton Powell* was a one-man show. And only one man was watching.

Passing through the lobby to the adjacent theater, Uli came across a pair of double doors and pushed on them, only to find them locked.

"That theater's empty," the elderly ticket taker/candyman said. "The third play is that-a-way." He pointed to the last set of double doors at the end of the lobby.

"Thanks."

"I should warn you," said the antique fellow, "this play is 646,212 pages of staged transcription with only one performance. It began three days ago."

"When does it end?"

"Two weeks from Wednesday, and the only intermission is in four days."

This would've been a good place to sleep last night, Uli thought. He entered the rear of the theater and counted six other heads scattered about in the darkness. Most of them had seats next to them filled with food, blankets, and other knickknacks.

"Article six, subparagraph two distinctly prohibits the building of these brassy skyscrapers and you know it," stated one of the actors playing a Councilperson, waving his hand majestically in the air. "You, sir, are an upzoning menace!"

Uli glanced around and saw that there was someone next to a theatergoer in the back row who he had initially thought was alone. He found a comfortable seat near them and waited to see if the duet could be his targets.

"Developer John McLeod, you're a monster." An actor playing the real estate mogul's young apprentice was performing a monologue. "You fired me because I didn't ignore the landmark preservation laws of this fair city. Then you just went ahead and built your monstrosity, disregarding six civil ordinances! I'm fired? No sir, your ethical duty to the architectural integrity of this city is fired! No amount of shabbily slapped-together men's shelters can pardon inorganic styles, no volume of recessed public spaces can compensate for a wildly seesawing skyline!" Uli realized from the stylized dialogue that the play couldn't have been written just from transcripts.

One of the two theater patrons in the back row stood up and began applauding. Uli then discerned that his possible agents were actually a pair of seniors.

Heading out to the lobby for the last time, he found the ticket man fast asleep. Before leaving, he pressed his right ear against the locked double doors to the fourth theater and thought he heard a faint swooning. Peering to his far left, he spotted another narrow passage that looked like an entrance to the actors' dressing rooms. The snoring ticket seller had a large ring of keys hanging from one of the belt loops of his baggy pants. As Uli silently unclasped the key ring, he noticed a rusty steak knife under the box office desk and slipped it into his back pocket.

He quickly located a small key that fit the lock of the dressing room door. Opening it just a crack, he saw that the room was dimly lit and empty. A black velvet curtain separated the little room from the fourth stage. Uli entered and peaked under the heavy curtain into the small black box theater.

Upon a bare mattress on the dark stage, Uli made out two nude figures clinging to each other as though to life, feverishly kissing and fondling. It was definitely them. In the dressing room, he found a heavy drawstring and an empty wine bottle, probably from a cast party of some municipal melodrama past. The bottle looked just thick enough. With the steak knife he was able to cut roughly six feet of the thick string, which he wound up around his hand and slipped in his pocket. Sneaking back into the dark theater, Uli listened to the women in their ever-rising throes of lovemaking. He crept down as close as he could get without being detected and waited until he heard a particularly sharp gasp of ecstasy, then shattered the wine bottle across the back of one of their skulls. He jumped onto the sweaty body of the other woman, who turned out to be Deer.

"You cocksucker!" she shouted, as Uli spun her thin naked body facedown. Three fresh gashes, each one with four long clawlike scratches, ran down her upper back. Sitting on her lower back, he twisted her right arm up. Catching the other hand, he bent it behind her as well and bound her wrists together with the thick string.

The other woman, Kennesy, stirred when he flipped her away from the broken bottle onto her belly. On the right cheek of her skinny butt, Uli noticed a green tattoo of a hog—an insignia of her true Pigger loyalties. Uli lashed her wrists behind her back as well with the remaining string, but not before Deer struggled to her knees and started screaming. Uli kicked her back to the floor. Finding her flimsy T-shirt next to the mattress, he twisted it into a tight strip and used it as a gag, tying it firmly behind her head.

Glancing down, Uli gasped. A shrunken penis was bobbing between Deer's legs—she was a man, just like Dianne Colder!

"You're a transvestite!" Uli announced. When she failed to respond, he grabbed them both by their lashed wrists and yanked them to their feet. He pushed the naked and cursing Piggers through the black velvet curtains and into the changing room, where he flipped on the overhead light and shoved Kennesy facedown on the floor. A small trickle of blood was seeping down the back of her neck from the broken bottle. Still in a daze, she just lay there. Uli snapped his wedding band from off her neck and put it back on his own finger.

He then tossed Deer backwards into an old armchair in the corner and removed her gag. "Who cut your back?"

"A nasty little whore."

"Okay," he pressed on, "it's very simple: You're going to tell me where Mallory is."

"Fuck you!"

Although he didn't have the live electrical cord that she and Underwood had used on him, he did have the old steak knife. "Let's say I cut out your girlfriend's eye, would that change anything?"

"You don't have the balls!"

"After you electrocuted them, I feel them every waking moment."

"Slice her open, see if I care."

"How about I pop out *your* eye?" Uli put the tip of the rusty knife to the corner of her eye.

"You'll do it anyway," Deer said—he was clearly one tough little prick.

Uli took her shirt and regagged her. Despite her kicking and twisting, he was able to flop her over and bind the young man's ankles together.

Grabbing Kennesy, Uli brought her back into the auditorium where she couldn't see her beloved. He pushed her onto the mattress and tied her ankles together so she couldn't run. By the time he returned to the dressing room, Deer was struggling to get the thick curtain string off from around his skinny ankles. Uli tossed him on his spindly back and sat on him.

"Wha are you doin?" he mumbled through his gag.

"One last time, where's Mallory?"

"Fug you," Deer cursed through the cloth.

Taking out the steak knife again and exhaling deeply, Uli thought of Oric's cruel death and jabbed the tip of the blade into the young sadist's face, then made a quick sharp incision down his right cheek.

"Top it! Oh gog!" Deer screamed and started gagging. When Uli pulled the shirt from his mouth, he howled out in pain.

"WHERE THE FUCK IS MALLORY?" Uli held the knife back up to Deer's eye.

"Leave him alone!" he heard Kennesy shouting from the next room.

"Torturing people is illegal," Deer said, controlling his pain. Blood rushed down his face and neck.

"Not according to Underwood."

"You're outside your jurisdiction. You're answerable to a greater authority!"

"Who do you think I am?" Uli demanded.

"Siftwelt said you were some big FBI hotshot."

"Where's Mallory?" He returned to his immediate concern.

"Dead, fucker."

Uli cracked him across the mouth, causing him to howl.

"I'll kill you!" Kennesy screamed from the next room.

Deer groaned out to his lover, "Don't tell him shit!"

When Uli clasped his hand over Deer's mouth, the cruel transvestite bit him. Dropping his weight firmly on Deer's skinny chest and tightly clamping his mouth and nose, Uli waited as his captive desperately struggled before finally passing out. Then Uli artistically smeared the young man's blood around his eyes so that they appeared to have been cut out of their sockets. He returned to the theater, where Kennesy lay struggling.

"What did you do to him?"

"Come see for yourself."

He undid the knots around Kennesy's ankles and led her back into the changing room.

"What the fuck did you do?"

"If he would just have told me where Mallory is," he responded, "he would've saved his sight."

"Is he dead?" Kennesy asked trembling, staring at her lover.

"No, and I'll prove it."

Uli pulled out his bloody steak knife. When he pressed it delicately into Deer's exposed groin, Kennesy shouted, "Stop! I'll tell you!"

"Where is Mallory?"

"I don't fucking know!" Kennesy replied.

Uli forced opened Deer's limp legs, ready to turn him into a transsexual.

"Just hear me out!" Kennesy cried. "Word has it a local Pigger gang is holding her."

"You better come up with more than that if you don't want your friend pissing through a catheter."

"Some drug den up on 4th Street and C. They grabbed her from St. Vinny's."

"Why wouldn't they take her back to Queens or the Bronx?"

"The Crappers closed all roads off the island."

Uli remembered getting frisked on the bridge, and the roadblocks checking all cars. "Did they kill her?"

"No."

"What are they going to do with her?"

"I don't know. She's part of some elaborate new plan."

As if arising from death, Deer suddenly sprang up with his hands free and snagged the knife away from Uli, then brought the blade tip down, catching the top of Uli's collar bone. When Uli jumped away, Deer leaned forward and, with a sharp yank, cut the cord restraining Kennesy's wrists. Apparently Deer had only pretended to be unconscious and had wiggled his narrow wrists loose from their bind.

Uli dashed into the empty theater as Deer pulled on his panties. Uli located a small broom behind the door and stressed the wooden stick over his knee until part of the grain splintered out. Then he snapped it so that the end came to a sharp angle. He sprinted back into the changing room to see Deer still sawing the ropes around her ankles.

"Watch it!" yelled Kennesy.

Deer threw the steak knife across the room, missing Uli's head by inches.

Uli bolted forward and thrust his spear up into Deer's bony neck, shoving it right through his jugular. The tip of the broomstick came out behind Deer's throat, sending the young man gagging with a stream of blood shooting upward. Kennesy threw herself across the room and grabbed the steak knife. When she swung it around at him, Uli blocked her elbow, shooting the long blade squarely into her sternum. The Pigger agent fell forward to the ground, thrashing back and forth.

"I assure you," Uli said to her, "your death is far more compassionate than what you put that poor retarded man through."

As the two Pigger agents lay dying, Uli inspected his small laceration. Though sliced, the skin over his clavicle was barely bleeding.

He passed through the lobby and up to the aged ticket seller, who was still snoring. He quietly clipped the ring of keys back on the belt loop of the old fellow's pants and left the theater.

The wind had started kicking up again. According to Kennesy, Mallory might be in some Pigger safe house on Avenue C. True to the socioeconomic trends of old New York, the further east Uli walked, the more run-down the buildings became. Through the wind and sand, Uli could hear a dull throbbing beat down Avenue C. He followed the percussion to one of the few buildings that wasn't sealed up with cinder blocks, a dilapidated ash-colored brownstone.

Inside, a pack of people were moving haphazardly to a pulsing beat. A thick wave of choke smoke obscured the rear of the place. Semi-clad bodies flopped and slinked. Most everyone appeared intoxicated. Ancient Middle Eastern music was blaring through massive amplifiers. Croak, choke, homemade liquor, and things he'd never heard of were being peddled.

With the remote possibility that Mallory was being held somewhere on the premises, Uli roamed around discreetly. He found that most of the upper floors were uninhabitable and there was no basement. After ten minutes of careful searching, he was convinced that she was not in the building. He decided to lay low and try to spot more

Pigger agents to mine for information. But judging by their flamboyant dress and convivial behavior, Uli sensed that many of the wild-haired youths were libertine leftovers from the Foul Festival.

After about ten minutes, Uli observed a strange white-wigged man in a black turtleneck and his memory released another bit of hostaged information: "You're Andy Warhol!"

"I'm afraid you're mistaken," said the man's companion. "This is the artist Danny Varholski."

"And who are you?"

"His dealer." The oddball artist didn't move a muscle or utter a sound. "Are you interested in buying a silk screen?" Uli shook his head no and the dealer and his artist promptly exited.

"Hey! You!" a large Afro-haired man shouted at Uli. "You're that asshole who threw up on Allen Ginsberg yesterday."

"It was an accident," Uli answered, "and if *he* could forgive me, maybe you should try." The man gave Uli a disgusted look and walked away.

Finding a solitary spot on an old futon couch, Uli sat down, exhausted, to collect his thoughts. In a moment, he closed his eyes. Despite the droning music, the filthy stench of the sofa, and his incomplete mission to find Mallory, his mind clicked off and he passed out almost immediately.

11/5/80

10:32 a.m.

Uli awoke to something hard rubbing against his face. A hiking boot was pressing gently across his nose and cheek. Three large, scary men were standing over him, all wearing turquoise shirts and green do-rags around their heads. One of them, who had a deep and jagged scar running across his face, was rustling through the pockets of Uli's army jacket. His head felt cold and he realized that his wig had popped off.

"You fellows with the Verdant League?" Uli asked, hopeful of their green gang colors.

"This is what they call a disguise," said one.

"It's also ironic," added the scarred man. "We're looking all over town for you, and we find you hiding out here."

"I'm afraid you've mistaken me for someone else," Uli replied tiredly. The apparent leader's scar was too perfectly proportioned to be an accident. It looked like a lightning bolt starting at the top right corner of his forehead and jaggedly cutting down his right eye, across his nose, ending at the bottom of his left cheek.

"Special Agent Uli," said the man on his left.

"You've mistaken me for—"

The disfigured man crushed down on his kneecap. Uli screamed in pain.

"That ain't cool, man," said a hippie lounging nearby, who everyone ignored.

Uli swung his leg back, upending the scar-faced leader. One of the other thugs pulled out a large knife that looked like an artifact from the Bronze Age and placed it against Uli's throat.

"Don't!" Scarface yelled, grabbing the blade away. "They need him for something with Mallory."

"Was she elected?"

"Oh yeah."

When Uli tried to get to his feet, Scarface knocked him back down and a second man kicked him in the face.

"ASSHOLE!" the leader yelled at his comrade, shoving him away. Then he inspected Uli's scalp. "If you've bruised him so they can't use him, I swear I'll give them *you*."

Uli was dizzy and blood was coming out of his mouth and nose. He felt himself being flipped over onto his belly and his arms being yanked back painfully. A pair of plastic handcuffs were snapped on his wrists. He heard the familiar sound of the tightening loop as it zipped along the hard plastic catch. A few minutes later he was pulled to his feet and shoved out the door of the run-down brownstone. They marched him westward down 4th Street. Despite his aches and pains, what bothered him most was the searing morning sunlight. Two men walked in front and Scarface followed as they moved wordlessly down the street.

When the group crossed Avenue A, Uli glanced around for someone who might be of help. After all, this was a Crapper borough. A lot of the locals were out shoveling sand from yesterday's storm.

Spotting a Council sand inspector, Uli momentarily hoped the man might intervene, but all he did was compensate the collectors loading the heavy cloth bags into the back of an official gray dumptruck. Everyone else who noticed Uli being led, handcuffed, through the streets, politely ignored him.

As they crossed an unswept intersection, a car turned

the corner and skidded on the layer of sand, slamming right into the two goons who were leading Uli. They flew up over the hood and onto the pavement. The car screeched to a halt twenty feet ahead. Uli was about to dash off when he felt the leader's large hand clamp onto the back of his neck.

"Oh fuck!" screamed the older blond motorist, visibly shaken. The two gangcops rolled in pain on the ground behind her.

"You stupid fucking bitch!" shouted Scarface, who now held Uli tightly by his cuffed arms.

"My god, what did I do?" The woman stepped out of her dented car to see if she could assist the two injured men.

"Get back in your fucking car!" the asshole leader shouted.

"Come on," the woman said to Uli, ignoring the command. "Help me put them in the backseat. We can get them to the Beth Israel Clinic."

"You stupid cunt!" Scarface yelled. She tried lifting the more injured of the two, until the leader pulled out the huge prehistoric knife.

"Watch it!" Uli tried to warn her as the man raced over.

Without missing a beat, the woman swung around, pulled out a small pistol, and pumped a single bullet into the man's broad chest. He dropped the knife and fell backwards into a seated position.

"Fucking bitch!" Scarface looked down at his chest.

"Uli!" she shrieked.

Inspecting her closely, Uli realized it was the blond man who'd protected him from the angry mob at Greenwood Cemetary . . . but he was now a woman.

"Let's get the heck out of here! Forget about these Piggers," she urged, leading him to her car.

"Wait a second! I think he knows where Mallory is," Uli said.

People were collecting on the curb now, staring benignly at the man with blood soaking the front of his shirt. His two large assistants were still rolling in agony.

"You sure?" she asked, and picking up the large knife that Scarface had dropped, she cut the plastic bands off of Uli's wrists.

"Yes, come on!"

Together they each lifted under an armpit and dragged the semiconscious leader into the backseat of the blond woman's car. Uli got in next to him and compressed his chest wound as the woman sped off north.

"I don't want to be rude, but when I met you before—"

"I was undercover as a man," she replied.

"How do I know you?"

"I'm your sister, Karen. Remember?" She peered at him intensely in the rearview mirror. In shock, he dropped the rag he was holding against Scarface's chest. A small fountain of blood shot out. He grabbed it back and continued compressing.

Uli saw the striking similarity—to himself. He instantly remembered that he had a twin.

"How the hell did you get in here?" she asked.

"I don't know. I found myself stumbling along a street in Queens without any clue of who I was or why I was here, but then I saw your face at that funeral in Brooklyn . . ."

"I was working undercover. Listen, do you know anything about Vartan?"

"Who?"

"My son!"

"I don't even know my own name. Maybe I came to rescue you."

"Not likely," she replied. "You put me here."

"I what?"

"About four days ago," she said, "I had this dream about some white-haired guy giving me instructions to kill Dropt, and I realized it was Newt Underwood. I thought

I was hallucinating. Then I saw dogs racing at me and I knew I was connecting with someone, but I didn't know it was you."

"*You* were the one who told me to run," he said, remembering the mysterious voice in his head.

"Yeah, but it wasn't until I saw you at Father Berrigan's funeral in Brooklyn that I knew it was you."

"Why didn't you meet me at Rock & Filler Center?"

"Oh, believe me, I tried. There were tons of Piggers in that funeral crowd. One of them heard what I shouted to you and I got delayed. I have an office at 30 Rock & Filler. I've been tracking you ever since. I sensed you hanging unconscious in some barnhouse and tried to wake you up. Then I thought they were holding you in the Bronx. While I was there looking for you, I felt this intense burning pain here and here." She pointed to her chest and lower region.

"I was tortured at Rikers."

"Here on the reservation, it's not unusual for twins to have a psychic connection," she explained as they sped uptown.

"Why did that preacher scream at me in Brooklyn?"

"You tried putting him and his brother away ten years ago."

"I did?"

"Yeah, and when it was discovered that you had set them up, a jury acquitted them. But after the Manhattan bombing, they got detained here."

He wondered what kind of a person he really was. How could he send anyone, let alone his own sister, into this hellhole?

Suddenly she slammed on the brakes, screeching to a stop on 16th Street in front of Beth Israel Clinic. Uli helped her as she pulled the severely wounded man out of the backseat. His shirt and pants were soaked in blood. Together they dragged him through the double doors of the emergency room.

The putrid stench hit Uli immediately as he entered the lobby. Just as Ernestina Eric had said, the conditions of the hospital looked completely medieval. The unwashed mix of dried blood and dirt covering the floor was a perfect breeding ground for endless bacteria. Off to one side, near the receptionist's window, Uli noticed a blood-smudged spool of tickets that patients were supposed to grab upon entering. The rows of benches were packed with the sick and injured. Others were lying on the floor bleeding from assorted wounds and orifices. Some must have been dead.

Ignoring everyone, Karen pulled out a gold badge and explained to the nurse on duty that her patient was top priority.

Within minutes, a man who Uli figured was one of the few real doctors on the reservation came down to the reception area and began treating Scarface's chest wound. The bullet had punctured his lung and was lodged in his right atrium. With a Crapper gangcop guarding the victim, Karen used the phone at the nurse's station.

"We have a very tiny window of opportunity here!" Uli heard her shout. "Once the Piggers realize he's in our custody, they're going to either move Mallory or kill her!"

As she continued talking, Uli spotted a blood-stained newspaper on the lobby floor. The headlines of the daily screamed, *Assassin Assassinated!* To his surprise, there was a photo of his missing coworker, Patricia Itt. According to the article, she had shot and killed Daniel Ellsberg while he was being led out of the Astoria police headquarters.

The doctor stuck an IV drip into the patient's arm, while an aide strapped a mask over his scarred face.

Five minutes later, the Pigger was carried into a small operating room upstairs. A team of Crapper gangcops arrived and further secured the area. Soon, four strange men rushed into the room, pulling on rubber gloves and surgical masks. There was something about them, in their dress and demeanor, quite unlike all others in Rescue City. Two of them were evidently nurses. One took surgical tools from a large plastic box and laid them out on a linen-covered tray. The other injected Scarface with painkillers, attached him to three portable monitors, and jerked his head back to slip a breathing tube down his throat.

"No," the apparent leader of this medical group stopped him, "you can't interrogate someone with a tube down his throat."

Without even cutting the patient's hair, the leader proceeded to run a small bone saw along the crown of his skull. Uli was about to mention that the bullet was in his chest, not his head, when he realized they weren't trying to save the man.

"I didn't know you had neurosurgeons here," whispered Uli.

"We don't," Karen replied. "Technically they're scientists: cleavings, incisions, and amputations."

Uli grasped that her words formed the acronym *CIA*. "Where'd you find them?"

"They occasionally send these experiment memos to Pigger and Crapper headquarters. A couple months ago they put out a surgical memo to both gangs that in exchange for testing their latest procedure, they were willing to extract vital information from any hostile witness who is going to die anyway."

"I guess that's why they're not worried about keeping sterile."

One of the scientists opened what looked like a small wooden cigar box. Inside was an instrument that resembled a stainless steel yarmulke with dozens of long, thin needles pointing downward. Dozens of intricate wires shooting out of the top end were weaved together like a braid that ended in a single complex plug. The scientist secured it into the back of a small black control panel. The steel points were delicately inserted into the ruffled contours of the Pigger's exposed gray matter.

"Revive the subject," said the lead scientist to the one controlling the anesthesia and oxygen levels. Within moments, the patient started coming to.

"You can question him now," the leader said, as if to do so himself would be somehow unethical.

"Where is Mallory? . . . Where is Mallory," Karen inquired softly.

"Be more aggressive," the scientist coached.

"Where the hell is Mallory!"

"Fuck you!" the guinea pig spat back with his eyes still shut tight. "I— Fuck you— She—"

Another scientist standing behind the control panel read a display of vital statistics as he flipped switches and turned dials.

"You're not hurting him, are you?" Uli asked.

The surgeon confidently shook his head no.

Uli watched as another scientist monitored the physical reactions on the dying subject's gray semiconscious face. Uli saw that the needles were having some kind of effect on the man's motor neurons, as his arms and legs involuntarily shuddered and twitched.

"Where is Mallory?" Karen asked firmly.

"No fucking way . . . I . . . gonna tell you shit—"

One of the other scientists flipped another switch that seemed to take things up a notch. Scarface's eyelids started fluttering.

"Where is she!"

"No, I'm—" Scarface cringed, shutting his eyes again. "Stinking-fucking-Island! No!"

"Where?"

"No way! The dumps! No fucking . . . to the dumps. No fucking way . . . The fucking dumps!"

"What dumps?" Karen asked, as a technician fine-tuned the control panel.

"Stinking-fucking-Island!"

"The city dump?" she asked.

"His vitals are dropping," the lead scientist warned. Within a matter of seconds, all the portable instruments beeped and flatlined.

"—And he's gone."

As the scientists congratulated each other on their success and started packing things up, Karen pulled Uli out of the room. In the hallway, a dozen Crapper gangcops were mulling around.

"What'd you find?" one asked.

"He died before we could get anything." They all looked dejected.

"Let's go," Karen whispered to Uli.

"Shouldn't we ask those gangcops to help us?" he asked as they headed out to her car.

"No, we have a serious mole infestation. We still have a small chance of getting out there before they move her."

They jumped in her car and headed south. Moving down Bowery, Karen had the dispatcher put her through to her second-in-command—a Sergeant Schuman in midtown. After asking half a dozen questions about the manpower and carpower of the present shift, she instructed him to assemble an initial crew of twenty gangcops, divided into five squads. Each four-man group would be assigned to new cars with bulletproof armor. Karen verbally compiled a list of supplies that included guns, bullets, walkie-talkies, spears, arrows, machetes, a hundred feet of rope, fifteen sandwiches, five gallons of water, cotton swabs, masking tape, and a box of nose pins.

"We're also going to need a medic, some new clothes for Mallory, and some basic medical supplies in case she's injured."

"Sergeant Jack is just going off-duty with his squad,"

her lieutenant informed her through the car's speaker phone.

"Put him on."

Within a minute, five more armored cars were added, doubling the motorized armada to ten. They were instructed to meet Karen and Uli at the Manhattan side of the Staten Island Ferry Bridge as soon as possible.

Roughly half an hour later, the line of ten squad cars arrived. Karen parked her own car and they got in the front vehicle, leading the convoy.

He could feel the car sinking and rising as they drove over the wobbly bridge. The awful smell hit them like a bucket of cold water. Uli, Karen, their driver, and the two gangcops with them immediately slipped on their nose pins.

"This stink was the price for establishing order here," Karen said, peering over the waste water lapping against the sandbags of Manhattan. "The entire place used to be so dangerous you couldn't go three blocks in any direction without having some gang attack you."

"I heard that the guy who saved the place was some Indian mystic."

"That's a load of shit," Karen replied. "Jackie Wilson started out a ruthless ganglord. He was the top lieutenant in a small gang in Hell's Kitchen. When his boss got killed, Jackie took the gang into the desert. Actually, they were hardly a gang—thirteen warriors. They spent forty days in the desert circling the city so that they wouldn't be caught by other gangs. Then they invaded the area that later became JFK Airport, which at the time was really just a big empty lot. There was nothing out there. Everyone thought he was crazy when he spent six months securing it like a goddamned fortress.

"Late one night, after he finally locked it up tight, he went into Brooklyn and hijacked a bunch of trucks. He filled them with as many logs and rocks and bags of concrete as they could carry and dumped everything on the big drain below Staten Island—trucks and all. That's where we're heading now. Then he blasted the retaining walls along lower Staten Island that held the sewage water back, immediately flooding the borough. Within a week, the airfield there, which was the only functioning airfield in Rescue City, was under five feet of sewage. Roughly two weeks later, Feedmore switched from piloted planes to the first unpiloted drones, which began landing at JFK—just as Wilson knew they would. Suddenly *he* was in charge of all the food and supplies for the entire city. Some gangs tried invading, but he was ready for them. He had his hand around the throat of this place. To his credit, he was fair, he treated everyone equal. People basically liked him. But if you wanted supplies, you had to do things his way."

"Who created the political parties?"

"Two of Wilson's lieutenants started rival factions, but he unified the city by establishing laws and the two-party system, along with elections. Wilson became the first official mayor here."

"Why didn't he fix the drain after taking control?" Uli asked, looking out over the putrid waters of Staten Island.

"Oh, he tried. He spent a year or so employing an army of people to pull out all the debris and build back the retaining walls, attempting to make things like they were before. They erected this beautiful coffer dam to divert the water around the blocked sewage tube while trying to unplug it. Then they tried to bore a new hole through the debris and into the old drain. Between tunneling explosions and strange diseases, a lot of people died, yet they were never able to reconnect with the original tube."

After passing the rows of sunken and uninhabitable houses, the pavement below them narrowed into a particularly pitted stretch of Hyman Boulevard. Uli saw large gashes in the blacktop and the twisted remains of strange rusty vehicles.

"Those were the personnel carriers from when the army was still here bringing in supplies," Karen explained. "People started attacking them, blowing them up on route from the airport."

"Where did they get the explosives?"

"Old artillery depots had been left behind, and ammonium nitrate was being shipped in to make bombs."

"Why were people attacking them?"

"Everything started to go wrong. Electrical blackouts, food shortages. People didn't like their housing assignments. Then, when the government discovered that some terrorists had been inadvertently swept here, they turned off phone service. When people began killing soldiers, the army withdrew all its troops."

"Was this when that reproductive disease struck?"

"The EGGS epidemic? No," she replied. "That set in after Wilson flooded Staten Island."

When the highway forked off in several directions, the convoy stayed to the east with the river to their immediate left. Roughly halfway down the length of Staten Island, during one long descent, the bilious brown water curved west, completely washing out the torn and twisted road. At the point where the river was at its widest and shallowest, they were able to carefully drive across. With windows up, the entourage of cars slushed through dark waves of toxic water that came up to the doors, almost flooding the engines. Then they sped along the rising edge of the lumpy brown river until they came to a fork of five roads. Unsure of where he was going, the driver stopped.

"That way," directed one of the two gangcops in the backseat, pointing to the narrowest path.

"What the hell's over there?" the driver responded.

The gangcop had worked for the Council's Department of Sanitation and explained that this was the way to the city dump, the southernmost point of Rescue City.

"You're sure?" Karen asked him.

"I drove down here every day for five years," the cop replied.

The caravan soon came to what looked like an endless sprawl of smoldering garbage dunes. It was here that most of the nonbiodegradable trash from the city was deposited. Along a wide, damp field of filth, a number of tire fires sent up ribbons of thick black smoke. Robust little animals darted around. Inspecting them closely, Uli identified them by their beautiful coats and large ears—they were chinchillas.

That morning's squad of garbage trucks was parked off to the side with teams of sanitation workers still unloading them. Two small tractors shoveled the trash about. Karen and the two gangcops stopped and rounded up a dozen or so workers. Swarms of black flies buzzed everywhere.

"Have you seen anyone out of the ordinary around here in the past day?" she asked them, as gangcops from other vehicles scoured the area for any signs of their missing leader.

"Two cars I didn't recognize sped down this road not ten minutes ago," said an older supervisor. Others confirmed this.

"Is there anything down there?" Karen asked.

"A couple of old abandoned buildings."

A stray dog began barking at a large rattlesnake slithering away from a nearby garbage pile.

In another moment they were all back in the cars heading down the barely identifiable path. A few more dogs appeared from nowhere and started barking at the convoy. The vehicles followed the road downhill. Several minutes beyond was a small, neglected cemetery with broken wooden crosses and a few toppled headstones.

As the cars rose up a steep hill, they came across a pair of old wooden buildings sagging sideways. They looked like they had been erected long before Rescue City was built. Five cars came to a halt in front of the smaller structure, while the other five stopped at the larger one.

Two gangcops kicked in the door of the first building. A moment later, Uli heard someone shout, "Shit!"

He followed Karen inside. A lukewarm glass of tea and the thick aroma of choke indicated it had only just been evacuated.

Suddenly, a burst of gunfire erupted from the second building. Karen and Uli exited the smaller structure to find that a gangcop had been shot through the head as he was trying to climb into a second-story window. The gunman had raced downstairs quickly enough to shoot a second cop, then had retreated back upstairs.

"This guy's alone, he doesn't have Mallory!" Karen shouted to some of the others. "Come on!" Sprinting back to the car, she got behind the steering wheel herself. As others stayed back to shoot it out with the lone Pigger barricaded in the top floor, Uli and two others jumped in with her. Karen sped about a quarter-mile before the road slumped down into a small lacuna where the dirt turned into soft sand, marking the beginning of the true desert.

Uli stared out over the dunes to their left and thought he saw a small cloud of sand. "What's that?"

Karen swerved the car up over the first dune and they immediately saw it. An older model solarcar was stuck in the desert about five hundred feet out. Its wheels spun uselessly, sending up a thick geyser of dust. Uli could make out two men trying to push its rear bumper as a third steered. But glancing back, he realized that besides Karen and the two gangcops, they were alone.

"We're not going to have a big element of surprise," Karen said, checking the bullets in her pistol. She drove halfway to the vehicle before their own car got stuck in the sand. She threw open the door and ran ahead until the taller of the two men pushing the vehicle turned and spotted them. He slipped back into the car, while the other Pigger pulled out a pistol and started blasting. The two gangcops with Uli and Karen immediately returned fire, hitting the man repeatedly.

Within seconds, one of the two remaining Piggers pulled a dazed but conscious Mallory out of the backseat and jammed a gun to the side of her head, which had been shaved bald. "Relax!" he screamed.

"Just back the fuck up!" yelled the other Pigger as he climbed out of the driver's seat holding a bottle. With wild eyes, a scraggly beard, and sweating profusely, he appeared to be some kind of addict.

"We can talk this out," Karen called back to them.

The bearded man poured his bottle of clear liquid over Mallory and held open a Zippo lighter. "Back up or she goes up like a dry Christmas tree!"

"Can we just—"

"Back your fucking ass up!!"

In one swift motion, Karen pulled out her pistol and fired a shot, hitting the man in his neck.

"Kill her!" the bearded man coughed out to the thin Pigger holding the gun.

"Do it and you're dead," Karen warned, seeing that the young man was trembling.

The wounded man struck his lighter and dropped it onto Mallory, whose dress erupted in flames. As fire spread across her body, Mallory dove face-forward into the sand as though it were water.

"Holy shit!" cried the thin gunman.

Mallory had vanished into the ground. The bearded man crawled over and grabbed the gun out of the other man's hands and shot twice into the mound of sand in front of them. Before he could fire a third bullet, Karen shot him four more times, dropping him to the ground for good. As the thin man grabbed the gun, Mallory's head suddenly popped out of the sand gasping for air.

"Back up!" the Pigger yelled shakily. He reached down and pulled Mallory up, smoke still streaming from her.

"Look," Karen reasoned, "I know you don't want to kill anyone. You're young, and you have a choice. You can spend the rest of your days in unbelievable agony or you can have a privileged life."

"That's far enough!" the man spat back at Karen, who was inching closer.

"Fine." She stopped and held up her hands. "I can help you."

"No you can't!" shouted the kidnapper, holding one arm over Mallory's neck. His other hand held the gun to her skull. "I let her go, they're going to torture the shit out of me and you know it!"

"We can get you out of here!"

"No way!"

"I got Mnemosyne!" Karen barked.

"Bullshit!"

"If I show it to you, and promise you that we'll have you out of here before this day is done, will you release Mallory?"

He stared at her furiously.

"It's in a bag in my glove compartment," Karen said to one of the two Crapper gangcops, who jogged back to the car.

The other vehicles in their convoy were finally speeding over toward them. As the first gangcop raced back to Karen with the bag from her glove compartment, the second went to hold off the rest of the team so as not to exacerbate the situation.

Karen removed a shattered plastic box from the bag. To Uli's surprise, he recognized it as one of the items he had found in Dianne Colder's hotel room.

"Where's the Charon oxygen tank?" the kidnapper demanded.

"What's going on?" Uli asked.

"If I let her go," the kidnapper said, "you'll—"

"We'll take you to the hole in the pipe and slip you down there right now."

"And I'll—"

"You'll be in stasis for however long it takes you to be flushed out to the Colorado River, or the Pacific, or wherever the hell that tube drains. You'll be a free man."

"And how do I know you won't kill me?"

Karen moved as close to the man as she could before he started flinching and said, "I'm in charge of all this. You just have to trust me."

He put his gun down and let Mallory walk away. Karen held out her hand and he gave her his pistol. Then together they walked back toward the rest of the group. Mallory hugged Karen.

"You better hurry up, cause there are two other gangs around here somewhere," the Pigger kidnapper said.

"Where exactly?" Karen asked.

"They were going to meet us on the other side of the dunes, so they're probably looking for us now."

Karen signaled everyone back to the cars. After frisking the Pigger to make sure he wasn't hiding another gun or a knife, she had him sit in the second car of the convoy and kept Mallory in her own car, which was now sixth in the line. Sergeant Schuman, whose vehicle had been the last to pull up, said they had spotted a group of cars behind them as they entered the lacuna.

"We better get the hell out of here *now!*" Karen announced.

The convoy turned around and started driving back in the direction of Manhattan. Getting Mallory—the new mayor—back to safety was the first order of business.

"What did they do to you?" Uli asked Mallory.

"They were going to do some kind of brain surgery on me," she said groggily. "Try to turn me into a zombie."

"How do you know?" Karen asked.

"I woke up in some operating room in St. Vincent's and found that they had cut off all my hair. They were about to operate, but then they discovered they didn't have the right tools or equipment." Mallory bent forward, revealing some strange markings on her scalp. "They had those fucking CIA guys come and inspect me."

Suddenly, renewed gunfire erupted in front of them.

"Everyone's okay," a voice informed over the radio, "but there's a gang up ahead, so we're going back down to the bottom of the hill."

All vehicles switched direction again and returned to the sandy lacuna. The front car had a line of bullet holes running from its hood to its right fender.

"We were lucky," said the lead driver. "What could've been an effective ambush was ruined when we almost crashed into them. Three cars. They got out and started shooting. We were able to turn around quickly."

"How many men did you see?" Karen asked.

"Maybe twelve or so."

"If we continue up the other road," chimed in the former sanitation worker, "there used to be a route to the drain, but it was more of a footpath."

"I was just at the Verdant League headquarters, so I might be able to remember the way there," Uli said.

"That sounds like our best bet," Karen said.

No sooner had the new lead car proceeded twenty feet up the far hill than a volley of gunfire shattered the windshields of the first two vehicles. The driver in the second car was immediately killed. The cop riding shotgun managed to grab the wheel, throw the car in reverse, and steer it backwards down to the bottom of the dusty lacuna.

"We're boxed in," the driver reported to Karen.

When one of the cars tried bypassing the ambushers by driving off the road, the tires quickly sunk into the soft sand, spinning pointlessly. They simply couldn't circumnavigate around the two blocked roadways.

Multiple attempts to call for additional help failed since their cheap radios couldn't transmit beyond two miles. The terrain in the area was barren, without so much as a bush or tree, and the sergeant pointed out that if they tried storming up the hill, they would be picked off before they made it anywhere near the summit.

"There seems to be less fire power from the south," the sergeant observed. "Let's try to bust out that way."

One veteran gangcop suggested sending two of the armored cars up the hill side by side. When they approached the Piggers, the cops could bail out and try to secure a forward position amid a cluster of rocks at the top. From there they could provide cover for subsequent teams joining them.

"The longer we wait, the more tired we'll get," Karen responded. "Unless anyone has any better ideas, let's get a move on."

The sergeant asked for volunteers. Eight men boarded two armored cars; each one was given a handgun and a dozen bullets. As the two vehicles climbed up the slope toward the southern pass, heavy gunfire from both sides of the road burst through the reinforced windshields. The car on the left drew more fire, and when the driver was killed, the shotgun cop steered the wheel, trying to at least provide protection for the car on the right. From the backseat of the left vehicle, the two gangcops shot back until they too were picked off.

When the two vehicles got within thirty feet of the enemy line, Molotov cocktails were tossed onto their hoods. Fiery gasoline spread through the broken windshields and into the cars. The tires of the car on the right were shot out, and when the driver took a hit, the three remaining cops bailed out. They rolled for cover, under a hail of bullets.

Meanwhile, the shotgun driver of the car on the left—the only surviving passenger—managed to keep his burning vehicle straight and slammed into the rock formation fifty feet above the other vehicle. It looked like a solid position for cover.

A third car zoomed up the hill, driven by the former sanitation worker. The vehicle drew fire, allowing the surviving cop in the first car to get a better position. All watched as he was able to shoot two Piggers, whose bodies came rolling part of the way down the hill. The Piggers seemed to pull back, and for an instant there was a wave of optimism among those below.

Before more cars could join in the attack, a flurry of gunfire erupted behind them. Eight Pigger gangcops were racing down another hill behind them into the sandy lacuna with guns blazing. Three Crappers were killed and two more were wounded before a defensive line was formed to repel the attack.

Meanwhile, the beleaguered first group of Piggers seized the opportunity by attacking and shooting the sole cop perched at the top of the rocks. Then they lobbed down more Molotov cocktails, creating a blinding wall of flame around the second Crapper position below. Three Pigger gunmen rushed forward and shot freely into the group.

One Crapper gangcop managed to race through the flames, but he was immediately beaten, doused with gasoline, and set on fire. A marksman from below who tried shooting his burning comrade to put him out of his misery was ordered to cease. At that range it was a waste of valuable bullets.

"Shub himself has to be behind this," deduced a Crapper gangcop. The amount of bullets being fired at them was simply too costly for it to be a splinter gang.

"What now?" asked another.

"Wait until dark," suggested a senior guard of Mallory's security staff. "Then half of us can hold out here while the mayor and the other group head into the desert. They can loop around and hopefully reach Brooklyn by tomorrow afternoon."

"These fuckers aren't stupid," Karen said. "And there's no place to hide. We go into the desert, and even at night they'll pursue us. Only we'll be half as strong and have no cover at all. We're either going to break out or die trying."

At 4 o'clock Karen instructed the sergeant to move the vehicles to an isolated clearing to avoid sabotage. Everyone was divided into two groups to guard the perimeter. The sergeant ordered two trenches to be dug in case of a night attack coming from either direction.

Just before 5 p.m., while most of the entourage were still making preparations, scooping out packed sand with their bare hands, a barrage of gunfire sounded on the northern peak before them. Screams and cries could be heard over the hill.

"This is it!" one of the Crapper gangcops yelled. All the men jumped into the unfinished trenches.

"They're coming!"

"But it doesn't make sense," Uli said to the cop next to him, pointing out the long rays of the setting sun over the surrounding hills. "Why would they give up their advantage and attack us in daylight?"

Everyone waited, but no Piggers came. More yells and gunshots were heard, but nothing was visible beyond the sandy bluffs.

"They're screwing with our heads," one cop hypothesized.

"No, bullets are way too expensive to use as distractions," an older cop replied.

A few minutes later, another exchange of gunshots and cries echoed in their little valley. This time, however, it was coming from the road back to the city, behind them.

"What the fuck is going on?" a terrified gangcop shouted.

In the distance, two fat Piggers in broad-rimmed hats came dashing madly down the hill, holding their arms in the air in apparent surrender. Uli watched as some naked man jumped up behind them and stretched out a long bow. An arrow tip popped out through the front of one of the

Piggers' chests along with a widening circle of blood. Another man wearing little more than a loincloth sprinted down, knocking the second Pigger to the ground. Unsure of whether or not it was some strange trap, the Crapper gang-cops held their ground and witnessed as the nearly naked man pulled out a knife and slit the Pigger's fat throat, then calmly proceeded to scalp him.

"Holy crap," Uli said, realizing what was up. "Those are Tim's people!"

From both the north and south sides of the road, roughly thirty men—members of the acid-head tribe bivouacked behind the Staten Island terminal—strolled down the hill toward Mallory as her guards cheered them on. Uli looked for Bea, but there was no sign of her. In a moment, Adolphus Rafique himself appeared at the rear of the pack.

"Welcome to Greater Staten Island," he called out to Mallory. "I heard you died."

"If you came here an hour or so later, that probably would've been the case," she grinned. "How many Piggers were up there?"

"About twenty or so. Five of them had rifles. Unfortunately, none of the Piggers on our side survived," Rafique said, then called out to the leader of his second force coming down the far hill: "How many on your end?"

"Fifteen," the white-faced chieftain answered. It was Tim, the former Harvard professor. He was wearing a white and green football helmet—the colors of the New York Jets. "Lucky we brought our bows and arrows. Most of those damn bullets that the lobbyist gave you were duds."

"I'll be glad to reimburse whatever bullets this cost you," Mallory said.

"Call it Staten Island courtesy," Adolphus Rafique said with a smile. "It's our city too—and Shub just made his concession speech. Congratulations."

"It's been a long time since we were screaming at each other in City Council meetings," she reminisced.

"What are you doing down here anyway?"

"They kidnapped me from St. Vincent's Hospital after I got pulled from the bombed headquarters."

Another volley of shots hailed down on the parked vehicles, but the only victim was the surviving kidnapper being held in the backseat of one of them.

Turning around, Uli spotted Bea emerging behind the commotion. When she smiled at him, he instantly recognized the tableau from the vision he'd had in the basement of Rikers Island. In that dream, she'd had her skull blown open. Now, he tackled her instinctively, to prevent the premonition from becoming reality. A bullet screamed over their heads and slammed into Rafique's chest.

One of the gangcops dashed forward to protect Mallory, the mayor-elect, but he fell backwards when another bullet blasted into his face. Bea shoved Uli off of her, grabbed Mallory by the elbow, and swung her behind the nearest car. Half a dozen Crapper gangcops and VL tribe members ran up the hill looking for the shooter. A freshly fired pistol was found, but other than a badger scurrying away, there was nothing else around.

"I was supposed to be guarding him!" Bea screamed, racing over to the fallen VL head.

Mallory stayed by Rafique's side as Tim and his tribe attempted to save him.

Karen offered to drive Rafique back to VL headquarters.

"He's not going to last that long," Tim's second-in-command replied.

"Is there something I can do?" Mallory asked.

"More than anything," Tim said, "he wanted you to see the blocked sewer. Fixing it was his greatest wish."

"How far is it to the sewer?"

"Only about thirty minutes further. I'll take you," Tim volunteered.

"It's too dangerous," Karen replied.

"No, I'm never coming back here again," Mallory said. "Let's do this now."

Uli was off to the side waiting for Bea, who was standing over Rafique's unconscious body.

"Hey, this is your big chance if you still want out," Mallory called over to Uli. "Come on, let's get moving!"

"What?"

"We made a deal, remember? You get out of here in exchange for speaking to Rafique."

"What deal?" asked Bea upon overhearing the exchange. "You were supposed to help *us!* It's part of the vision and—"

"Can you give me a moment?" Uli said to Mallory, then turning to Bea, he explained, "You asked me to trust my instincts. Well, they tell me that I can't do any more here than what I've already done."

"Why did you push me out of the way?" she asked accusingly.

"I saw that you were going to get your brains blown out. I didn't know the bullet would hit Rafique." He gave her a hug, then climbed into the backseat of Mallory's car next to Karen. While the rest of the Burnt Men stayed with Rafique, Tim squeezed in the front seat of Mallory's car and the surviving members of the convoy departed up the hill and out of the sandy lacuna. With the sun low in the western sky, they headed south.

Tim navigated the circuitous twists and turns through the barren landscape that was neither wetlands nor pure desert. The terrain eventually rose slightly and then sloped forward, becoming more marshlike.

"So what exactly is this way out?" Uli asked Mallory in the silence of the car.

"That hypodermic needle you found in Colder's room is something called Mnemosyne," she said. "They call it the escape drug. It's one of the experimental CIA pharmaceuticals. The theory is that you inject yourself and then drop into the hole of the sewer pipe."

"No one has ever confirmed that it works," Tim spoke up.

"That's true, but about eight years ago one of our people found some Mnemosyne and our doctor was able to test it on someone. Their heart stopped and they didn't breathe for a full hour before coming to."

"The sewer pipe out of here would take a lot longer than an hour."

"It's a gamble," Mallory replied, slightly perturbed. "We don't know the dosage or potency, but we have reason to suspect that it works."

"What reason?"

"Shub has dispensed it to countless soldiers and loyal friends to escape from here."

"How many people has he given it to?" Uli asked.

"We don't know exactly, but lots."

"How about the toxicity level of the sewer water—wouldn't that alone kill anyone who enters it?"

"I remember a study that was done when my husband was mayor. They discovered that the water that made it all the way to the pipe had already been considerably filtered through the rocks. It was much cleaner than the black sludge in the river."

"You don't have to go if you don't want to," Karen said softly to her brother. "It's your choice."

"It's the wong choice, but he's going anyway," said Tim confidently.

"How do you know?" Uli asked.

"Because that explains why I was told to bring this," Tim answered, removing his football helmet. Another divine gift from the prescient Wovoka, the alleged god and former mayor of Rescue City. When Uli failed to respond, Tim added, "If this is your choice, then this is your destiny."

After five more minutes of navigation, they came to a place where the brown waters expanded vastly before them, turning the western desert into a huge dung-filled swamp.

Tim suggested they park the vehicles, as the wheels were beginning to get stuck in the wet sand. Pointing to a large basin of still water, he explained, "This is the northern rim of the sewer drains. We can walk to the hole from here."

They all parked along the swamp's edge and everyone got out. Four of the older cops agreed to stay with the convoy and the others grabbed some food to eat as they walked.

"If he really is going down the hundreds of miles of piping," said Sergeant Schuman, "there are a few things I think you should consider."

"Like what?" Karen asked.

"Well, it might not offer much protection, but I have a sleeping bag in my trunk and a can of grease for the car."

"Good thinking," Karen affirmed. "The Mnemosyne might keep you from drowning but the ride is long and that water must still be pretty corrosive."

Uli thanked Schuman, collecting the sleeping bag and can of grease from him. One of the other gangcops grabbed the rope. Karen took the small oxygen tank from the trunk of her car, and the group proceeded with Tim on their hunt for the elusive hole that Jackie Wilson had dug into the earth years before when trying to repair the damage he had done to the drain.

The group silently hiked fifteen more minutes uphill through a smelly, soggy stretch filled with strange-looking cattails and other leafy foliage able to survive in the toxic desert marsh.

"So how did Rafique know we were in trouble?" Karen asked Tim.

"I told him."

"How'd *you* know?"

"Wovoka told us."

"Too bad he didn't mention that Rafique was going to be murdered," Uli said solemnly.

"Actually, I told him there was a good chance it would happen."

"How'd you know that?" Uli asked.

"Because Wovoka reminded us that everything is paid for with sacrifice."

"Who?" Mallory asked severely.

"Mayor Wilson," Tim clarified.

"The Jack Wilson I knew and worked with ten years ago wouldn't piss on you if you were on fire," Mallory replied.

Tim didn't say anything, he simply looked off into the distance.

Along the trail, Uli felt as though they had walked back in time to the Mesozoic era. In the primordial sludge, Karen pointed out percolating bubbles of carbolic acid produced by decomposing bodies. Eviscerated rib cages, like driftwood, were caught up against mossy rocks and had fused into a vast disintegrating organic mass.

"Were you really going to give my Mnemosyne ticket to Mallory's kidnapper?" Uli asked his sister.

"Sorry," she replied, "but the guy could've killed Mallory. And she is our mayor-elect. That means a new era for the next four years. I just couldn't betray him after that."

"For the record," Mallory said, "I'm hoping that you will try to win our freedom on the outside and come back here to tell us if there is any way out of this godforsaken place."

"Of course I will," he said. "And by the way, I worked with that woman who was arrested for killing Ellsberg. Her name is Patricia Itt and she's mentally incapable of pulling off that crime."

"I'll look into it," Mallory replied with exhaustion.

As Tim led them along, Uli could see through the tall weeds across the river to a pulverized and crumbling wall that was overgrown with strange vegetation.

"There!" Tim called out. "That's the monument that brought us from the brink of anarchy to this miserable joke of a democracy." It was the site where Jackie Wilson had dynamited the vast wall and dikes that held back the river.

As Tim brought the group around the reservoir of fetid waters, the sun slipped further down the western sky, lighting the distant dunes a fiery orange.

Uli glanced back at a cluster of low-level buildings emerging behind the sandy foreground. Though from this vantage it resembled a Middle Eastern city from ancient times, it was just southwestern Brooklyn, Nevada.

Tim led them onward to higher ground. Three menacing dogs appeared and started barking and growling at them. Tim shot one of them dead with an arrow and the other two dashed away. Ten minutes uphill, beyond the basin and the massive sealed grate, they came to a group of rising rocks.

After a sweaty duration of carefully footing and clawing up the rocks, the group came to the clump of large, jagged boulders that Uli had seen at a distance with Bea. It wasn't until he felt the cool wind rise in the midst of the hot desert that Uli realized they were close. One of the only indications that other human beings had ever been there was faded spray paint on a large boulder that read, *The Hol'-in-da Tunle*—another dumb play on a New York landmark. Between the rocks, a narrow crevice yielded a steady cool breeze.

The circular crack in the earth didn't look much more than three feet in diameter. Someone had crawled down and carefully chiseled through the thick rock, leaving a serrated hole. Staring into the bottomless abyss, Uli could hear a faint gurgling. Some water was apparently still escaping into the great drain.

Uli unrolled the sleeping bag.

"You have to cover your entire body in grease," his sister instructed.

As Uli stripped down, it was clear that his eagerness to escape eclipsed all modesty. Naked, he opened the small bucket of grease and proceeded to rub gobs of it over his face, neck, chest, arms, legs, and backside. When he smoothed the gel over his seared groin, he felt a degree of relief.

One of the gangcops knotted the ends of two ropes around the top flaps of the sleeping bag and rubbed grease along the outer side of it so it wouldn't get stuck during the rocky insertion.

Karen reminded Uli that he had a small oxygen tank with roughly ten minutes of air. Once he awoke from his chemical slumber, he would have to turn the dial, put the tube in his mouth, and breathe, exhaling through his nose. With masking tape, Karen secured the tank around his back. Uli could see the word *Charon* printed on it—presumably a brand name.

"Listen, if you start hallucinating when you wake up," Tim said softly to Uli, "there are two syringes between the cushions of this helmet. Inject them into one of your veins if you want to have *any* chance of surviving."

"I'll consider it," Uli replied.

Tim started moving around in a tight jerky hop, chanting. Uli realized the odd man was performing one of his ghost dances.

"This is it," Mallory said, as she took out the Mnemosyne-filled syringe and tried to straighten out the bent needle.

Uli gave his sister a final hug. "Sorry for putting you and whoever else into this hellhole. Once I'm free, I really will try to get all of you out." He embraced Mallory as well.

Uli held up his bare forearm, squeezed out a vein, and Karen injected him. As he climbed into the sleeping bag and laid down, he immediately felt woozy. It was a strangely peaceful sensation as his breathing grew shallow. After a lifetime largely unremembered and a frantic week of chaos in Rescue City, the tranquility was truly glorious.

"I haven't seen my big brother in nearly ten years," Karen said with tears in her eyes. "And now after just a day, he's gone again."

One of gangcops put his finger on Uli's jugular and said, "I don't feel a pulse."

"Either you're dead or it's working," Mallory muttered serenely.

Uli wanted to tell her he was fine, but he couldn't so much as bat an eyelash. It was over. Although he didn't feel panicky, it was very strange not being able to breathe. He could still feel his sister preparing him—taping his nose, ears, and lips with grease-covered swabs of cotton. He tried to lift his arms and help Mallory as she fit a pair of goggles tightly over his eyes, but in another moment he couldn't feel much of anything at all.

Mallory slipped the oxygen tube near his mouth and Tim's New York Jets football helmet over his head, fastening the chin guard to secure it.

Uli heard a muffled voice say, *"Okay, he's ready."* Darkness spread inside him as several gangcops lifted the bag upright. They loosely tied the top of the bag with a piece of the rope, then lowered Uli down through the rocky fissure and deep into the windy chasm. A few times he got stuck sideways and they had to re-lift and re-lower him. He never actually felt water, simply a dark rushing force that bent his body sideways.

Suddenly, the rope was cut and he felt like a kite blown high in the air. The current swirled him around and he was utterly joyous. Experiencing a strange sensation without breath or light, he found himself focusing on the pigeon, then on his sister's face. His body seemed to be shaping the direction it was moving, with the pipes forming around it. *He* was the force around himself.

From this unbelievable velocity, a single fugitive memory broke loose, and from it, backwards through vast convolutions of reasoning, an awesome deduction occurred:

She set up the Pigger ambush! She's the one who planned the attempt on my life and blew up the truck in midtown! Building on his reasoning, Uli thought, *I must've been sent here to arrest her.*

The memory producing this was his and his alone. With his body bending, slipping, shooting, looping through the vast underworld of massive pipes, he knew now that ten years before, the person who had detonated the dirty bombs throughout lower Manhattan was none other than his own sister—Karen.

The more he remembered, the greater the rush of thoughts both devoured and propelled him through the blackness of words and voices: *"dkadhja akdala dand a kdncka then slaughter of and New York no longer . . . missile attacks . . . New York State World's Fair . . . Times Square . . . fucking hippies . . . . . . Armenians forced out of their homelands and into . . . . . . I . I . I . I . I . . . I. Have. To. To. To. Go. Back . . . To! Get! Back! Up! . . . . . . To! Warn!! Mallory?? . . . New York's gonna get hit again . . . . after ten years it's nearly scrubbed down . . . . that's why you were on that drone . . . . Did Hanoi slip weapons-grade plutonium into New York? . . . The fluoroscope machines! . . . . They were connected with the first gang . . . . . . Who? . . . . The bastards that hit New York in 1970 . . . . that was when you found the old man . . . . the one who hated his goddamn brother . . . . when the senile old bastard mentioned Karen . . . . his sister and the plan . . . . Robert Moses . . . Paul Moses!!"*

AUTHOR'S NOTE

This is a work of fiction embellishing certain historical events and figures. Of course, Nixon didn't finish his second term, nor did Ronald Reagan win the presidency in 1976. (However, if Nixon hadn't been forced to resign due to Watergate, Reagan might've been in the White House four years earlier.) Although I don't know of a military simulation city in Nevada, German Village—designed for rehearsal of the bombing of Berlin—does exist out in Utah. Jack Wilson was supposedly a Paiute mystic—later renamed Wovoka—and is accredited with having created ghost dancing. Dates and events have been revised to serve the story. Anyone who is interested in the actual historical events embellished in these pages—and I genuinely hope you are—should go to a library or bookstore, anywhere but here.

Further adventures to be announced

11/6/08

www.akashicbooks.com

Thanks to:

Johnny Temple
Kara Gilmour
Arthur Jackson Temple
Johanna Ingalls
Ibrahim Ahmad
Aaron Petrovich
Sohrab Habibion
Dan Mandel
Joseph Burke
Kim Kowalski
Patrick Nersesian
Burke Nersesian
Delphi Basilicato
David Platt
Chris Leung
Hrag Vartanian
Sylvia Rascon
Alexis Fleisig
Rick Froberg